Deepest Red

ISSN 1463 1350
ISBN 0 9526947 2 7

Editors
Mat Coward, Andy Cox

Production & Publishing
TTA Press, 5 Martins Lane, Witcham, Ely, Cambs CB6 2LB
tel/fax: 01353 777931
email: ttapress@aol.com

Shadowlink Website
http://purl.oclc.org/net/ttaonline/index.html (Lawrence Dyer)

Copyright
© TTA Press & contributors 1999

Subscriptions
2 volumes: £11 · Eur £13
RoW £15/US$22
4 volumes: £20 · Eur £24
RoW £28/US$40
Cheques should be made payable to 'TTA Press'. Subscribers abroad may pay by foreign currency cheque at rates equivalent to those listed — this method is preferred to foreign cash. Published biannually in June and December

Submissions
Unsolicited submissions of short stories are welcome. Please study the magazine before submitting and always enclose return postage (overseas submissions should be disposable and accompanied by two International Reply Coupons or simply an email address). We are unable to reply otherwise. Always enclose a covering letter and send just one story at a time. There is no restriction on the length of short stories. Letters are welcome via email but all other submissions should be made via post. No responsibility can be accepted for loss or damage to unsolicited material, howsoever caused

Advertising
Call or write for details

Printing
Black Bear Press, Cambridge

Distribution
For details of wholesale, retail and mail order distribution in Great Britain and other countries across the world please contact the publisher

One question people often ask me is, "Those amazing readers' letters you print in CW: they're made up aren't they?" My answer is that we don't actually print any readers' letters in CW, least of all amazing ones, and that therefore though they are, indeed, made up it's not a job that takes very long.

No, most of my time as co-editor is spent making up biographical notes for our contributors. I'm not sure many people outside the business understand just how very boring the life of the writer is. As the very word 'writer' might suggest, a writer spends every day, all day, filing things, filling in tax returns, chasing cheques, returning phone calls to people who aren't there, or aren't there any more, and trying to get a spare part for their two-year-old fax machines. Think about it: that's what 'writer' means. It's from the Greek, as you know.

So, fair enough, even if they had anything to write about in their biographical notes, they wouldn't have the time – the sheer bloody time – to do it. Or vice versa. When asked for a couple of paragraphs on their life and times, CW's writers usually respond with a variation on "Oh, man, I hate doing this kinda stuff. You know? Okay, man, I'm like a writer and like I live in a house and I've had a bunch of stories published in like all the usual places. Yeah? Think you can cobble something together from that, man?"

Of course we can, lovey. No probs. Leave it to us.

Which is why TTA Press has recently invested in a massively expensive new software/hardware/string thing that is designed to produce, in less time than it takes to read the instruction book, biographical notes which are essentially random chains of letters and numbers but which look as if they might mean something provided you don't read them. We hope you will notice a great improvement in that department, starting with this issue.

You might wonder why we bother having biographical notes, when they involve such a lot of trouble and expense. Fair question. The answer is simply that they add verisimilitude. We don't want people thinking we make up all the stories, along with all the amazing readers' letters.

Mat Coward

PS. Mr JG of Rotherhithe: you want to try greasing it first. Okay now?

ILLUSTRATIONS
Wendy Down (& front cover), David Checkley, Roddy Williams

THE GOOD BOOK
PETER CROWTHER

a Koko Tate tale

James Axelrod Baker's study looked as if it had been put together for a *Life*
magazine article or a 1967 psychedelic album sleeve. It smelled of paper, stale
pipe smoke and memories, in almost equal amounts, while, underneath, it reeked
of the twin fears of death and progress.

My first thought was it should have been sealed up and opened in a thousand
years so that our descendants might know what we were about. *These were the
people that put a man on the moon?* They may well ask.

Three of the walls were fitted with floor-to-ceiling bookshelves, the books stacked
and racked both vertically and horizontally. At the edges of the shelves, in front of
the books, were items of bric-a-brac and memorabilia. It looked like a kindergarten
'lost and found' office, with Disney figurines, die-cast metal toy cars, and elastic-
banded sets of bubble gum cards sharing cramped space with Halloween monster
masks, baseball caps and pieces of surreal pottery.

The window ledge boasted more of the same, and stacked against the wall below
were piles of folders and books, plus twin towers of old *Saturday Evening Post*,
Esquire and *Playboy* magazines *plus* numerous boxes bearing faded writing I couldn't
read. Fixed to the wall above the storage radiator by the door were a series of framed
comic books: *Batman and Robin, Casper the Friendly Ghost, Superman, Donald
Duck,* and some I didn't recognize. I never was big on comic books. I fell in love
with reality at an early age. It was weirder.

In the center of the room stood a large desk which held, among other things, a
computer, a keyboard, a printer, two angle-poise lamps, a magnetized paperclip
mountain, a mess of matchbooks, three ashtrays, a Sellotape dispenser, a stapler,
two pipe racks, an array of pens and pencils, four large tins jammed full with *more*
pens and pencils, a couple of *National Geographic* maps, several more piles of
books, and a lot of dust. It was spread so thick in places I half expected to see a
cow skull partially buried beside a dried-up waterhole.

In the middle of it all was a Fisher Price clock that had been customized so that
it told the real time. As the big, yellow-arrowed hand moved over the 12, the study
door opened and a tall man wearing a wide, gap-toothed smile walked into the
room. It was quite an entrance, and punctual, too. At first I thought it was Terry-
Thomas, and I'd been caught up in an old British black-and-white movie.

"Mr Tate, I'm Jim Baker," his voice boomed around the paper and mementos,
seeming perfectly at home. He looked every inch the eccentric: a narrow, academic
face, thin-lipped mouth, and pinched cheeks leading up to a wiry thatch of unkempt
Einstein-style brown hair. And his clothes…tweed jacket complete with leather edging
and elbow patches, a frayed-collared, checkered shirt with a bootlace tie held tight
with a brass Madonna — and not the one who wears her top clothes underneath her
hosiery — a pair of scuffed, brown brogues, and obligatory odd socks into which he
had tucked the legs of a singularly shapeless pair of bottle green denim pants. He
made the neighborhood five-and-dime look like Saks Fifth Avenue.

I took hold of the hand at the end of the outstretched arm, noticing the cracked
and tobacco-filled fingernails, and shook it firmly…if a little distastefully. "Quite a
collection," I told him. I didn't think for a minute that my four-minute appraisal
would come as any surprise, but he did me the courtesy of raising his eyebrows
briefly and nodding eternal gratitude.

"Thank you, Mr Tate," he said politely. "Please, sit."

I sat in one of the chairs behind the desk, keeping my eyes fixed on the top of
his head for signs of small beaks looking for bugs and watched as he lifted a pipe
from one of the racks. He tapped it into his palm and then jammed it quickly into
the corner of his mouth. "I'll come straight to the point," he said around the stem.
"I've had a most unusual burglary."

"From in here?"

He nodded again and removed a small leather tobacco pouch from his jacket
pocket. He proceeded to extract long strands of what looked like brown crab grass
and drop them into the bowl.

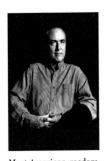

Most American readers
will recognise Pete
Crowther's name, and
some may even be
surprised to learn that
he is a British writer,
since so much of his
work is set in the USA.
In fact, he and his wife
live in Harrogate, and
you can't get much
more English than that.
Pete used to work in
corporate
communications,
before becoming a
prolific and celebrated
anthologist, columnist,
short story writer and
novelist: *Escardy Gap*,
co-authored with
James Lovegrove, is
available in the UK and
US. He writes in many
different genres, and in
all of them is noted for
the humour and
warmth which typify
even his darkest works.
That, and an unhealthy
fixation with popular
culture.

Illustrations:
David Checkley

I waved my arms and gave him my best in incredulous expressions. "You mean there was *more* than this in here?"

Baker smiled as he flicked open a matchbook, struck it, and held it to the bowl, all with one hand. Maybe he used to drive a yellow cab. Maybe not. Cab drivers could also drive a car, hit innocent and inanimate objects and people without ever damaging their own vehicle, hurl abuse out of the open window, and watch what you were doing through the rear mirror at the same time. I didn't think Baker was that good. And, anyway, he spoke English and probably knew where the Empire State Building was. He puffed on the pipe and disappeared in a fog of smoke.

I waited, memorizing the route to the door in case I lost my bearings, and took out my ever-ready yellow Post-it pad and chewed pencil stub. Ever the professional.

"One item," he said at last, wafting away the smoke and then holding an index finger aloft in case I had trouble with the concept. "A Bible."

"A Bible?"

"It wasn't just *any* Bible, Mr Tate." He reached into his inside jacket pocket and, amidst a spray of crumbs and lint-balls, pulled out some Polaroid photographs. "Here, take a look at these," he said, handing them over.

I took them and looked while Baker spoke.

"It was a St James version, printed by George E Eyre and William Spottiswoode of Fleet Street, England, in 1856. Black leather, tooled covers — front, back and spine — and brass-bound at the edges and corners. As you can see, the brass is very decorative and extends to a hinged clasp that keeps the book closed when not in use." He puffed on his pipe and watched me thumb through the photographs. "Full Morocco gilt to page edges and a predominantly red marbling — excellent condition — to the inside covers, both front and back."

It was a good description of the book in the photographs. "When did the theft take place?"

"It was here on Monday."

Today was Wednesday. "When did you notice it was missing?"

"About three o'clock yesterday afternoon. I called the police; they came around a little after four."

"What did they say?"

"They suggested that I might have misplaced it." He laughed at the sheer absurdity of such a suggestion.

"And is that possible?" I asked, laughing along with him.

"All of my books are carefully recorded in my files when I buy them and then placed on an appropriate pile to await filing." He shifted his pipe to the other side of his mouth as he watched my face. "As a system, it works, Mr Tate."

I looked to the shelves and let my eyes drift up and down, left and right, then looked around the room. "How did he get in?"

Baker shrugged. "No signs of breaking in anywhere."

"Are you alarmed?"

"I'm afraid not."

"Might be a good idea to give it some more consideration."

"My only concern now is to find the Bible."

I nodded agreeably. "So, the book went missing sometime between…?"

"I last saw it around ten o'clock on Monday night. I was in here doing some reorganisation."

I wondered if the room realised it had been reorganized. I doubted it. "Okay, between ten on Monday night and three yesterday afternoon. Did you have any visitors yesterday?"

He shook his head.

"Monday night, after ten o'clock?"

"Nobody."

I smiled correctively. "You had *one*, Mr Baker. Whenever it was, you had one."

"Mmmm."

"Was the Bible valuable?"

He shook his head. "Normally, this particular edition would be worth around two hundred dollars, maybe three. The only unusual feature of my copy was a small crest — a coat of arms, I suppose you'd call it — engraved on the clasp." He leaned over and fanned out the photographs. "Here," he said, pointing to one of them.

I was looking at a small design of blimps and squiggles, like preschool doodlings or vintage Andy Warhol, scratched onto the metal that spanned the closed pages. "You say 'normally'. Does the crest make it any more valuable?"

"A little."

"How little?"

"Maybe another fifty, a hundred at the most."

"What is it?"

"What is what?"

"The coat of arms."

"It's a personal mark indicating that the book is from the personal library of Charles Waring."

He had said the name with such implied significance that I felt like a hayseed for needing clarification. I mentally shifted the grass stem with my tongue, tried not to think about stalking jackrabbits through the swamps, and asked anyway.

"Charles Waring was one of *the* great bibliophiles."

"Was?"

"Yes, he's dead."

"Oh," I said, just to keep things ticking. Baker sat without moving, watching me. I felt there was something more. "Is there something more?"

"Well, not really. He died about two weeks ago...tragic, really."

"Tragic? In what way?"

"An accident. He was working in his library when he fell and hit his head."

"And that was it? It killed him?"

Baker nodded, his face filled with the mock concerns of someone who really couldn't have cared less. "He was an old man, Mr Tate. He hit his head on a table and" — Baker snapped his fingers — "that was that."

"Who found him?"

"His assistant, Elicia Barnes. Look," he said with a deep sigh, "I asked you here to investigate the theft of my Bible, Mr Tate."

I nodded. "When did you buy the Bible — before his death or after?"

"After."

"Who sold it to you?"

"Well, I knew of its existence, of course, and when I heard of Waring's unfortunate accident, I waited a few days — for appearance's sake, you understand..."

I waved away any hint of ghoulish opportunism.

"...And then I got in touch with Waring's daughter."

I shuffled my little pad and made ready my trusty pencil.

"Ella Thornley...she's in the book under that name."

I wrote it down under the other names. Soon I'd need to start another sheet. "So she sold you the book?"

He shook his head. "No. When I phoned her, she said she had already sold all of her father's historical and theological books to a dealer. In fact, she sold the entire collection to various dealers and private collectors before her father was even buried."

"And you bought it from him?"

"Yes."

I held the pencil ready. "And *his* name?"

"Edgar Hooper. He has a store down in the Village...one of the unnumbered streets, I don't remember which one." He coughed chestily and then swallowed. I made a mental note to skip lunch. "Hooper heard about the death almost as soon as it had happened, and not being one to observe many of the social graces, he got in immediate contact with Waring's daughter."

"How immediate?"

"Oh," Baker said, looking to the ceiling for inspiration. "The following day, I think. The call was ostensibly to offer condolences, but still managing to offer to take some of the collection off her hands. She took him up on it straight away, and he bought the lot — all that he wanted — that afternoon."

"How do you know all this timing?"

"Hooper. He's a braggart."

"So, the daughter...she needed the money?"

Baker smiled. "Constantly."

"Are there any other children?"

"No, just Ella. Ella Waring was a disappointment to her father, Mr Tate. She married beneath her, and her father never forgave her. Jimmy Thornley has been involved in one money-chasing venture after another. None of them worked out. The pair of them were in constant need of money."

"How much did Hooper say he'd paid her?"

"Eleven thousand dollars."

I whistled. "Taking his mark-up into account, that's a lot of books."

"I would say so, yes."

"How much did you pay? For the Bible?"

"Four hundred and fifty dollars." Baker removed the pipe from his mouth and pursed his lips, moistening them. It made me feel queasy. "It was a fair price," he added, placing the pipe on the table in front of him. "A very fair price."

"What's so special about books from Waring's collection?"

"Items from the Waring collection always fetch a slightly higher price. Waring had a habit of personalising his books with a mock coat of arms he appended to the fly leaf by means of an inked rubber stamp. As you can see from the photographs, the difference in the case of the Eyre and Spottiswoode is that the coat was actually engraved onto the clasp. But even then, the Bible is only worth around four or five hundred dollars — what I paid for it, in fact." He picked up the pipe again, jammed it back between newly wetted lips, and held his lighter over the bowl. And just when my tear ducts had sealed up again.

"Still seems like a lot to me," I said.

"That's the point," Baker said through a pungent cloud of smoke. "In terms of rare books — and certainly in terms of the books you can see in this room — the thief could have taken a handful worth several thousand dollars. Instead, he took only one. A four-hundred-dollar Bible."

I pulled out one of the photographs and shuffled the others together. "Okay if I keep this one?"

"Absolutely," he said with a grand wave of his arm, as though he were giving me something really valuable.

I put the photograph in my pocket, handed the others back to him and stood up. "From what you say, wouldn't it be easier to just go out and buy another copy? It should be easy to replace, at least if you're prepared to do without the engraved clasp. And it would cost you less than hiring me to look for it."

"I agree, but the money is not important. There is only one Waring copy, Mr Tate, and that is the copy that I want. And I want to know who would be prepared to steal to get it."

"And why?" I suggested.

Baker nodded. "And why."

The fat man was reading a Bible and muttering to himself. I looked over his shoulder at a block of yellow, highlighted print. "Good?" I asked quietly.

His shoulders started, and he looked around, shielding his eyes against the glare. "You startled me."

I nodded proudly. "It's these shoes," I explained. "Bought them from a guy named Cranston. Laughed a lot."

Edgar Hooper grunted and snapped the Bible closed. "Deuteronomy 14," he said, as if it meant something to me. It didn't. "I read it every day," he added.

"You figure you'll ever finish it?"

He squinted up at me and shook his head, the folds of skin hanging from his jawbone swinging like a turkey's gullet in a cyclone. "Did you want something here?"

I shifted my Juicy Fruit gum from one side of my mouth to the other, as if I meant business. "Looking for redemption." I pointed to the Bible trapped beneath his folded arms. "Maybe I'll find it in Deuteronomy."

Hooper leaned over and pushed the Bible into a shelf. "I don't think you would find anything in there to interest you, mister…"

"Tate," I said. "Koko Tate." I held out my card.

"Mmm, private investigator. What can I do for you, Mr Tate?"

"I'm investigating the theft of a book from the private collection of Mr James Baker." I pulled my pad and the photograph out and held it in front of him. "A Bible. Recognize it?"

"Yes." He said it with a slight tremor.

I sat on the edge of the table to Hooper's left before he got the chance to stand. "I understand that you sold him the book?" I returned the photograph to my pocket, watching Hooper's eyes follow it all the way.

"That's correct."

"You remember it very easily."

"Well, I… I only sold it to him last week."

It was hot, but not that hot. Telltale trickles of sweat coursed down the sides of Hooper's face. I held off asking another question and studied the scribbles on my yellow pad, looking up every few seconds. The trickles were getting thicker. "How did you know about Charles Waring's death?"

"Wha… I thought you were here to talk about Baker's burglary?"

"I am," I said. My mention of Charles Waring had startled him, but not in any defensive way. "It's just that Mr Baker told me about Mr Waring's death and I… well, I wondered how you'd managed to find out about the accident so fast."

Hooper shuffled in his straight-backed chair and smiled. "I have my contacts, Mr Tate."

"Police?"

He frowned, but allowed a small smile. "There's no law against that, is there?"

"None that I know of." I looked back at the pad. "You specialize in this kind of book?"

Hooper closed one eye and rubbed it. "Well, yes, theological and religious works…and some history."

"You keep other types of books though?"

"Oh yes, I keep all types, except fiction." He spat the word out as if it were infested with maggots.

"How much is the book worth?"

He turned up his mouth and shrugged. "Four, five hundred dollars. What Baker paid me for it."

"Could it be worth any more?"

"I don't follow you." Hooper's top lip was glistening now, and he licked at it with his tongue.

"I mean, could you have made a mistake? Could it, maybe, be some kind of special edition that made it worth even more than you charged Baker?"

He shook his head, then rubbed his eye again.

I folded my pad and slipped it into my inside pocket — with the photograph — gave a big smile and made to move. Hooper returned the smile and moved forward in his seat. As I stood up I said, "Has anyone ever made inquiries for such a book? Either before Waring's death or after?"

The eye gave him more problems. He shook his head again and added a croaky 'no', just for good measure.

I thanked him and told him to give me a ring if anyone did. Or if he remembered anything that might prove helpful. I left him beamed in a smile that looked as though it might fall right off his face at any moment. I wished I could have been there when it did.

Charlie Bieglemann was eating when he answered the phone. The word he said sounded like 'Beeklemop', and I half imagined I heard the soft *plop* of a wedge of Yonah Shminel knish or blueberry cheese bagel landing in the mouthpiece. Charlie's was a very staple diet.

"Charlie, it's Koko."

"Hey, how's it hanging, Koke?" he said around munches.

"Limp," I said. "Charlie, a favor."

"You ever call me for anything else?"

"The Charles Waring case. You handling it?"

"The Charles Waring *case*? I miss something? Where's the case, Koke? Guy falls off of his ladder, takes half of the top of his head off on the corner of his table." I heard him drinking. "That's it. The guy's history."

"You involved?"

"I got out there, sure. What's your interest?"

I told him.

"I think you're out of the grounds on this one, Koke. Old dame finds the guy—"

"Elicia Barnes?"

"She the assistant?"

"Yes. What's she like?"

"Granny Slocum in nice clothes." He did another *sluurrrp*, and went on. "Yeah, she finds him sprawled on the floor beside the table, blood everywhere, including the corner of the table. That's it."

"Nothing missing?"

I could sense him shaking his head. "She checked. Everything had a place and everything was in it."

I tried to imagine it. Guy falls off a ladder, lands on the corner of the table. "The table, Charlie. What kind of a table?"

What kind? How do *I* know what kind of a table? It was a table."

"You see it? When you went out there?"

"Yeah, I saw it. Blood on the corner. Sharp corner. Covered in books — "

"Covered in books? Waring or the table?"

"The table," he snapped in exasperation. "Apparently Waring used to pile books on the table, ready for filing them into the main collection."

"What did they look like? The piles of books?'

"Just piles of books. What're you getting at here?"

"Any of them fallen over?"

Charlie Bieglemann went quiet. "No," he said at last. "They were all just the way he'd piled them up." He suddenly sounded tired. "Can I finish my lunch now?"

The woman who answered the door wore a smart bottle-green two-piece over a lime-green ruffle-necked blouse, smart green suede shoes, and a cheek that looked as if it had stopped a Willie Mays fly ball. The bruise had closed her right eye and spread all the way around to her ear. I had to hand it to her as far as color coordination was concerned. I figured it was about a week old. A few days earlier she would have worn purple. "Don't tell me," I said, "you fell over making an omelet."

"Who're you?"

"Tate. Koko Tate. It's short for Kokorian."

She frowned.

"It's Transylvanian. But don't worry, I only bite at night."

"What do you want?"

"Are you Ella Thornley?"

She looked at me.

"I'm a private detective, Mrs Thornley. I wonder if I might come in and ask you a few questions."

"What about?"

"A burglary. Can we talk inside?"

"Do you have any ID?"

I pulled out a card, which she accepted without reading. She opened the door and nodded for me to go in. I went.

"How did you get it? The bruise."

"I fell over making an omelet." She smiled.

"Kitchens," I said, shaking my head. "Dangerous places."

"You do a lot of cooking?'

"Only when I'm hungry."

She sat on the back of a Parker-Knoll suite that looked as though it cost someone a year's salary, and lifted her foot onto the edge of a coffee table. Suddenly, she had a lot of legs. "You hungry now?"

"Not while I'm on duty, ma'am."

She laughed gently and threw back her hair. "What do you want, Mr Tate?"

I smiled and pointed to her leg. "Well, for starters, I'd like it if you took your foot off the table. Those things mark easy. *You* should know that."

She removed her foot and walked across the floor to a breakfast bar that separated the room we were in from the kitchen. The two-piece fitted where it touched, and it touched a lot of places. As she walked, I lost about ten pounds. She picked up a pack of Chesterfields and shook one out. "You're here to talk about my father?" She lit the cigarette with a match and made a big deal out of shaking it dead. "Or my husband?"

"What makes you think it might be about your father?"

She smiled the kind of smile you give at the supermarket checkout when you've spotted that you've just been shortchanged. "The cheap crack about the coffee table."

"Oh, you got that."

"I got it."

"Sorry."

She laughed again. "Don't mention it." She moved back toward me and let out a genuine smile. "Look, come and sit down. Tell me what it is you want to know."

I walked to a chair you could have held a small party in and sat, crossed my legs. "I'm trying to find a book for my client, Mrs Thornley."

"Ella," she corrected. She plopped down on the couch up alongside of me.

I nodded. "A Bible. One of your father's books. My client bought it from a dealer name of Hooper. Now the book's gone AWOL. You know Hooper?"

"Yes, he telephoned me the day my father died. He bought a whole load of books from the collection."

"How come they were yours to sell?"

She blew out a column of smoke and frowned. "Pardon me?"

"I mean, how come you were able to sell the books so quickly? Didn't you have to wait for the will to be proven and all that stuff?"

"Oh, I see." She stubbed her cigarette out in a large bronze ashtray. "My father had made it so that the books immediately went to me. I always said I'd sell them straight away. He knew that and said he wouldn't mind because he wouldn't be here."

"Did you...did you and your father get on...Ella?"

"Very much. We didn't always see eye-to-eye about a lot of things, Mr Tate, but then that isn't unusual."

"One of those things your husband?"

She nodded and shifted her gaze down to her feet. "Daddy always felt that I was worth more."

"And were you?"

She looked up quickly. I couldn't tell what she was wanting to say.

"He do that?" I pointed to her cheek.

She reached up and gave it a gentle rub. "Doesn't hurt anymore," she said.

"But it did."

"It did, yes."

"Why?"

"Why did it hurt?"

"Why did he do it?"

"Because I'd sold some of the books. Because I'd sold them before I'd discussed it with him. He said that if we'd waited, we could have got a better price."

"Why *did* you sell them so quickly?"

"Because I knew he needed money."

"But won't there be a lot of money from your father's estate?"

She shook off her shoes and tucked her legs beneath her on the couch. "Yes, but that will take time. Jimmy doesn't have a lot of time...at least not as far as this particular transaction goes."

"What — "

"I really don't want to say anything more about that, Mr Tate. I've probably said too much already."

I lifted my hands to say that was okay. "Did anyone else ask about the books?"

"Oh, a lot of people. People who had been on at Daddy for years. I sold everything within a week. Got a good price, I think. Anyway, I didn't want things hanging around."

"Anyone ask about one particular book?"

She shrugged and then shook her head. "No, they were all dealers — there were a couple of collectors, but even they just bought whole shelves full so they could use the books in trade." She ran her fingers through her hair and grabbed at one thick strand. "My father's collection was highly sought after."

"So I understand."

We sat for a minute, her looking at me, me watching her fiddle with that strand of hair.

"You sure you're not hungry?"

"Yeah," I said, "I'm hungry." I stood up. "Guess I'd better go get something to eat."

She followed me to the door and held it open for me. As I stepped out she said, "Thanks for calling, Mr Tate."

"Thanks?"

She smiled at me. "You made me laugh. I don't laugh very much, Mr Tate."

"Call me Koke," I said.

She nodded a soft slow nod and let the smile become embarrassed. "See you sometime."

"Yeah," I said. When the door slammed, I was halfway down the corridor, looking for a cold shower.

When the first call came in, I had just turned on the television. I'd been waiting for this movie all week — one of my favorites, and my *absolute* favorite western, *The Man Who Shot Liberty Valance*. I'd missed the beginning so I wasn't in the best of moods. But I was starting to feel better. I was halfway through a Sbarro pizza laced with double anchovies, and working my way through my second Lone Star beer. Jimmy Stewart had just picked up John Wayne's steak and slapped it on the table and everyone was pissed off: Wayne because he wanted Lee Marvin to pick it up; Marvin because he wanted Wayne to pick it up; Stewart because he thought they were both a couple of kids; me because the goddamn telephone was ringing.

"This better be good," I barked. It was a little before eleven.

"It *was* good," Charlie Bieglemann said. "Now it's gone all to hell in a hand-cart."

"Charlie?"

"I thought you'd like to know. I finished my lunch."

I laughed. "What else?"

"You got me thinking. I had Forensic check the table. No grain damage, no tissue, no nothing. Hardest thing it had been hit with is a napkin."

"What about the blood?"

"Smeared on."

"The thick plottens," I said.

"This isn't good, Koke. We should've checked all this stuff out a couple weeks ago."

"Hey, you're doing it now, Charlie."

He grunted. "I'll be getting back to you if I get anything more." He waited. "You do the same, huh?"

"Count on it," I told him.

"I am."

When the second call came, Lee Marvin had just worked over Edmond O'Brien and things were hotting up.

"Jesus Christ!" I snapped into the mouthpiece.

"No, it's Ella Thornley," Ella Thornley said.

It was one of those moments when you wished you could have the last thirty seconds back and then you could go dig a hole and bury them. "Just a second, you want Koko," I said, and I turned away from the mouthpiece and yelled my name as loud as I could. Then I turned back and said, "Koko Tate?"

She was laughing.

"Sorry," I said. "I'm making a habit of apologising to you."

"I like it," she said, still laughing. "Listen, we had a call earlier tonight. I picked up the phone because I didn't think Jimmy had heard it." She paused.

Jimmy Stewart was strapping on a gun. "Yeah, I'm listening."

"It was Hooper."

"The dealer?"

"But he was ringing Jimmy. He was telling him he had something that he thought Jimmy wanted. Jimmy heard me on the extension and told me to get off the line."

"He said that?"

"He said, 'Get the fuck off the line, Ella'."

"Sweet talker."

"You don't know the half of it."

"So you don't know what else he said... Hooper?"

"No. But Jimmy paced around here for a while, drank a couple of Scotches and then went out."

"How long ago?"

"About a half an hour. I waited to make sure he wasn't just going to come right back in before I called you."

"He say where he was going?"

"No. Well, for a drink, he said."

"Okay, thanks."

"Does it mean anything?"

"No, but I never let a little thing like that stop me when I'm hot on the scent."

"That's one you owe me," she said. "Next time you call, bring your appetite."

When I replaced the receiver, I was opening and closing my mouth like a goldfish.

The night streets in the Village were a lot like the one Jimmy Stewart was walking down when I switched off the television — hot, oppressive, and dangerous. I pulled my Toyota onto a piece of sidewalk in front of a huge roll-up metal door bearing the words IN USE DAY AND NIGHT and got out. There was nobody around.

Hooper's Books was a single-window store along the street on the left. It looked closed and deserted, but then so did the rest of the street. Somewhere over the buildings I heard a police car, its lonesome wail joined by several car horns. I waited until the sound died away, heading uptown, and then walked along to the store.

Right away I could see things were not good. The door was partially open, stopped from closing by a solitary book whose pages had foxed and bent in a wedge beneath the door. Inside, the store looked dark and intimidating. I picked up the book and looked at the spine: *The Modernist Impulse in American Protestantism* by William R Hutchison. One of the many that hadn't made the *New York Times* best-seller list.

I looked behind me, then pulled out my .38 police special and checked the clip. Leaning against the side window, I pushed gently at the door and watched it drift open. Beyond was pure blackness, giving nothing away. I stepped inside and moved to the right. Moving to the left would have put the window behind me, ideal for target practice. I strained to hear anything, but there was nothing. I waited.

It must have been ten minutes later that I said, "Hooper?" as quietly as I could. There was no response. I said it louder. Nothing. This was it. I slipped the gun back in my waistband and pushed the door closed, hard. A little bell on the top jingled, but there was nobody there to hear. Walking crouched down, I moved along in front of the window to the far wall. The floor was littered with books. "Hooper? You in here?"

I stood up and backed along the wall until I felt a box suddenly jab into my back — light switches. I ran my hand down the switches and watched the spectacle unfold before me.

It looked like Berlin must've looked just before the war, when they dropped truckloads of books onto spare ground and burned the lot. Hooper's store was like that; all that was missing was a guy with gasoline and matches.

The store was divided into four corridors, or, at least, it had been once. Now it was a shambles of books and shelving scattered across the floor and partially burying the crumpled body of Edgar Hooper. At first I thought he was watching me, then I wondered why his face looked so strange. As I stepped over toward him, I saw that he was eating a book. I pulled out a handkerchief, crouched down, and wrapping the handkerchief around my hand, I prised the book free. As I pulled it out, a thick pool of blood bubbled once, up into his mouth, and spilled over his cheeks and his chin. The book was *The Literary Man's Bible* by WL Courtney. Who said humor was dead?

I lifted the books from him gently and carefully, the way I figure he'd have wanted me to — not for his sake but for the books'. After a while, I saw that someone had pulled down his pants and his shorts. Checking him over, trying to ignore the number of bruises and the swelling of his battered genitals, I noticed that, although he was lying flat on the floor, his body was arched in the middle. I removed a few more books and turned him over. The book lodged in his backside was *The Social Gospel in America*, edited by Robert T Handy. I pulled it out with the covered hand, trying not to look at the mess it had made, and laid it with *The Literary Man's Bible* over by the door.

A few minutes later, Hooper's dignity restored, I climbed back into my Toyota and started the engine. Beside me on the seat was a book-size, handkerchief-wrapped package. Ahead of me Hooper's store was again in darkness.

He opened the door and glared. "Who're you?"

"Koko Tate," I said.

"Tough shit," he snapped and slammed the door in my face.

I rang the bell again. The door opened, and he took a step into the corridor. "Look, you got a problem, fella?"

I shook my head and smiled. "Uh-uhh."

He looked me up and down, hesitating at the package I held. I did the same with him. He was wearing a white shirt, open at the neck, a pair of expensive light-tweed pants, and what looked like Gucci loafers. But then anything made out of leather looks like Gucci loafers to me. I double-checked the pants for any telltale bulges that might prove troublesome later. There were none. A gold identity bracelet hung from his wrist. I leaned forward and tilted my head on one side. "Jim-my," I read. I straightened up and said, "Hey, I used to have one of those, but now I remember who I am all the time."

Ella Thornley appeared at the door behind him. When she saw me, she said, "Oh, Mr Tate, come in."

I brushed past her husband while he tried to think of something cute to say and went into the apartment, checking over my shoulder to see if there was anything jammed into his waistband at the back. All clear.

Her face was bruised on both sides now, her top lip puffed out and hanging over the bottom one. It looked sore. I turned around as Jimmy Thornley was closing the door. "You do this?" I asked him.

"What if I did?"

"Don't you know it's not polite to hit a lady?"

He smiled and punched his right hand into his left. If it hurt him, he didn't show it. "You want I should hit you instead?"

"I want you should try," I said.

"Jimmy," Ella Thornley said, "please. Mr Tate was here earlier to ask about a theft."

"A theft?" His eyes brightened up. I had the feeling it was maybe one of the few crimes he genuinely knew nothing about. He let his arms drop to his sides and ruffled his hair. "Look, I'm sorry..." He searched for my name. I let him search. "It's been a real tough night, and I had a few drinks, you know how it is," he added with a conspiratorial all-guys-together smile.

"I'm learning," I said.

He shrugged, ruffled his hair some more, and walked over to a well-stocked bar. As he reached for a bottle of Jim Beam, he said, "So, a theft, huh? How can we help?"

"You know a fella name of Hooper?"

I was impressed. His hand never faltered. "You want one of these?" he asked, eyebrows raised.

I shook my head. "He's a book dealer."

He took a sip of the whiskey and frowned. "Hooper... Hooper. No, I don't believe I do. Should I?"

"I guess so. I just been over to see him. He's had an...accident."

He ran a sad look at me. "That's too bad. Serious?"

"He wasn't laughing when I left him," I said, watching Thornley take another drink. "But he did say a few words."

Thornley looked up sharply and a thin trail of whiskey ran down his chin. I nodded to it and said, "You should try a Tommy Tippee catch-all bib. They're real good. I used to use them myself...about thirty years ago."

"You're real funny, Tate. I'm beginning to worry these pants'll never dry."

"I try," I said, turning to shrug at Ella Thornley.

"So, what'd he say, this...Hooper?"

"He says he rang you to tell you a book you'd expressed an interest in had turned up after all. He'd managed to get a copy for you. Special book."

"Yeah?" He nodded to the package. "That it?"

I held up the two books in my handkerchief, and Ella Thornley gasped. The handkerchief was kind of discolored. "These?" I shook my head and rested them on my left hand, opening the handkerchief with my right. "No, these I took from Mr Hooper to help his breathing and...and the general passing of air. But now that I've done that, you have a problem."

Thornley took another sip, realized the glass was almost empty, and reached for the bottle. "I've had it with you, Tate," he said. "I think you'd better go. Now!"

"No!" Ella Thornley snapped the word into the air, and both Thornley and I turned to face her. "I want to hear about my husband's problem."

"His problem is this, Mrs Thornley. I think your husband killed Charles Waring. I think he battered his head in with an antique Bible, then he set the body up to look like he'd fallen from the ladder and hit his head on the corner of his desk."

Thornley stood, watching me impassively. I caught him glance across at his wife once, then take another sip.

I turned to face Thornley and went on. "You smeared his blood over the corner of the desk and put the book back on the shelf. You couldn't take the book with you because you were worried Waring's assistant might notice it was missing. Then she'd know his death wasn't an accident. You figured you'd go back for the book later." I turned to Ella Thornley. "He had to go back because, although he probably wiped it clean, there's always a danger it'll hold traces of blood and tissue. Particularly this book, Mrs Thornley. It has metallic corner guards attached to the leather and...well, things could have got trapped in there."

I put my own two books on the arm of one of the chairs, undid my jacket and stepped to my left, away from Ella Thornley, still talking to her, but now watching Thornley. "So, he's done the murder, and he gets out of the way setting up alibis, just in case. When he gets back, you've already sold some of the books, including the murder weapon. This does not make him happy." I jabbed my finger into my cheek and gave her a quick glance.

"So he goes around to see Hooper and looks through the piles of books he bought from you. The Bible was the only one of your father's books that Hooper had sold, so that had to be what your husband was looking for. And, worst of all, Hooper recognized him." I stopped for a second. "How'm I doing?"

"Pure *Twilight Zone*," Thornley said and drained his glass.

I checked the room. One door behind me — the one I came in at — two doors over on the far wall, breakfast bar over on my right. I took a breath. "At this stage Hooper gets greedy, figures he maybe screwed up on the Bible, and it was worth a lot more than the four-fifty he charged Baker. He knows Baker won't sell him the book back, so he decides to steal it. This he does. He checks and checks the book, can't find how it could be worth more than he originally estimated. He looks and he looks. Eventually, the inevitable happens and he realizes why the book is valuable to your husband. I'm sorry, Mrs Thornley."

She shook her head, her finger jammed between her teeth to stop from crying. Maybe stop her doing other things, too.

"So, tonight, he calls your husband. Tells him he has the book and that it's for sale, at the right price. Jimmy here goes around to try persuade him to let the book go for no money at all. He batters the guy to a pulp. Jams books down his throat and up his ass until Hooper tells him where the Bible is. He leaves him for dead." I turned to Thornley and wagged my finger side to side. "Your first real mistake, asshole, and it happens more than you'd realize," I said, leaning toward the wall. "Right now, he's over at St Vincent's, getting emergency treatment to his rectum and larynx, talking to a friend of mine who wears a badge and eats kosher pizza."

Thornley put down the glass and rubbed his hands together.

"Jimmy," Ella Thornley said.

How could so much exhaustion, so much disappointment, and so much hatred get itself tangled up in one little word?

"Where's the Bible, Jimmy?" I said. "Time to make your peace with God."

Thornley moved fast.

He leaped forward, pulled the two books I'd brought around off the chair, and in one fluid movement tossed them straight at me. I was already moving toward him. I ducked and one of the books missed me completely. The other hit me right on the bridge of the nose, and I went down seeing whole galaxies. Somewhere off to one side, Ella Thornley screamed, and I rolled over fumbling for my gun. There was a crash and a sudden, overwhelming smell of whiskey. Everything went quiet for a second, and then the floor alongside me shook as Thornley came to keep me company. I opened my eyes and looked into three or four images of his face, all of them desperately trying to pull themselves together.

Thornley's face was a little below mine, his eyes closed, his hair soaked in a mixture of alcohol and blood. I turned around and looked up at Ella Thornley, standing beside the chair, swaying slightly, the jagged neck of a Jim Beam bottle in her right hand. Just a couple of seconds later, we were all on the floor.

First dates can be hell, but wakes can be worse.

This was a little of both.

The damage to Ella Thornley's face had healed up, and I'd taken her up on her suggestion that I unleash my appetite, but only after pacing around my apartment, glaring at the telephone for more than a week.

Jimmy Thornley had never regained consciousness, and I'd told her it was probably for the best. Saved the taxpayers a little money, at least. She'd hit him a good blow across the side of the head, fracturing his skull right on the temple — transected an artery. The clot started to compress the brain. They tried to operate, but it was hopeless; less than forty-eight hours after he'd been crowned with Jim Bean whiskey, Jimmy Thornley moved on to a new address — cause of death, subdural hematoma. He died with her at his side.

I told her to tell people it was drink that killed him in the end.

James Baker got his Bible back and immediately arranged for a specialist to remove the brass binding for cleaning. He was delighted, and his check showed it. Time to celebrate.

The Mon Hueng Seafood House is tucked away on a little side street off Canal Street. Once I'd decided on Chinese food, it had been a toss-up whether to go for Mon Hueng or Sam Wo's — Woody Allen rated Sam Wo's crabs so highly that he even shot some of *Manhattan* there, but the footage ended up on the cutting-room floor — but, in the end, I'd gone for Mon Hueng's.

We'd both started off with snails in garlic and black bean sauce — she said she would if I would, and I said I would if she would…which made me excited and nervous, both at the same time — and then I'd had stir-fried crabs Cantonese, with minced pork, more black beans, and soft egg gravy. She said one plate of fish — "Snails...*fish*?" I said — was enough and went instead for a deep dish of 'jeah jeah' chicken — the 'jeah jeah' is the sound it makes as it's sauteed — with mixed Chinese vegetables.

Over our impressively empty plates Ella Thornley said, "You know what day it is?"

"My lucky one?"

She smiled gently. "Father's Day."

"Oh."

"Yeah, 'oh'." She moved her finger around the rim of her glass and made a soft, far-off hum that sounded like fairies singing. "Is your father still alive?"

"Nope."

"You miss him?"

"I never really think about it...missing him, I mean. But, sure, yeah, I guess I miss him. You only get the one."

"I was thinking about that film, Kevin Costner...it was about baseball, but it wasn't, if you know what I mean."

"*Field of Dreams*," I said. "Good movie, great book."

"It was a book?"

"*Shoeless Joe*. It was written by a guy called WP Kinsella."

"Lovely movie."

I nodded and mashed my napkin into an even smaller bundle.

"That was all about his father, wasn't it?"

"Yeah, about fathers and relationships and generally growing older. All those things." Her eyes avoided looking at me, but I could still see the shine of the lights reflected in their moisture. "It's right you should feel sad," I said. "Particularly so soon after and it being a special day."

"That's just it," she said, leaning toward me. "Every day should be special while they're here."

"They should, but they're not. You take them for granted. You know what they say: you don't miss your water till your well runs dry."

She didn't respond. Just sat there. Outside, a siren wailed.

"Let's have a drink to them."

"Our fathers?"

"Sure, why not?"

She shrugged. "Seems silly. Morbid."

"Needn't be. Death is only morbid to the living. To the dead, it's a way of life."

Her laugh was a long time coming, but when it arrived, it brought the tears with it.

Over coffee and bourbon we sat and talked until past one, when the waiters sat down at one of the little Formica tables over by the window and ate from bowls — containing delicacies that might have looked good to me about four hours earlier — as if they were in a race, chopsticks traveling the two or three inches from dish to mouth, and clattering in time to their incessant chatter.

We talked more about fathers and the special places they hold in your heart. We talked about their silences and their sternness, about how they guided us and helped us, and I told her many things that I hadn't told anyone else before... things I should have remembered earlier.

Then we talked some more about our favorite movies — turned out she was a big fan of Jimmy Stewart, so I knew we were off to a good start — and how something had to be done about the Park in the summertime...and, later, in a mixture of silence and the gentle movements that only two people who really know each other can do, we talked about the kind of jazz that cools down hot apartments.

We never mentioned books once. ∎

A crowd armed with staves gathered in front of St Mary's Church, Oxford. Men wearing hats strung with green ribbon handed out leaflets depicting the Catholic Duke of York with horns and a tail, setting fire to London. One of their number ascended the steps to address the crowd: "Shall England be subject to the whim of Louis? Shall proud English men be slaves to the will of France and the Devil that sits in Rome?"

"No!" the crowd replied.

"No slavery! No popery!" the men distributing the leaflets prompted the crowd. Immediately they took up the chant, "No slavery! No popery!"

"Look!" said the man at the top of the stairs, pointing. An ornate coach came into view, heading towards Christchurch, where the court was in residence while Parliament met in the university city. The sole occupant of the coach was a woman. Chestnut ringlets framed the heart-shaped face beneath her large round-brimmed bonnet, a copy of the latest style from France. Her dress was copied from the French court's style as well: wine-red satin with a white lace collar, cut low. Around her neck she wore a chain of pearls set in gold. At the sight of her, the crowd went berserk. "It's Madam Carwell herself! The Catholic whore who poisons the mind of the king!"

Someone shouted, "Death to the Catholic whore!" The mob surged towards the coach, repeating "Death to the Catholic whore!"

The coach was quickly surrounded; the crowd rocked it back and forth, baying for the blood of the Catholic whore. The woman inside it took a deep breath and opened the window. "I pray you good people, be civil," she said. "I am the *Protestant* whore."

The man closest to the window shouted to those around him, "Stop it, you fools, it's Nell Gwyn!" He turned back to the woman in the carriage, "Please forgive us, Mistress Gwyn. We thought you were the Duchess of Portsmouth."

The crowd stepped aside and allowed the carriage to continue on its way.

It was the 28th of March, 1681.

Nell walked into the hall at Christchurch, made her way up the stairs, and paused outside the king's private chamber. She knocked on the door, ruffled her hair, and struck a dramatic pose, gasping for breath and clinging to the wall.

The door was opened by Louise Renee de Keroualle, the Duchess of Portsmouth, dubbed Madam Carwell by the common people who could not pronounce her name. "Mon dieu, Nellie," she said, "You do look a mess. Have you been back at your old profession?" She turned to the king, who was lying asleep on a sofa on the other side of the room, dressed in red knee-length velvet breeches and nothing else. A long black wig hung from a hook on the wall; the king's head was bare, revealing the close crop of his own hair, which was now more grey than black. "Charles, the ageing orange-girl is here to see you."

The king opened his eyes; he leapt up and rushed to the door. "Odd's fish," he said, placing one arm around Nell. He led her over to the sofa and had her sit down beside him. "Nellie, what happened?"

"I was nearly murdered by a mob, Sir."

"What?"

"It's true, Sir. They wanted to tear me limb from limb."

Charles pressed her face into his bare shoulder and gently patted her head. "There, there, my poor darling. It must have been dreadful for you."

Across the room, the Duchess of Portsmouth drew her mouth into a thin line and crossed her arms. She cleared her throat loudly.

Nell raised her head and looked straight into Charles's eyes, her own open wide and sparkling with mischief. "No Sir, indeed I thought it quite wonderful, really." She indicated the Duchess of Portsmouth with a tilt of her head. "They thought I was her."

"Nellie, for shame," the king said, stifling a laugh. Louise de Keroualle ran from the room, slamming the door behind her.

"Now that's done it," Charles said. "There'll be no peace in court for a week."

Molly Brown writes in genres including science fiction, fantasy, mainstream and crime. Her novels include *Virus*, a science fiction thriller for teenagers; *Cracker: To Say I Love You*, a novelisation based on the Granada television series *Cracker*, by Jimmy McGovern; and *Invitation To A Funeral*, a humorous historical whodunnit featuring Aphra Behn and Nell Gwyn. A feature film based on her short story 'Bad Timing' is currently in development at Twentieth Century Fox, and she is webmistress of a multiple award-winning online tour of Restoration London (www.okima.com/). 'The Lemon Juice Plot' was originally published in *Royal Crimes*, edited by Maxim Jakubowski and Martin H Greenberg (Signet, 1994).

When Nell returned to her own room, her maid presented her with a sealed envelope, addressed to Mistress Eleanor Gwyn. Though the message was brief, Nell spent several minutes staring at its contents, frowning in deep concentration. Completely illiterate when she first came to court, she still found reading a slow and difficult business. Finally, she threw the letter on the fire and instructed her maid to pack her belongings immediately, she was returning to London.

It was a moonless night. Two men carried a sedan chair through the twisted streets and alleys off Drury Lane, preceded by a linkman with a lantern. Young boys carrying long hooked rods scattered, exposed by the light. Passing beneath an open window, the chair was splattered with the contents of a chamber pot.

When the chair turned into Lewkenor's Lane, the lantern became the cause of much consternation and cursing from the shadows — more than one couple hastily rearranged their clothing at the approach of the chair. The chair came to a stop, and Nell Gwyn stepped out, her face hidden by a mask. "Wait for me," she said.

She approached one of the houses and knocked. The woman who answered the door reeked of strong ale and old perspiration. "Lost your way, dearie?"

"I wish to speak to Madam Ross."

"Looking for a job, dearie? We'll have to see what's underneath that mask first, won't we? Your figure looks well, but your face may be scarred by the pox for all we know."

A short, thick-necked woman came to the door and pushed the other aside. "Come in," she said, "we can talk upstairs." The thick-necked woman's hair was grey and so thin her scalp showed through it; in length it barely reached her shoulders. Her nose was large, threaded with blue and red veins, her eyes were bloodshot, and she had no teeth. Nell followed her through a noisy front room, crowded as any tavern. The air was heavy with a mix of cheap perfume, smoke, and the smell of raw sewage. Raising a small lace handkerchief to her nose, she struggled to hold her breath.

As she passed, one man, who already had a woman sitting on one knee, called out that he had another knee ready and waiting at her service, and knees weren't all he had to offer. "Your loss," he muttered as she kept walking.

"Why the mask, Nellie?" the thick-necked woman asked when they were alone in an upstairs room, furnished with nothing but a bed and two chairs. "You were raised in a house much like this one. Are you too grand to be seen with the likes of us now?"

Nell removed the mask and flopped into one of the chairs. "Too grand?" She shook her head. "No, not I. But there are those who would use my visit here against me if they were to learn of it. I should have travelled to Windsor with the court now Parliament is dissolved, but I begged his Majesty to allow me return to London as a dear friend was ill. So please, Madam Ross, tell me what matter of life and death is so urgent that I must lie to the king and jeopardise my position at court."

"Just a minute. I must fetch someone first." She left the room and returned a few moments later, accompanied by an old man. His knee-length frock coat and breeches were made of coarse, dark brown cloth; his stockings and his shoes were caked with mud. The fingers of his right-hand glove were nearly worn through. The man's grey hair was lank and greasy, hanging well below his shoulders, but his posture was straight and his eyes were alert and intelligent.

He smiled broadly, revealing a full mouth of tobacco-stained teeth. "If it isn't little Nellie! My, what a fine lady you've become."

Nell stared at him blankly.

"You haven't forgotten me, have you? Thomas Shaw? I knew your mother when you were a child."

"Thomas? Of course I remember! I must have been five or six years old, and my father was in prison and my mother had no money, and my sister and I might have died of the cold had you not brought us coal for the fire and socks for our feet. How could I ever forget such kindness?"

"Madam Ross said you would not forget an old friend and she was right."

"What can I do for you, Thomas?"

"I would never ask you for money, though a few shillings from one in your position — who surely must have pounds to spare — would not be unappreciated. No, there is another reason for requiring your presence so urgently. I have something to tell you of great importance: Madam Ross and I believe we have uncovered a plot."

Nell rolled her eyes and threw up her hands. "God's flesh, not another plot! His Majesty is sick to death of plots. I am sick to death of plots. *Everyone* is sick to death of plots! Thanks to Lord Shaftesbury and his informer, Mr Titus Oates, we've heard of nothing but plots and conspiracies for three years now! What, pray tell, are the Pope and the Duke of York up to this time? Thanks to good Mr Oates, we now know the Papists set fire to London, and we know they were responsible for the plague. So what will their next trick be? Are the Jesuits secretly draining the Thames dry? Or perhaps the French plan to invade by digging a tunnel beneath the Channel! Surely that's no more ridiculous than anything the Whigs would have the people believe."

"Hush, Nellie, and listen," said Madam Ross. "Thomas has found something in a book."

"A book? Is Thomas a man to read books?"

"I have it here," said Thomas. He reached into his coat pocket and handed a small leatherbound book to her. The cover was charred black and the pages within were singed at the edges. "I'm afraid it's slightly burnt."

"Why? What happened to it?"

Thomas cleared his throat. "When I first came upon it, the pages within were blank. I thought it worthless and tossed it on the fire. The book fell open and in the heat I saw writing appear on the pages as if by magic, so I fetched it out again."

Nell raised one eyebrow. "Magic? The traitor Coleman used lemon juice."

The old man shrugged. "Just look, and you will see why the writing was hidden."

Nell slowly made her way through several pages, moving her lips and pointing to each word with one finger. On the first page were inscribed the words: 'To my most kind patron, a record of my experiments.' The rest was in the form of a diary, with scribbled entries beneath each day's date. Much of it was incomprehensible; it appeared to be written in a foreign language. Other pages were covered with nothing but rows of numbers and strange symbols. But then she came upon a roughly-sketched map of Whitehall and the words: 'Have made contact with one in her service. Price 200. Obtain from L.S.?' There were two X's, a short distance apart on the map; Nell recognised the locations they marked. An entry dated 18th March read: 'Parliament to Ox. C. remains London. Meet C. tonight.' Under 20th March were the words: 'C. instructed in knife. Before king and others? Best way to avoid suspicion. Must wait for return of court.' The final entry was for 26th March, the previous Saturday: 'To my sister in Essex. Back Friday to meet C.'

Nell Gwyn

Nell looked up, her lips pursed in thought.

"Don't you see, Nellie?" said Thomas. "They plan to kill the king. With a knife, in the very heart of Whitehall palace! See how they've marked his quarters with an X?"

"Surely such intelligence is worth something," said Madam Ross, "and there's the proof in writing. Is not the king generous to friends who would save his life?"

"If this is what you think, then why summon me? Why not take this to a magistrate?" Nell asked, removing several coins from her purse.

"A magistrate would ask me where I got it."

She held the coins just beyond the old man's reach. "And do you really believe I will not ask the same question myself, Thomas?"

The next morning, Nell took a coach to the home of the playwright Aphra Behn.
Nell sank into a thickly padded sofa while Aphra studied the charred diary at a

desk beside the window. At the age of forty, the playwright's light brown hair was already streaked with grey and her once-round face had begun to sag, forming deep creases on either side of her mouth.

Nell closed her eyes and found her thoughts wandering back to the days when she was the seventeen-year-old toast of the Drury Lane stage whose face and wit had captured the heart of a king. She was thirty-one now, and suddenly she felt very tired. Her eyes fluttered open at the sound of Aphra's voice, "I use blank books such as this to do my own writing. But the contents of this journal are most strange. Wherever did you come across this curious volume?"

"I was given it by an angler who sent me a message through Madam Ross, begging me to return to London at once."

"An angler? One of those rogues who push hooked rods through open windows? Let me understand this. A common thief summons you to London and you abandon the King of England to keep the appointment?"

"He believes the book refers to a plot..."

"A plot! That's original," Aphra interrupted dryly.

"...against the life of the king," Nell continued, ignoring her, "and Madam Ross agrees with him."

Aphra threw her hands up. "If a thief and a brothel-keeper believe it, then it must be true."

"But the layout of the map concerns me," Nell carried on, again ignoring the interruption. "Those X's on the map don't mark the king's apartments."

"Whose apartments do they mark then?"

Nell curled her upper lip. "Squintabella."

"Who?"

"Louise, the Duchess of Portsmouth."

Frowning, Aphra opened the book to the page with the map and carried it over to Nell. "If this X is her apartment, what is this X over here?"

"That's her kitchen — all the kitchens in Whitehall are separate from the residences. The king is building her a house, over here," she pointed at another part of the map, "because she says the twenty-four rooms she has now aren't good enough and if the king doesn't build her house exactly the way she wants it, she'll sob and she'll weep, and she'll make him pull it down and start all over again. That's what she did the last time. The king's rooms are over here, by the river. And this passage leads directly from His Majesty's bedchamber to those of the Maids of Honour. The Queen," she dragged her finger dramatically across the page, "lives at some distance, over here." She looked up expectantly. "What should I do, Aphra? Should I take this to the king?"

"This is all very thin, Nell; there's not much here at all. Page after page of gibberish, then a map and a few scribbled notes. We've already had the Popish Plot and the Meal Tub Plot, would you go to the king with a Lemon Juice Plot?"

"But it does mention a knife."

"So? We all own knives, my kitchen is full of them. Perhaps this is nothing but innocent scribbling, though there are other possibilities you might consider. Perhaps your supposed friends are not your friends at all. Perhaps they mean you harm and this is a hoax meant to discredit you, or even to incriminate you. If this book was truly obtained in the way you describe, are you not in possession of stolen property?"

"I do not believe Thomas and Madam Ross would treat me so ill. They both knew me from a child."

"Perhaps they are but unknowing pawns to another who plots against you. Are there none who resent your influence over the king? None who would be glad to see you banished from court?"

"There is one name that springs to mind. But though the weeping willow may have the desire, she has not the wit."

"But we must not forget one final possibility. Perhaps your friends are right, and the king is in danger."

"It makes me dizzy to consider so many possibilities."

"Then you must reduce them to only one: the truth."

"That I would do gladly. But how do I discover the truth? I have not the slightest idea how to gather intelligence. I have no experience of investigation." She paused for effect, watching Aphra's reaction. "But you do."

Aphra shook her head violently. "No," she said. "I cannot help you."

"But you were a spy in the war against Holland."

"And what did it benefit me? Nothing! My intelligence was ignored and I was never paid. I have sworn I would never be so used again."

"I'll do everything myself," Nell pleaded. "Just tell me where to begin."

"No," said Aphra. "Instead I will tell you where to stop. Here. And now. Suppose there *is* a plot? No one will believe you. And no one will thank you."

"They will believe me when I present them with proof!"

"That's what I thought, once. To be a spy is a thankless task, Nellie. I know this from cruel, hard experience."

"I care not what thanks I may receive. And I care not whether experience be cruel or hard. I care for the king, do you understand? Charles is surrounded by those who care only for what he can give them; be it position, power, money. I care only for the man. I love him, Aphra."

Aphra sighed and shook her head. "Let's get started then, shall we?"

"Is that the house?" Aphra asked as their coach pulled to a stop in front of a small house only two floors high, and extremely narrow.

Nell opened the window and stuck her head through. "I believe so," she said, turning back to Aphra. "This is the address Thomas gave me. He said he was here with his rod late Saturday night."

"I see a small window still open...up near the top," Aphra said. "Your friend Thomas's rod must be a long one."

"I assure you I've never seen it," Nell answered quickly.

"According to the diary, whoever lives here went to Essex on Saturday last and does not return until tomorrow. Let us see if this is true."

The two women disembarked from the coach and walked up to the door. Aphra knocked, and getting no reply, examined the downstairs front window. "No fear of running into servants. The shutter is filthy."

They walked through a narrow passage alongside the house. It led to a tiny back garden, planted with rows of herbs, surrounded by a high fence. The gate swung open at Aphra's touch, and she walked down a path to the house's back door. She ran one gloved finger along the frame. "Perfect," she said.

"Aphra!" Nell said, horrified. "I pray you're not thinking what I fear you're thinking?"

"In broad daylight, with the whole street having seen us and a coachman waiting out front? I wouldn't dream of anything so foolish," Aphra assured her. "We'll come back tonight."

At midnight they shared a jug of wine for courage and at half past the hour they left Aphra's house, dressed in clothing borrowed from the wardrobe of Aphra's late husband. Passing as men, with their breeches and long jackets and wide-brimmed hats, they travelled the dark streets on foot, unnoticed — something they never could have done in women's clothing. They walked the long way around, avoiding Covent Garden, which they knew would be full of brawling drunks, and eventually came to Holborn and the lane where the little house stood. The only light anywhere came from the upstairs window of a tavern a short way down and across the road.

Moving stealthily in near total darkness, they crept unseen into the passage and entered the high-walled garden. "There's still time to change your mind," Aphra whispered. Nell shook her head. Aphra reached into her pocket and took out a long thin piece of metal which she slid between the door and its frame.

They entered through the kitchen, wrinkling their noses at the smell. Some vegetables lay rotting in a basket on the floor; a joint of meat sat on a table, covered in

Frowning,
Aphra opened
the book to
the page with
the map and
carried it over
to Nell...

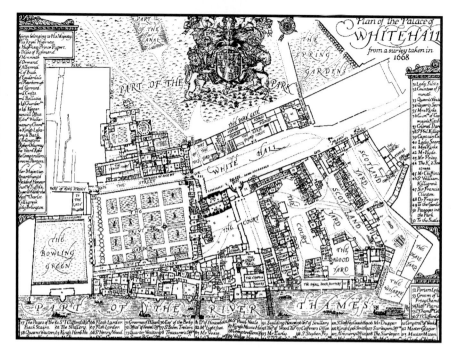

green mould, but the overpowering odour was not one of decaying food. Carrying lit candles, they walked past a rusting metal bath tub and into the tiny front room. The only furnishings were two wooden chairs and a sofa that had one corner propped up with bricks where there should have been a leg. They entered the hallway behind the front door and walked up creaking steps to the upper floor, the bad smell that permeated the house getting stronger.

In the rear they found a small bedroom; in the front they found a laboratory. The walls were lined with shelves, some piled high with thick leatherbound volumes, others displaying rows of glass bottles and jars, at least three deep. There was a table in the centre of the room, crowded with more bottles and jars and various arrangements of glass tubing. Nell held her candle up to one of the jars on the table and grimaced in disgust. It held a dead toad suspended in liquid. A label on the jar read 'venin de crapaud'. Other smaller jars were labelled Arsenic, Monkshood, Foxglove, Vitriol, Antimony, Prussic Acid.

By the window there was a desk, cluttered with notebooks and more bottles. Here they found the source of the smell: the bottle nearest the window had tipped over and shattered, spilling its contents over the desktop. The spillage had since dried, but it still gave off an acrid odour that burned the women's lungs.

"That's thanks to your friend Thomas and his hook," said Aphra, indicating the broken bottle. "So our friend the plotter is a chemist. That explains the pages of seeming gibberish — they were chemical formulations."

"I have seen a chemist's laboratory before; the king has one at Whitehall. But it is nothing like this! How can someone work in such a place as this?"

"I've seen worse," Aphra said glumly, examining the papers on the desk before putting them to one side and opening the top drawer. Inside, she found a collection of anti-Papist leaflets and satirical cartoons — and several letters addressed to Jeremiah Hopkin. The letters were unsigned and partly written in a crude form of numerical code, but their meaning was clear: the Duchess of Portsmouth was the plotters' target, not the king.

"Squintabella!" Nell exclaimed. "Who'd want to kill the weeping willow?" She slapped her forehead. "Stupid question! Who *wouldn't* want to?"

"Quiet! Would you have us go to prison? I have been there Nellie, and I can tell you there is no place worse."

"Sorry," Nell whispered.

"So what would you do now?" Aphra said. "The plot appears not to be against your beloved king, but against your worst enemy. You've always said you'd give anything to be rid of her, and now someone seems prepared to do your bidding. This seems a plot to your advantage, would you still wish to snare the plotters?"

Nell threw both hands up to her face. "I don't know."

"If you wish to pursue this no further, only say the word. We will return to our separate homes and forget the entire matter. My silence may be relied upon."

"Oh no, Aphra! Loathsome she may be, but I cannot stand by and let her be murdered. Let us snare these plotters, if we can."

Aphra shrugged. "I was afraid you'd say that." She reached into her coat, producing a small volume identical to the one nearly destroyed by the angler — except that this one was blank and showed no sign of having been thrown on a fire. She bent back the spine and ruffled the pages to make it look used, then she placed it on the desk, next to the window. "Nothing must be missing, nothing must appear to have been disturbed. Jeremiah Hopkin must suspect nothing, or he will cover his traces, and there is much more we need to know if we would trap him. Now let us risk no more time here. Our purpose for tonight has been accomplished."

They returned to Holborn the next morning, again disguised as men. "We can watch just as well from the tavern over there," Aphra said. "The view should be clear."

They entered the tavern slapping their thighs, winking at the barmaid, and completely overdoing their portrayal of two men in search of a hearty breakfast. The two 'men' sat at a table by the window.

A short while later, Aphra stood up. "Look," she said, pointing across the street.

A tall, bespectacled man was getting out of a hackney carriage. He was extremely thin and dressed entirely in black: black hat, black coat, black breeches and black stockings. He wore no wig and seemed to have little if any hair. He walked up to the narrow house across the way, carrying several bags which he placed on the pavement while he searched for something in his pockets. Then he took out a key and went inside.

Aphra turned to Nell and smiled. "The prodigal son returns."

According to the diary, Jeremiah Hopkin was to meet his co-conspirator, 'C', upon his return on Friday. So they waited — sometimes inside the tavern, sometimes leaning against the wall outside — and watched. It was nearly dark when a ginger-haired young man knocked on Jeremiah Hopkin's door and was admitted.

He left half an hour later, followed by Aphra. Nell stayed behind to watch the house. Fifteen minutes later, the bespectacled chemist walked out into Holborn, heading east.

Nell could hardly believe it when she saw the house Hopkin had entered: it was the residence of Lord Shaftesbury, leader of the Whigs. She waited outside a while longer, and saw a man whose small eyes and large chin she recognised at once — the man whose testimony had begun the anti-Papist hysteria: Mr Titus Oates.

When Nell arrived home, Aphra was waiting with the news that she had followed the ginger-haired man back to Whitehall Palace and discovered he was a servant in the Duchess of Portsmouth's kitchen. "What will you do now?" she asked. "Inform the king?"

"I will," Nell assured her. "I will. When the time is right."

She came upon Charles in the woods outside Windsor, a hooded falcon at rest upon his arm.

"Nellie!" The king's face lit up when he saw her. "Is your friend recovered from her illness?"

"Yes, Sir." She scanned the faces of the courtiers surrounding the king. "Is Louise not here, Sir?"

"I believe she's in her chamber; you know she cares not for sport. And what will you do, Nell? There are many diversions here for you to choose from."

"If your Majesty has no objection, I'm most anxious to visit dear Louise. I've missed her so."

Nell found it hard not to laugh when she saw the shocked faces and raised eyebrows that surrounded her on all sides.

"If you wish," said the king, a puzzled expression on his face.

Two days after the court returned to Whitehall, Nell accompanied Louise to the afternoon performance at the King's Theatre. They took their seats in the middle gallery during the interval between the second and third acts. A row of girls stood below them in the pit, holding baskets of fruit on their arms and calling, "Oranges, will you have any oranges?"

"Wouldn't you be more comfortable down there, Nellie?" Louise asked, tilting her head towards the orange girls with a mirthless little smile. "I'm sure you could use the money. The king gives you so little, and it does show." She shook her head in mock sympathy. "Mon dieu, that dress!"

Nell turned to her and smiled, shaking her own head. "Mon dieu," she said, imitating Louise perfectly, "that face!"

In the pit below, a dark-haired man approached one of the orange girls. From where she was sitting, Nell couldn't see exactly what happened, but she heard the girl squeal as though she'd been pinched. The man swaggered away carrying several oranges, a smug expression on his face. He was heading towards the middle gallery.

"Hide yourself, Louise," Nell whispered, raising a hand to cover her face, "it's that horrid Samuel Pepys."

"Oh no," Louise groaned, raising a hand to her forehead and resolutely staring into her lap. "First you, now him! How can this day get any worse?"

"All the actresses laugh at him and his airs. But he's still one to watch; his hands wander as much as his eyes. Do you know when I was an actress, he used to come backstage into the tiring room to watch me dress!"

"The poor man must have been desperate."

Without a word or sign of warning, Louise stood up and headed for the exit halfway through the third act. Nell leapt from her seat and followed her up the aisle.

"No need for you to come," Louise hissed.

Nell ignored her, walking close behind and scanning the crowd for any sign of suspicious movement.

They walked out the door and into Drury Lane, where Louise's coach was waiting.

"Why must you follow me everywhere I go?" Louise asked as Nell climbed into the coach and sat down beside her. "Why constantly plague me with your presence? Why won't you leave me alone?"

"I merely wished to see the play, Louise."

"Then why leave before the finish?"

"It wasn't very good."

"You're planning something," Louise said, her voice rising to a hysterical pitch. "You think I don't know you're plotting against me? My maid saw you in the hall outside my quarters at three this morning. Why?"

"Perhaps I find it hard to sleep," Nell said.

That evening, the guests around Louise's supper table included the king, three members of the privy council, and Nell. Nell was the only one who hadn't been invited. "Dear Nellie," Louise had said with a forced smile as the others arrived, "I'm sure you have important business elsewhere and I wouldn't dream of keeping you from it. If you wish to take your leave, I assure you no one here will take offence."

Nell had refused to take the hint.

She was enjoying Louise's little party, and she was particularly enjoying the fact that every word she spoke caused another little line of tension to form on the other woman's face. Louise was so obviously uncomfortable, squirming and seething and struggling to hold her temper in front of the others, that Nell began to wonder why she'd never thought of tormenting the woman this way before. "A toast to my dearest friend," she said, raising her glass and barely suppressing a giggle.

A young man entered the room, carrying a large silver platter. The king slapped the table. "Ah, at last here's the meat!"

Nell narrowed her eyes and took a deep breath. She recognised the man with the platter. She watched intently as he placed the platter on a sideboard and with a large knife, began to carve the meat and serve it to the guests.

Everyone had been served except the Duchess of Portsmouth; the ginger-haired servant paused to wipe the blade with a cloth. Then he prepared a final slice, put it on a plate, and served it to the duchess.

For a few brief seconds, as he placed the plate in front of her, he was only inches away from her rival. Nell tensed, ready to jump into action. But nothing happened. He put the plate down and moved away. He'd left the knife on the sideboard.

Of course Nell knew it would be madness to stab Louise in front of all these witnesses, but the diary had specifically mentioned a knife — and that he'd been instructed in its use. Then she remembered the part that read: 'Before king and others? Best way to avoid suspicion.' Whatever he was supposed to do was meant to be done in front of the king and other people — something they would all witness yet never suspect. But what?

She thought again about the knife — he'd cut several slices of meat, wiped the blade with a cloth, and then he'd cut Louise's slice. She thought back to the toad suspended in liquid, the labels on the jars she'd seen in Holborn: Arsenic, Monkshood, Foxglove, Vitriol, Antimony, Prussic Acid. All poisons!

Louise de Keroualle

Louise speared a piece of meat on a three-pronged silver fork and raised it to her mouth. "Stop!" Nell shouted, leaping from her seat and knocking the fork from Louise's hand.

"Mon dieu! Have you gone mad?"

Nell pointed after the young man, who had already bolted from the room. "Seize him!"

"Calm down Nellie," the king said, embarrassed.

"Seize him! The meat is poisoned!"

The privy councillors gagged and dropped their forks.

"Not yours, hers!"

The councillors ran from the table and sounded the alarm. Guards and servants rushed in all directions.

"The poison was on the cloth," Nell told Louise. "He wiped the blade with it before slicing your portion."

Outside, there were running feet, shouting voices and blowing horns. Inside, there was Louise, sobbing. "Oh, Charles, I've never been so frightened. Someone tried to kill me."

The king took her in his arms, cooing and patting her on the head. "There, there, my little Fubs. Charlie's here and he won't let anything happen to you."

Nell rolled her eyes. Fubs. She hated it when the king called Louise Fubs. "Excuse me, Louise, but did you perchance notice I just saved your life?"

"Charles, I think I'm going to faint."

Charles, keeping both his arms around Louise, began to lead her towards another room. "Poor darling, let's get you tucked into your bed."

"Wouldn't Your Majesty like to hear how I single-handedly uncovered a dastardly plot to murder one of your court?"

"Later, Nell," said the king, closing the door behind him.

The next morning, Nell took a hackney coach to Aphra's house. She found her in the front room, writing in one of her little blank books. "Well?" said Aphra, looking up.

"You were right. It was a thankless task." ■

Simon Morse: Losers

Sedgfield waved one of his stubby, camouflaged arms feebly back in the direction of the Registration Hut and whined, "I reckon they'll be over there. I reckon we've passed them."

"Oh, *do* you now?" snarled Thompson, the words whipping fatso's confidence out from underneath him.

Sedgfield's face was a picture, it was classic. Like a kid who's been spanked on the arse and the pain hasn't connected with his head yet. We did it all the time round the office. It was our sport.

"Er...yeah. Look, listen to me, I reckon we've passed them," Sedgfield said, desperate to make us take him seriously. I glanced over at Williams, who was smirking as usual. I smirked back, but then realised I envied him the baseball cap he'd brought to augment his camouflage fatigues: HMS Ark Royal, Falklands Conflict 1982. The flash bastard. He wasn't even ten years old in 1982.

Thompson clamped hold of Sedgfield's shoulder and did some pointing of his own — in the opposite direction, over the brow of the hill and down towards the scattering of copses at its foot. "For your information, Sedge, they're all *down there*. D'you wanna know how I know? I'll tell you. The team from Edwin Electrical left *there*," he said, pointing back at the Registration Hut, "at three o'clock; Reynolds & Davison Printers left at ten past three; Cranby Sales And Marketing left at three twenty; and we, the young high-flyers, the stout yeomen of the Bishops Hall Packaging and Distribution managerial team, left at half past three."

Williams and I were barely able to stifle our guffaws. Sedgfield was losing it badly, his pig face bright red and his bottom lip trembling. Strictly speaking, we were all on the same rung of the corporate ladder, and so he shouldn't have been taking this shit from us. But old habits die hard, and when you're in for the kill you've got to go all out for it. All out or nothing. Those are the rules.

Thompson shoved his watch right under Sedgfield's nose. "Can you tell the time? Sedge? Can you?"

"Piss off," he whined.

"I'll teach you. The little hand's on the...eight, and the big hand's almost on the...four, so what time is it, Sedge?"

Sedgfield tried to bat Thompson's arm out of the way but he brought it back up again, closer to his face this time. "Piss *off*," he moaned. Then Thompson pushed the watch *into* his face, squashing his nose with it. When he pushed Thompson away he finally had the bright idea to step out of range. "Piss *off,* piss *off.*"

Now the three of us chuckled to ourselves. "It's twenty to four, Sedge," said Williams.

Flustered and sweating, despite the cold Peak District wind, Sedgfield grabbed at his belt and pulled out his pistol, aiming it with a shaking hand at Thompson. "Stop fucking taking the piss out of me or I'll fucking shoot you. I'll shoot the lot of you," he blathered.

"Yeah, yeah," I said, "put the weapon away, Sedge."

"It might only be paintball pellets in here," he said, "but you heard what they said — they can *sting.*"

"Ooh! Ow! Steer clear!" mocked Thompson.

"All right, come on," said Williams. "Look, are we in this game to win or what?"

"Yeah, let's get some fucking strategy going here before we freeze to death," I said. "Put the gun away, Sedge."

He did as I told him to. He looked angry, but with Sedgfield it was never going to go anywhere. He just wasn't the type.

"Okay, let's take a look," said Thompson, and we all surveyed the surrounding countryside. Try as we might, we couldn't see any of the other teams. No suspicious tree movements, no flashes of fading afternoon light glinting off metal or glass, nothing.

"I'm drawing a blank," said Williams.

"Me too," I said. "I can't see fuck-all. They must be dug in or something."

"Fuck off," said Thompson. "Dug in? What are they gonna dig with? You didn't see them handing out shovels at the hut, did you?"

"Yeah, okay Thompson," I said.

"We're in a good fucking position to see them though, if they do move," said Williams. "I can't believe people would give up such a cool vantage point as this. They must be fucking morons."

Sedgfield hmm'd. No one took any notice.

"Nah," said Thompson. "Go in, go deep — that's the way. They're in there somewhere, in those trees."

"So let's go," I said. "Go in, guns blazing, blast 'em out. *Force majeure.*"

They all looked at me like I was mental.

"You can if you want," said Williams, "but if they've got territory like that they're gonna take positions around it and wait for arseholes like you to come to *them.* Fly in the spider web: they'll pick us off one by one if we play it that way. Cos they're playing the long game. Waiting for someone to trip up. No, I say superior intelligence is what'll secure our victory. Find out precisely where each team member's hiding, and surgical strike — *zzzziiiipp!* Ninja-style."

"Yeah," Thompson nodded with an entertained, evil grin. "I like the sound of that."

Sedgfield did too. "Ninja," he repeated.

"Who the fuck asked you?" said Williams, smacking him right down so well I felt like giving Williams a high-five right there.

"We can't give up this place though," I said, trying to add some depth to our plan, some texture. "I say — go for both."

"Okay, I'll go along with that," said Williams. "We split up. Two teams of two. Morris, you stay here with Sedge and keep lookout."

"Cool," I said.

"Me and Thompson will go in."

"I wanna go in," grizzled Sedgfield.

"Get to fuck," spat Thompson, "they'd pick you off in a second."

"He's got a point," I whispered to Williams. "Know what I mean?"

"Er, maybe we *should* let Sedge have first crack, Thompson," Williams said. "He's observant, so...let him observe."

Simon Morse was born in Swindon, Wiltshire, in 1969 and spent his childhood in Swindon and Bristol. Between 1983 and 1990 his parents ran pubs in London (off Regent Street), Southend and Brentwood. It's from those places and some of the people who frequented them that he got his knowledge of everyday, shitty-nosed, weasel-faced, squirming, petty, life-altering crime. He left all that to do art college, gaining a BA in Liverpool and an MA in Chelsea. Since then he's worked for an advertising agency in Blackfriars (awful), for Rupert Murdoch in Wapping (all politics aside, a vision of hell), and is now working in interactive television. Simon currently lives in Dublin and, occasionally, London.

Photo: Ruth Rogers

Illustrations: David Checkley

Thompson got the message, and the three of us swapped collusive glances, ending with big smiles in Sedgfield's direction. "Uh...let's go for it," he said.

"Let's," said Thompson, and pulled Sedgfield away with him towards the right of the hill where there was a dry stone wall they could crawl down behind.

"Get off me," whined Sedgfield.

"Don't piss me off, Sedgfield, or I'm warning you," said Thompson.

"Rendezvous back in twenty," Williams called after them. He and I watched as Thompson repeatedly bashed Sedgfield on the shoulder, then grabbed his gun off of him. "Always baiting," he said.

"Yep," I said. "But you gotta admit, the podgy bastard deserves it."

My eyes followed them as they reached the wall and disappeared behind it. My only thought was I was glad I wasn't in Thompson's shoes.

For the next ten minutes Williams and I lay in the grass looking down the hill for anything that could be construed as human life, but there was nothing. We were in a stand-off situation definitely, I told myself, and at that point it looked like we were going to use up what little daylight remained and then some if the situation stayed deadlocked. "We're the only fuckers taking the initiative here," I complained to Williams.

"If I'd wanted to go birdwatching, I would have gone birdwatching," he concurred. "As it is, I'm here for some full-on paintball action. But what do I get? Three teams who think they're fucking Napoleon. It makes me sick how gutless some people in middle management are today. No balls."

"There's cautionary tactics, biding your time, planning your strategy, stealth — "

"Stealth, *yes*."

"And then there's this," I said.

"Piece of shit," he said.

"Piece of shit," I agreed.

We continued in the same vein for a few minutes, and then we caught sight of Thompson emerging on all fours from behind the dry stone wall. "Why's he crawling?" asked Williams. "He's behind the ridge of the hill, none of the enemy are going to see him."

"Ever the fucking professional," I said, and Williams laughed.

It took Thompson a couple of minutes to reach us like that. When he flopped down next to us he was wheezing like an eighty-year-old. "What's the matter — can't stand the pace?" I said.

He didn't respond. He just lay there on the grass, face-down.

"Come on, you lazy bastard. What's going on?" said Williams.

"Yeah. Where's fat boy?"

At that, Thompson rolled over onto his back. His face was flushed red, there was a terrible, fearful, crushed look in his eye, and his front was spattered with yellow paint.

"Oh great, you've been shot," moaned Williams. "Fantastic. You're out of the game, idiot!"

"No," gasped Thompson.

"What?" I said.

"No, I'm... I've not...been shot."

"What the fuck's the matter with you?" said Williams.

"Guys...guys, I can... I can trust you...can't I?"

"Leave out the amateur dramatics, Thompson," I said.

He grabbed my arm tightly. "Can I? Can I *trust* you?"

"Yeah," I shrugged. "So what?"

"Come with me."

Sedgfield's body was lying face-down next to a large clump of heather, halfway down the hill. At first I thought it was some joke Thompson and he were pulling

— an instinctual reaction, I guess. But when Williams kicked the body straight in the guts and there was no reaction I felt a streak of red hot something tear right up my spine to the back of my head. And there it stayed.

Bad.

This was *bad*.

"Oh, fucking hell man," I said to Thompson.

"Shhh, k-k-keep your voice down!" he replied, eyes wide like a madman's, taking in everything and nothing at once, his body starting to shake from the cold wind and the naked, ugly fear inside him.

I tried to get a hold of myself to stop my own body following suit.

"This was an accident, wasn't it?" stated Williams, the worry setting in to his voice too, raising it a couple of notes. "Tell me this was an accident."

He employed his foot again: this time he didn't kick the body but rolled it over so it was face-up. Sedgfield's fatigues were muddy — there was nothing unusual about that. What was unusual though was his face, and more particularly his open mouth. It was filled with yellow paint. Even in the bad light we could see it clearly. More than that, it was as if the paint was lighting up the inside of his mouth. Shining a searchlight on itself. Bright yellow, the paint smothered his lips too and leaked out and down his cheeks and chin, one dribble running backwards and pooling in the corner of his left eye, which like his right was open and staring up straight past us at the sky.

"Jesus Christ, Thompson," I said, quivering. "What the fuck did you do to him?"

Thompson dropped to the grass and leant against the wall. He clasped his hand to his mouth, his eyes fixed on the corpse. "I...he was just pissing me off."

"So you let him have it?" said Williams angrily.

"I..." Thompson held up his paintball gun. His hand shook violently. Seeing this, I considered getting out of the way, but I was rooted to the spot. "I didn't think...they're not meant to..."

Thompson was fucked.

"You put the gun in his mouth and executed him gangster-style, didn't you?" growled Williams. "Well, that's just fucking terrific. You think you're a gangster. Terrific. *Well, you're not on telly now, Ironside.*"

"Hey," I said, "take it easy, will you?"

"No way. This fucking arsehole's just...you see what he's done?"

"Oh God," bleated Thompson, clear tears welling in his reddened eyes.

"The guy's choked to death on the pellets," Williams said. "He's choked *to death*, Thompson."

Williams took a step over Sedgfield's body towards Thompson to start on him but I stepped forward and held him back. "Leave it," I said.

My body was trembling. I was scared. Really fucking scared. I'd only come out here because it was a works beano. Free afternoon. Fun. And now two of us were standing over the body of a dead workmate, and the other one was a gibbering wreck. And a murderer.

"We have to pretend it never happened," was my searingly brilliant plan. "Now let's stand away from the body and work out how."

"Sedgfield!" wailed Thompson.

"Oh shut up," I hissed, "you hated his guts. We all did. Now just forget about it and let's make sure none of us gets into any shit for it."

The icy wind blew around us and over us and through us for a moment. Then Thompson, with what little self control he could muster, nodded his head and mouthed the word, "Okay."

In extreme situations you revert to what you know best. That's what happened to us: we reverted to television.

While Thompson kept watch, Williams and I swapped his gun with Sedgfield's, wiped both guns as clean as we could to avoid fingerprint detection, and wrapped Sedgfield's stumpy fingers around Thompson's gun, with one on the trigger. We disagreed on where to leave the gun pointing: Williams thought the in-the-mouth position would be most convincing, but I maintained that away-from-the-body would be more natural and concurrent with a fall or flop of some kind. In the event we went with Williams's suggestion, and agreed that, if and when we were asked, we'd say we'd always had doubts about Sedgfield's mental aptitude and that he'd been depressed for some time. Which, in some senses, was true. But naturally we wouldn't own up to being the cause. We did all of this on automatic pilot, and when half an hour later we were back up on top of the hill trying to act as if we'd been there all the time I could scarcely believe I'd been that resourceful under such extreme circumstances. I made a mental note to lobby for promotion when I got back. Before the other two did.

"So when do you think we should call it a day?" said Williams. "I'm freezing my bollocks off out here."

"As soon as Thompson calms down a bit more," I said. We both looked at him. He'd stopped shaking so much, but that rabbit-in-headlights stare of his was a dead giveaway. My heart sank just to look at him, and in doing so I knew I was ahead in the coping stakes, and that felt good. We'd be out here a long time, but by just being patient, by watching and waiting, playing the long game, I was sure I'd come out on top.

Just then there was a movement from the left hand side of the hill. Coming up behind us was one of the other teams, breaking cover. "What are they doing? Are they mad, they're coming right towards us," said Williams. "We could get them easy."

"Just wait," I said. "Keep calm."

"I'm calm," said Williams.

"M-m-me too," spluttered Thompson.

"Jesus Christ," I said.

One of the team coming in our direction held up a handkerchief and started waving it about. "They're surrendering," said Williams. "Fuck me, we've got 'em."

I got edgy again. There was something I didn't trust about this whole situation. Understatement of the year.

"Hello," said one of the other team-members, the one waving the hankie, as they reached us. The three of us stood up. "We're Cranby Sales And Marketing."

"And you're surrendering," said Williams.

"Well, not quite," replied the man. "We've just noticed the time, and Johnson here's remembered he's got to be somewhere at seven."

"Hot date," the guy explained, grinning idiotically.

"So we thought, in the spirit of solidarity — all for one, one for all, that sort of thing — we thought we'd pack it in."

"Well, nice of you to, er, tell us," I said cautiously.

"Yes," said the man. And then he took a step closer. My body tensed. I cursed myself internally. I must have looked guilty as hell. As it was, I felt a complete arsehole when the man said, "We were wondering — would you like to buy our ammo off of us?"

"What?"

"You must be out of ammo by now," he said.

"Well," began Thompson.

"No thanks," Williams butted in, "we're fine for ammo. Haven't fired a single shot all afternoon, have we lads?"

"Not one," I sputtered.

"Ah," said the man. "Well...look: don't want to spoil the game for you or anything, but, er...we *could* let you know where the other two teams are. For a price."

"Fifty quid," said the idiotic grinner.

"Each," said the other team member.

The three of us stood absolutely transfixed. The man's expression changed. "Something wrong?" he enquired.

After a second I said, "We don't want to know."

"Suit yourself," he said, more than a little put out. "Just thought you might want to win, that's all."

"They look like they're losing anyway," said the idiotic grinner. "There's only three of them: one of them's obviously been shot already."

"He's not!" blabbed Thompson. "We didn't — "

"He's over there," I said quickly, pointing back down the hill, away from where the body was, "in those bushes. Taking a leak."

"Oh," said the man. "Funny — we came up that way. Didn't see him."

"He's very private," said Williams. "And he's in camouflage."

"Well," said the man, turning away, "he's certainly taking his time. You'll have to have a word with him. Cheerio." And with that the other team started walking off towards the Registration Hut.

"Hey," said Williams, "what did he just say?"

"What do you mean?" I asked.

"Under his breath as he turned away."

"I didn't — "

"Hey!" Williams shouted to the man. "Did I hear you right then?"

The man stopped and turned round. "What?"

"You just called us losers."

The man chuckled and carried on walking back.

"He did. Hey!" shouted Williams. Then he drew his gun and rapid-fired twenty or thirty pellets at the man, each falling short of their target.

"Don't do that, you arsehole," I said, grabbing at his gun.

"Fuck him," Williams spat.

"W-w-what's that?" said Thompson, turning round. Williams and I joined him. We peered through the dim light down the hill, and saw bushes at the bottom, by the start of the dry stone wall, rustling.

"There's someone down there," said Williams.

"Yeah — look!" I said.

There was a great roar as four men yelled and broke cover, scrambling up the hill towards us.

"They must have heard you shooting and shouting, Williams," I said.

"When they get, when they get half way..." Then Thompson stopped speaking. But we knew what was coming. ∎

The father was short and middle-aged, grey stubble shining on his face, hair cropped to silver spikes. He wore a beige raincoat not quite his size. His son was tall, mid-twenties, black hair slicked back to show a widow's peak. His trainers had been fashionable (and expensive) the previous Christmas, unlike his scuffed leather jacket.

They were seated at a table on the upper floor of a Princes Street burger emporium. The father had been trying unsuccessfully for some minutes to manoeuvre his chair into a more comfortable arrangement. "Bolted to the floor," he complained, peering underneath. "Do they think we're going to nick it?" He glared at the portion of burger and chips spread out on his tray. "Chips," he'd told his server. "Not fries, chips!"

Now he looked out of the window. His son knew exactly what he was thinking. They had different outlooks on life; nothing wrong with that. He'd been only too relieved to find a free table after the scrum downstairs: lead-up to Christmas, and everyone on the east coast had descended on Princes Street. Picking pockets had been the game — 'lifting', he called it. Only they hadn't had any luck so far, which was what was eating at his dad.

"Do you want that burger?" he asked, but his dad wasn't listening.

"Look out there, Marky. Best ruddy view of the castle you'll ever get, and it's from the window of a fast food shop." He turned to look at his son, who was busy with his food. He was impressed that Marky knew the score: had emptied his chips into the empty half of the burger box, made a nice little picnic plate of it. He'd tried the same himself, but the chips had fallen everywhere. No salt on the table; no sauce or vinegar.

"Your burger's already sauced," Marky had explained.

"Not doing my chips any good then, is it?"

"I can go downstairs and…"

IAN RANKIN

GET SHORTIE

But he'd shaken the offer away, gone back to picking the ice cubes out of his drink, stacking them in the tiny tin ashtray. All the tables around them: families with bulging shopping-bags, kids squawking and complaining. "I hate Christmas," he said.

"I know," said Marky, thinking back to when he was a kid and his mum was alive. The tree and the lights and the decorations: they were all down to his mum. His dad had sat there in his chair, can of beer in one hand, ciggie in the other, letting everything revolve around him.

"What time is it now?"

"Gone four," Marky said.

"They'll all be heading home soon."

Marky had a thought, leaned across the table and lowered his voice. "There's always the chocolate shop. Remember what I said."

His dad smiled. "'Soft target'," he recited. Marky let that sink in while he polished off his fries and drained his cola. The ashtray had become a little man-made lake, shimmering in the glare.

Suddenly his dad straightened his back, sniffed and looked around. The expectant look on his young son's face was enough to swing the argument. "Marky," he said, getting to his feet, "let's go to work."

Twas the night before Christmas, and Inspector John Rebus had been left holding the baby. He looked down at the sleeping infant, then handed it back to the reluctant constable. "Get on to Social Services," he ordered. "Their problem, not ours."

"Yes, sir. And meantime…?"

"Look on it as a test of your initiative."

Rebus offered a bleak smile and turned away, heading back to CID. But when he saw the Chief Super in the distance, he detoured into the toilets. The season of goodwill, and Rebus was washing his hands. In the mirror he saw eyes the colour of slush, cheeks as pale as a ghost's. "Humbug," he said to himself.

The Christmas Eve shift was never pleasant. Beggars begged to be arrested, so they'd have a hot meal on the big day. Despair and frustration took their hold on the housing schemes: it was the time of year when people torched their grim little flats in the hope of being offered something better. Add to this a baby abandoned on the station's doorstep, and suddenly the menagerie in Princes Street Gardens took on its proper perspective.

Rebus didn't know whose idea it had been: a live-action stable scene; donkeys and a cow, chickens and a pair of randy sheep. But the animals hadn't stuck to the script and were now on the loose, uniformed officers giving chase — to the delight of last-minute shoppers in the city centre.

Born in Cardenden, Fife, in 1960 (as was Rebus), Ian Rankin was a prize-winning poet and short story writer before turning to novels with *The Flood*, followed by *Knots & Crosses*, the first of his powerful Inspector Rebus novels in 1987. He is the winner of several prestigious awards and honours, the most recent being the 1997 CWA The Macallan Gold Dagger Award for Fiction for *Black & Blue*. His latest novel *Dead Souls* is out now in hardback from Orion (£9.99), as is the paperback of *The Hanging Garden* (£5.99).

"Cheer up, John," the Chief Super said, pushing open the door. "It's Christmas."

"I hadn't noticed, sir."

"Any idea yet who the nipper is?"

"Mary's boy child?" Rebus guessed, reaching for a paper towel.

Out in the corridor, he walked briskly to the CID room. His phone was ringing, but he ignored it. Poured himself a coffee and looked in vain for milk. There was never a runaway cow when you needed one. The phone stopped just as he was reaching for it. Rebus glanced heavenwards. "That's one I owe you, pal."

He sat down and turned on the monitor, hitting the video recorder's play button. In grainy black and white, two desperadoes in Santa beards were holding up a sweet shop. There was no sound, but Rebus had interviewed the shaken shop assistants, only to learn that the beards had disguised the men's voices as well as their faces — disguised them to such an extent that neither assistant had been able to understand at first that they were at the centre of a hold-up.

The men had wanted money, of course. The shop was about to close at the end of one of its busiest days of the year. Unfortunately for Butch and Sundance, the bulk of the takings had been lifted by a security van two hours previously, leaving them with about fifty quid and a fistful of continental chocolates.

The video footage was a couple of days old, and Rebus was watching it because he thought he recognised the older of the assailants — recognised, but couldn't yet put a name to the face. He had some notes in front of him: two more bungled robberies at a shopping centre. Descriptions: two men, one older and shorter than the other. A variety of disguises used: moustaches and glasses and hats. Scottish accents. Getting away with pennies and cheap presents. The younger one had tried lifting the charity-box from one shop's counter, but the elder had snapped at him, and the box had been left alone.

Rebus wondered about their relationship. Their only weapons had been anger and vague physical threats. He took a walk back down the corridor to clear his head. In the Comms Room, the desk sergeant was taking his shift with the baby, while a female officer opened a packet of white powder.

"I hope that's formula," Rebus told her.

"If it was cocaine, do you think I'd be hanging around here?"

They all had smart answers these days. "Any joy from Social Services?"

"One of the emergency team's on her way." She half-filled the bottle with hot water, shook it until the concoction turned into milk. "Poor little mite," she said, testing the temperature of the liquid against her wrist. "Not much of a start in life, is it?"

"Not much, no."

The desk sergeant was dandling the baby on his knee.

"Here," Rebus said, "I'll take him."

"It's a her," the desk sergeant said.

Rebus sat down, nestling the girl into his chest. There were bubbles at the corners of her mouth. Her eyes were dull blue, attracted to the ceiling lights. The woman PC handed over the bottle, and the baby started to feed. "She was swaddled up warm enough," the female constable said. "I think her mother must love her."

Rebus was thoughtful. "Have we checked local surgeries? An emergency call-out maybe."

The constable nodded. "It's happening, but slowly."

"Rounding up those bloody animals seems to take priority," the sergeant explained.

"How come?"

The sergeant shrugged. "We don't want animals getting hurt now, do we? Especially at Christmas." A call came in. The sergeant took it, and fed the details into the computer. He was chuckling and shaking his head. "I've heard everything now," he said.

"What?"

"Two Father Christmases have just had a go at one another."

"You're kidding."

"At the foot of The Mound. One thought the other was invading his turf."

Only halfway through her bottle, the baby had already dropped off. Taking her from Rebus, the constable explained that she'd made up a bed of sorts in one of the Interview Rooms.

"Are they being brought in?" Rebus asked the sergeant.

"Via the Infirmary."

"The Infirmary?" Rebus rubbed at his chin. "I think I'll take this call."

"Breath of fresh air?"

"Something like that," Rebus said, making for the door.

Accident and Emergency was the usual scrum. Drunks slouched sleepily in corners, faces and knees grazed from falls. Sober shoppers overburdened with packages sported similar injuries. One man had fallen and sprained an ankle while hiding presents on top of the wardrobe. Another had slipped on ice: suspected skull fracture. The tinsel and decorations did little to cheer the waiting area, and not even the appearance of two dishevelled Santa Clauses had relieved the gloom. For if Santa were not immune to the trials of the everyday, then who was?

Rebus had spoken to the constable who'd made the arrest and to the doctor who'd treated the combatants. Now he pushed open the curtain of one examination area. A Santa was seated on the trolley, legs swinging over the side. He'd discarded his hat and beard, but still wore the rest of the costume. One arm was torn, padding oozing from it. "Hello there, Chick," Rebus said.

The man looked up. "Mr Rebus."

"Thought you were going to keep out of trouble."

"I am. I was collecting for a kids' charity. I've got my badge and everything."

"Okay, Chick, calm down." Rebus lifted his hands in a pacifying gesture. The big man sighed and rubbed his forehead. He had a small cut above one eye.

"He just butted in, told me it was his shot now. I'd had a good afternoon, so no way was I giving up. Besides, I had my badge."

"And he didn't?"

"Only charity he was collecting for was himself. Didn't even have a tin, just a carrier-bag."

"So you had an argument?"

"It wasn't like that. He stood right next to me, hassling the pedestrians. So they started keeping their distance."

"And you got mad?"

"I'm not like that any more, Mr Rebus. But next thing I knew, he was grabbing my tin. Trying to make off with it. I couldn't let him do that."

"You hit him?"

"I was hanging on to the tin, we tripped and fell. That's where I got this cut."

"You want to press charges?"

"I... I'm not sure."

"Okay, Chick. Keep your nose clean, I'll be back in a minute."

Chick was wiping his nose as Rebus made his exit.

A nurse told him that someone was in with the other Santa. "His son," she said. Rebus nodded and asked her to check on recent admissions of young women. He waited till she'd gone before pulling back the curtain.

The second Santa, also minus beard and hat, was about a foot and a half shorter than Chick, and was lying stretched out on the trolley, face puffy and bruised, lip burst.

"Dearie me," Rebus said. "Had a disagreement with one of our little elves, did we?" The man turned his face away, but Rebus had already recognised him. "Is that you, Billy?" There was no reply, so Rebus smiled towards the son, who was standing beside the trolley, a carrier-bag in his hand. "Then you must be Mark." The young man twitched. "Your dad and me are old friends, isn't that right, Billy?"

There was a grunt from the trolley.

"Trying to nick a charity tin, Billy," Rebus said, shaking his head. "I'm disappointed in you. And only a couple of days ago, you stopped Mark here from doing the self-same thing."

Mark's eyes widened; Billy turned to peer at Rebus.

"We caught you on tape," Rebus said. "How long have you been back in town?" Neither man answered him. "Next time you try picking on a Santa, Billy, stick to ones smaller than yourself. That was Chick Waterson you went up against, amateur boxing champ and recently reformed hard-man."

Billy groaned. Rebus reached out a hand and took the carrier from Marky. It was heavy with coins. There were a few loose chocolates in there, too.

"We'll discuss this back at the station," Rebus said, turning to go.

The ward was long and quiet, its lights dimmed. There was a lamp on above her bed. She looked small, fragile, little more than a child herself. She had raised her knees beneath the sheet. Her hair needed washing, and there were dark rings of exhaustion around her eyes.

"Your baby's fine," Rebus told her, drawing over a chair. "Nurse tells me you're going to be fine, too."

She kept staring at the ceiling, tears dripping from her cheeks. Rebus placed the carrier-bag on her bedside cabinet, unwrapped two sweets: one for her, one for him.

"We can bring her in, let you take a look at her. She was sleeping last time I saw her."

"I…" She swallowed, lifted the tumbler from the cabinet and drank. Then she took a deep breath. "Maybe that would be okay," she said.

"There are people who'll help you, Mary," Rebus said quietly.

"Are there?" she said sceptically. "Funny, they weren't around earlier."

Rebus didn't know what to say, so sat there in silence for a few minutes. When he got up to leave, he forgot to take the carrier with him.

"Way things work," Rebus said, "you could be in here over New Year."

He was in an Interview Room with Billy McQueen. The baby was gone, but the perfumed smell of cleaning-wipes still lingered.

"It's not the boy's fault," Billy McQueen said. "He had nothing to do with it."

"We've got him on tape, Billy."

"Mr Rebus…" But Billy knew there was nothing to say. Rebus was a hard nut, everyone knew that. No breaks given, not ever. And being made to work the Christmas shift… Billy couldn't blame him.

"Only thing is," Rebus said, "a piece of evidence seems to have been mislaid. I don't mean the tape, I mean your carrier-bag."

A smile crept on to Billy's face. "What carrier-bag?" he said.

"Procurator-fiscal might be persuaded the case is a no-hoper."

"But we're stuck in the cells until then?"

"Call it a present, Billy."

Billy frowned. "Present?"

"Another chance. What better present can you think of?"

"Do we get a party at New Year?"

"With the trimmings: black bun, madeira cake, mince pies. Anything else you'd like?"

"Can't think of anything, Mr Rebus."

But as Billy McQueen was being escorted back to his cell, he did think of something. "Hey, Mr Rebus!" he shouted. "Don't forget — get shortie!" ■

Ian
Rankin

Out now in paperback

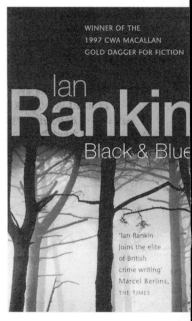

A one man crime wave

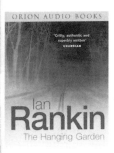

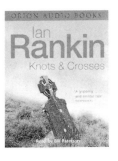

'Britain's finest detective novelist'
SCOTLAND ON SUNDAY

Ian Rankin
Dead Souls

Audio Books
out now

Out now in hardback
Available through all good bookshops

WATER WEARS THE STONES

Tom Piccirilli

Archetypal. That's the eight dollar word Claire would have used to describe how it played out in '68, when we drew away from who we were and dropped into other characters. We were all there in one fashion or another: the amiable loner; spurned lover; victim; Judas goat; Judas; and the revenge-bent possessed by sweet and heady insanity. Since December of '69 hit, along with the shrapnel of the fleshette mine outside Khe Sanh, I've taken on a piece of each role and made it my own.

But that's after the Judge's windows arched shattered and chiming in the leaf-strewn winds, when we used to listen to the 1AM freight rumble out of the Rude Bridge Hills, and the whippoorwills nested in McCleerey's Hollow, and Jenny could still count into double digits. Time shifts now, until the past can't always be distilled to its most honest form; everything is filtered through the Judge and Nam — which I hardly think of as a whole anymore — coloring events with tinges of what rage was to come.

Back in a season when I still had a face, and Mrs Grantham hadn't started hiding my fake legs yet.

Summerfell's population ranked lowest in the county with a census reading of eight hundred. I remember picking a battered copy of Jim Thompson's novel *POP. 1280* off Philly's dusty shelf and thinking how wonderful it must be to live in a town that large. His Fawcett Gold Medal mysteries and Marvel Comics collection proved a constant root of anxiety for his parents, who continued to pay for his wasted violin lessons. Summerfell sprang from the side of Cower's Valley like a Norman Rockwell painting freshly completed and running wet with Middle American sentiment. My friends and I were bored sick.

We must have talked like kids, about adolescent musings and the travails of high school, but I recall only meaningful conversations on Philly's back porch, where we sat like four Kantian scholars. Jenny, Claire, and I would drink his mother's bitter iced tea and listen to him espouse on the world at large; political fervor hadn't quite made it to the local news, but even stranded in our dust-locked town Philly knew it was coming. He was the most serious person I'd ever met, and he enjoyed that fact immensely.

Claire, having already finished three novels, carried notebooks stuffed with the abrupt squiggles of her script. She emulated O'Connor, Faulkner, even James Jones throughout her junior year. Most of it fell flat and we blamed ourselves for not living more exciting lives. Sunlit and sunburned, her fiery red hair spilled in a rushed mass of curls over her shoulders like poured flames.

Wearing shyness the way other girls wore rouge, Jenny was all the more attractive for it. You could see the timidity in her, ever-blushing cheeks and downcast gaze, lovely and diffident. Embarrassed by her beauty, she seemed to hate her own sensuous lips and boiling blue eyes, heart-shaped face framed by a boyish haircut. She swathed herself in loose-fitting clothes in order to hide her large breasts, incredibly curved hips, and lithe legs; it didn't help much.

Her father was Judge George Ray Solomon, who grew squatter and more toadish-looking each year, genetic faults miraculously skipping Jenny. My own father had gone to county jail for thirteen days because in a drunken, sorrowful rage he'd once broken thirteen dollars worth of windows at the mill. Judge George had that kind of sense of humor.

The afternoon came when Jenny sat on the porch trying valiantly to shield a black eye from us, flesh-colored creams and powders doing nothing but drawing more attention to her face. Claire, with five younger sisters, already proved adept in the art of matrons, and showed the good sense not to press for information. Instead they sat together on the love-seat, rocking gently, toes brushing the wild-flowers creeping along the railing.

Tom Piccirilli is the author of eight novels, including *Hexes*, *Shards*, *The Deceased*, and his Felicity Grove mystery series consisting of *The Dead Past* and *Sorrow's Crown*. He grew up on the south shore of Long Island, New York and attended a year at Suffolk Community College before moving on to graduate from Hoftstra University. Just across the street from SCC is Pilgrim Psychiatric Hospital, which became the basis for the chilling Panecraft Asylum featured in several of Tom's novels and short stories. He is also the creator of the cult favourite 'Self' tales featuring a modern-day necromancer and his demonic alter-ego. Tom divides his time between New York City and Estes Park, Colorado.

Illustrations:
Wendy Down

"What happened?" Philly asked, without glancing up from a new John D. MacDonald paperback. "Looks like you've got a shiner." He'd worked hard to get down a particular kind of timbre, full of whispery hiss and quiet wrath, but never belligerence.

Claire tensed, her cheek muscles tight, lips flat and bloodless, fingernails of her left hand lightly *scritching* at the corner of her notebook. One side of Philly's mouth edged towards a disarming grin. I was never sure if Jenny missed all the expressions and gestures, or if she simply let them slide by. She made a courageous attempt at a smile. "I was feeding the dogs when Malice leapt and his snout caught me just right."

"Just wrong," I said.

"Just," Philly said.

There are times when major decisions are made without any prelude. Philly and I might have let her get away with this kind of lie in the past — but at seventeen we'd both topped off our growth spurts and each wore an extra twenty pounds of muscle on our lean frames. Philly closed the MacDonald novel and held it to his nose, sniffing that fine novel smell. "Good ol' Malice. Amazing how a fourteen-year-old arthritic Retriever still has it in himself to jump like that."

"I think we should put the old pup to sleep," I said. "He's obviously become delusional."

"We couldn't do that," Philly argued, the other side of his mouth lifting a fraction until that grin was complete, heated and ugly. "Think about how Judge George would react, wailing and whining, clutching the beast to his breast as the vet dragged Malice off, the dog howling, his master weeping, the two of them forever parted by the whims of fate."

"Maybe the vet would take Judge George, too, as an act of selfless kindness. The weeping master would be willing to lay down his life in the name of a four-teen year friendship, wouldn't he?"

"I would."

"Any man would. Then they could die happily together as it was meant to be, wandering into the sunset, heroes walking hand in paw, vet in tow, whims of fate skirted."

"I like it," Philly said. "The Judge has class."

Claire stood and threw her iced tea over the porch rail, hands white as china. "Both of you shut the hell up."

We couldn't help ourselves; frustration had been taking a firmer hold all summer, adulthood pressing in like factory walls. The mill would get us both before long, and that set the full course for our lives. I adjusted my glasses and whispered, "All right, I'm sorry." Jenny sobbed silently, no sniffles or wrenched weeping. Philly got up and reached for her as she twisted on the love-seat; his hands groped and she slipped free, a strange dance being performed. He tried to make soothing sounds but couldn't quite do it, the noise in his throat coming out piggish at best.

As he moved, she squirmed, always in opposing directions, Philly's arms flashing, wildflower petals spinning against the shutters. Claire and I watched, and I could see the desperation to begin writing this scene down burning in her face. We were on the verge of something new, and understood we'd already started down different passages. Jenny dodged again, rose and stumbled from the porch, leaving Philly with his unhappy grin still stapled in place before he went back to his novel. He held the book up to his nose again and sniffed deeply, and I finished my iced tea.

That night Philly and I got drunk at the **Shore-Up Grille**, the same place where our fathers drank. Despite a few curious, sometimes warning glances from the regulars, as they watched another generation coming to do what they did, we found a worn and stained bench seat in the back. We'd already drank a lot of beer in our lives, but this was our first serious turn at whiskey. The waitress, Debbie Lee McCallister, had graduated two years ahead of us. Cut-off jeans one inch shy of covering her ass, Debbie Lee had more talk circulating about her than most.

She shot us bright smiles whenever we made eye contact, her black hair limp in an erotic postcoital kind of mess, belly only slightly bulging with her second child. That smile seemed as insincere as my ideas of heading to college, lighting up her face for only an instant, meaningless outside of gaining tips or lovers. When she wasn't serving men she draped herself over the end of the bar, smoking and rubbing her eyes, touching her top lip as if awaiting her mother's mustache.

Philly grew fouler as the night went on, the shots of scotch becoming less abrasive. "We ought to beat the bastard into the ground."

"That would solve our problems," I said, "but not Jenny's. Not anymore. You're right though, we ought to do something."

"I see what he's done to her. I watch it happening every day, and have for years, and he keeps scaring her behind all kinds of different walls, until she's terrified to even look in the mirror." His whispery hiss underscored his spite. "Can't bear to let another person touch her, in any capacity. There's no understanding what motivates the son of a bitch. What possible reason could he have to hurt her?"

"He doesn't need one."

"No?"

"No one really does, when you think about it."

"I won't. I can't." The burden of Philly's conscience played hell on his nerves. "It's not bad enough that he drove his wife to opening her wrists, or that his moods can keep people in jail for months. What's worse is that he's elected year in and out though everyone hates him. I can't believe we've been letting him put his hands on Jenny. That tin tyrant is coming down, I swear to Christ."

I agreed, though I knew nothing would be done.

Debbie Lee sauntered over, putting a little extra swag in her hips. Maybe she saw the whiskey working on us, and thought it would be easy to get our money or just a quick, ferocious lay. Her scent was a cloying mixture of sweat and lilac perfume. She dropped our shots in front of us with a hard snap of the wrist, giggling as if she'd found something grotesquely funny in the moment. Foam spattered my glasses, and Debbie Lee made a show of pulling my face down, down, to wipe them clean, so much further down into the apron around her waist. Her baby pressed against my cheek. "Let me help, honey. Here you go."

"Thanks."

"Don't you mention it none."

That smile wreaked as much havoc on me as what was happening to Jenny, or any of us. Debbie Lee kept it smeared across her face as she backtracked to her station. The drinks were having an effect; her belly appeared larger, as if we'd spent lifetimes going through these exact motions.

"Stop looking over at her," Philly said, slurring badly.

"I feel sorry for her."

"Why?" It wasn't a question, but a disgusted comment.

"Look, I know what's going on inside you lately because my gut's in the same state most of the time, but I don't need you on me for feeling a little remorse now and again, all right?"

"It's for old men."

"Maybe we are already."

He chuckled and shrugged, then took time to enunciate properly and did a pretty good job. "Not just yet. We've got more important things to do first. We're going to topple Judge George."

Instead, halfway home along the shallow creek path, he dropped to his knees and heaved until he passed out. Holding him in my arms, I stared at the slow trailing waters of the creek, hard-pressed and shifting a millennium of sediment. I carried him the rest of the way slung over my shoulder, neck creaking and skull stuffed with Debbie Lee's perfume. I dumped him onto the love-seat and listened to the 1AM freight chugging out of Rude Bridge Hills, and wondered if there was any way I could hop without breaking my spine, and if so, where it would take me and my familiar hate.

Of all places, not to Jenny's house — the Judge's house — which rested high on a perch at the north end of town. By far the richest home in Summerfell, a fusion of architectural types, the mansion spouted porticos and antebellum columns, colonial woodwork and an emerging modern taste for glass and skylights.

Judge George Ray Solomon sat in his den wearing a crimson velvet robe, kicked back with his feet on his desk. He smoked a cigar, toady-face set in its perpetual grimace. His hooded eyelids were semi-open in ecstasy as he puffed, rolling the wet cigar clockwise between his guppy lips, popping it out to blow smoke, and popping it back in. Crouched outside his window, my stomach turned and the last shot of whiskey rose two-thirds up my throat. His hands were the size of a young girl's, dainty and hairless.

Malice, who'd taken the brunt of lies again, lay in the dirt of a freshly turned azalea garden; the new lining bricks stacked near his head. He saw me, whimpered, and struggled to rise but the arthritis kept him down. I looked up at Jenny's bedroom.

I wondered if Philly had ever climbed the rose trellis and attempted to make his love to her. A year ago I thought he might have drawn her from her swathed sweater shell, but now his bitterness had gotten out of hand, along with the rest of ours, and Jenny would suffer for that too.

Wind splashed leaves against my legs. Sweat bathed my chest, dripping down the backs of my arms until I couldn't keep them at my sides anymore.

I tossed a brick through the Judge George's window and landed myself in county jail for thirty days.

The first thing I did when I got out was throw another brick through his window, and bought myself three months.

My mother pleaded with the bastard for weeks and he finally saw fit to let me out in just over a month, on the promise that I'd make a formal apology and paint his house.

County jail was a lot more Mayberry than Macon County, and the two deputies were both older brothers of guys I tutored after school. We spent time talking about Debbie Lee and other women, playing chess, eating the cakes my mother sent over every couple of days. Claire sat with me trying to get a hint of what she called the 'jailhouse experience', wanting to work it into one of her stories.

Finally, I'd managed to do something with the air of excitement. "Is there as much homosexuality in here as they say?" she asked.

"I've been alone except for when Gates Myrttle and Sammy Hocker got into a brawl and spent the night, and they never made a move on me."

"I'll have to use poetic license," she said, and I could just imagine what kind of bizarre scenarios she'd work onto the page.

Philly stewed every time he visited, his anger not entirely directed at the Judge. "Stop being thickheaded and apologize already. It doesn't mean anything. I'm all for stomping his ass into the ground, or some other kind of active retaliation..."

"Active retaliation?"

"...but this arrogant steadfast resistance is just wasting your life."

"Steadfast resistance?" Cronkite was beginning to filter into his syntax. "Thanks for mapping out alternatives. I've been considering a jail break."

The door was almost always kept unlocked.

"You're not too far behind in your schoolwork. You'll make it up in no time."

"I'm not sure that I want to," I said.

Disappointment marred his features, and I noticed his face had begun to sink in just like his father's. "I'll see you later."

When Jenny came she came alone, late at night, hoping I'd be asleep. I'd hear the door open and a few whispers pass between the deputies, and then she'd stand near my cot, smiling sadly. Sometimes we exchanged pleasantries but mostly we didn't, and that was fine. Once she put her hand on my inner thigh, an inept action that might have been meant to signify affection. Or some kind of repayment. We sat there for a while like that — perhaps with expectations — before she said, "Thank you," and left.

I was let out in the mornings to work on Judge George's home through the advent of autumn; I painted the porticos and trim, cut trees for firewood, and raked most of the four acre yard. I even buried Malice when his time came.

But I never apologized, so he threw me back in for another two months.

"You're a stupid little cuss," the Judge told me one afternoon. He almost didn't need a chair to sit in, his body always hunckered as if he were waiting to spring forward. Those guppy lips squirmed on their own, wanting to crawl off his chin.

"I like to think of myself as strong-willed," I said.

"Think of it any way you like, you're still breakin' your mama's heart."

"I'm doing a lot of things, but breaking my mother's heart isn't one of them. Actually, I get the feeling she's proud of me."

"You think so, huh? You could've gone to Daxton Central Prison. You've got lessons to learn, and you're making them harder than they have to be. Seems you're still under the wrongful notion that we're playing a game here, you and me, dancing or something. I gotta tell you, son, that's assuredly not the case."

"Trust me, Judge," I said, "I know we're not dancing."

He rose, if you could call that furled stance of his rising, and popped a cigar into his mouth. He bit the end off and spit it at my feet. "Have it your own way."

I turned eighteen in my cell — I considered it my cell, or on occasions my father's cell, having paved the path before me — and had just decided to quit school and look for work in California when they brought Thomas Martin in.

No one knew how Thomas Martin stumbled on us, but the word had been going around that he'd set up his trailer on the ridge outside Summerfell, surrounded by stands of Douglas Fir.

I'd heard of small towns decimated by World War II and Korea, where the odds played favorites and drafted nine out of ten men until the town dried up and blew off the map. Summerfell hadn't been touched by the Vietnam War in

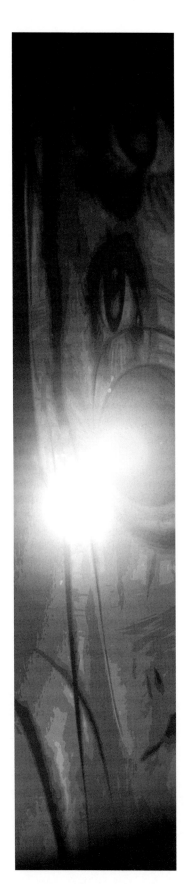

any manner. No one had enlisted or been drafted, and none of the other veterans — ten from WWII and seven from Korea — voiced opinions either pro or con.

Thomas Martin proved to be thin and clean-shaven, hair just slightly longer than military regulation. He wore glasses with lenses thicker than mine. The deputies were evidently uncomfortable throwing a man who'd served our country into jail, but Sheriff Stanton — whom I'd only seen three times my entire stint — growled adamant orders. Thomas Martin shook his head and chuckled occasionally, and sat in the cell next to mine.

"What happened?" I asked.

"I'm not certain I can describe it," he said. "Things have become hideously surreal lately."

"Okay. Want a slice of chocolate cake?"

"Sure, thanks. Just a small piece."

Ten minutes later, Claire ran in from a storm that had broken, gasping in an excited rush of giggles. I'd never seen her so giddy. Her wet hair flowed maniacally. I sat up. She smiled but stared solemnly at Thomas Martin. "Can I ask a question?"

"Please remember," he said, "this hasn't exactly been my day."

She went on without hesitation, pen in hand and notebook out. "Is it true you called Judge George Ray Solomon a 'third rate Ho Chi Minh' and smeared his face with dog shit?"

I burst out laughing and so did Claire. I couldn't help myself; she leaned up against the bars guffawing and I rolled on my cot.

"It's not that funny," Thomas Martin said deadpan. He turned to Claire. "You have the reddest hair I've ever seen."

"Thank you."

"In answer to your question, no. I called him a fourth rate Ho Chi Minh rat bastard because he kicked my dog, Barker, a fat basset hound that doesn't do anything besides eat, for absolutely no reason, and Barker, being trained not to take impoliteness lightly, snapped at the Judge's ankle. Judge slipped in Barker's recent droppings and went down to one knee. I never laid a hand on him."

"He's been upset since Malice died," I said. "The whims of fate could not be averted."

"Now what are you going to do?" she asked.

Thomas Martin took off his glasses and wiped the bridge of his nose. What I spotted in his eyes I'd never seen in before; they were separate pits of horror and humor, a marriage of the world and death. They told more tales than anyone would ever need to hear; certainly more than I wanted to know. Brown with specks of gold, shadowed yet clear, there was a lake of blood in them, and hatred, and twines of loss and gain, but most frightening of all was to discover that they held no fear. In that instant Claire, too, realized how childish and inept her questions were, and she took a step closer in awe and astonishment, slinking across the bars. Those eyes enveloped, lifted and carried me further than the fleshette mine would the following year.

He put his glasses back on. "Guess I'll simply take what comes."

I knew I'd apologize to the Judge the next morning.

He didn't show up for three days, and during that time — without asking — I got to hear a few of the long-driven stories from the life of Thomas Martin: he spoke of Vietnam in a glancing fashion, only mentioning it when talking of dead friends. He'd been on the Con Thien road and his unit had suffered forty percent casualties, and his best friend had been a hard-stripe sergeant who'd gone on Cong village sapper raids, bringing back hoochgirls. The war was simply a backdrop to anecdotes about his buddies, and he spent more time telling me of the garage band he'd belonged to in Detroit.

Thomas Martin said, "You know there's a girl who comes in here at night and just stares at us?"

"Yes. Jenny Solomon, the Judge's daughter."

"Beautiful kid," he said, "but in serious need of self confidence. The air around her shimmers with shyness."

I sat up. "'Shimmers with shyness?'"

"It's a lyric from one of my songs."

When Judge George showed his toady-face, I clambered off my bunk with a carefully formulated apology set to go — not too insincere but not penitent either. I never got a chance to say it because he'd already come over with the unnecessary key and let me out.

"Go on," he said. "We'll see each other again soon enough, I suspect."

"Me too," I told him.

He turned the key on Thomas Martin's cell, and gestured towards the front door without a word. I remember thinking how lucky Thomas Martin was right then to be a Vietnam veteran, that Judge George himself had paled before the glory of patriotism. When I got to Philly's house he'd just finished another John D MacDonald novel, and we got an early start on a binge, went out to the Shore-Up Grille and watched Debbie Lee waddle her girth across the floor, no longer smelling like lilacs now, and without even a smile left anymore.

Days passed in a blaze of stupid notions and vague ambitions; I dropped out of school and planned on moving west. My parents tried to talk me out of hooking up with the hippies, whom they expected me to join in an effort to take advantage of as much free love as possible. As my mother wept briefly, understanding there was no place left in Summerfell for me, my father pulled out a hidden bank book and forked over five hundred dollars.

Even without having attended classes the entire quarter I was able to help Philly with trigonometry and physics. He wore his broken grin, giving me long glances full of confusion and contrition. He questioned me relentlessly when he wasn't talking about saving Jenny and murdering Judge George. "So where are you heading exactly?"

"I don't know," I said, "exactly."

"And that doesn't bother you at all. You'll wind up where the highway takes you, hitchhiking until a stacked blonde in a muscle car skims by and screeches to a halt, checks you out sighing heavily, and lifts her sunglasses, one eyebrow raised, tongue jutting slightly from the corner of her luscious mouth, welcoming you into irredeemable acts."

"I hope so," I said.

"What are you going to do?"

I liked Thomas Martin's answer. "Guess I'll take what comes."

Other matters had grown unbearable, and they bled through whenever he tried to be conscientious. I knew he'd become more aggressive with Jenny, and that she'd rebuked him. She hadn't been around much lately, hiding more than usual, further proof of the wearing down of our friendship. "You just want to get laid."

"It is one of my many concerns," I admitted.

Claire had started a new novel entitled *Surviving the Big House*. She'd decided to read us winding, supposedly depraved prison scenes that lacked correct verb conjugation when Philly's mother walked onto the porch and told us that Jenny had fallen off a horse and been trampled.

A migraine instantly unleashed and my knees wobbled. Philly sucked wind and Claire groaned. One of us said, "That goddamn monster."

Being a few miles closer to the valley hospital, we actually beat the ambulance there, Philly driving his father's Ford in a neatly controlled panic. Only three doctors were on staff, and when the doors slammed open and Jenny was wheeled in they swarmed her. Judge George had outdone himself this time; both her arms had been fractured and her left knee looked three times its normal size. Philly fell back against a wall and began thumping his head. I started crying the second I saw her smashed nose and Claire held me close instead of the other way around.

Jenny's mouth ran rivulets of blood and she blew clots trying to breathe. She was awake and managed to fight the pain and tranquilizers they were administering enough to reach for me. She moaned something unintelligible, making pitiful noises so plaintive that I ran and grabbed the gurney. "What, Jenny?"

She'd swallowed teeth and her tongue needed stitches. "You got to...help... Thomas."

"Thomas Martin? Why?"

The doctor tried to shove me away, but I shouldered him in the chest. Jenny made feeble gestures. "...Go."

I glanced at Philly and watched him clunking his head and knew I was on my own, his impotence and lost love overwhelming him in the dim foyer. I hopped into the Ford and blew out to the ridge where Thomas Martin's trailer sat.

I parked and rushed up over the bank where Thomas Martin stood, Barker at his side, and the men around him just another group of ridiculous men the likes of which had wasted his time before. I ran as I would never run again, affixed on his grin, which stayed firmly in place until Sheriff Stanton kicked the basset hound. The deputies were rooted, dismayed. Thomas Martin shook himself as if from a dream, and flung himself forward. He opened his mouth to shout, making a rush while still foolishly believing — even after the war — that there were rules to be found...not quite understanding that the madness in those cruel corners of Vietnam was only slightly skewed from that of my hometown... where a jail cell could stay open and a man could slowly kill his child...even as Judge George lifted his rifle and shot Thomas Martin in the head.

Screaming, I caught the Judge with a roundhouse right, and they swiftly pounded me into the dirt, deputies putting on a show and giving me soft and clumsy kicks while the Sheriff and Judge made up a lot of lost ground. Ribs snapped and my nose wound up busted worse than Jenny's; it hurt but not as bad as it would've if I hadn't already been in shock.

After twenty minutes they left me there with Barker, who hadn't lived up to his name. He licked, whined, and when dusk fell he howled and curled beside me, the choking blood scent heavy in the air though they'd taken Thomas Martin's corpse with them. By the time I dragged myself home, heading into delirium, the mail was on my bed.

I'd been drafted.

Some tumblers take an immensely long time to click into place. I was with a whore in Saigon when it all came together; the shards of events snapping into place with a nearly audible clatter in my mind.

Despite the mortars and rockets hidden in the hills, the guns of CoRoc Ridge and the NVA .50 calibers blowing hell out of the Khe Sanh airstrip, it was a tiny fleshette mine — the force of the shrapnel being thrust upwards at a tight angle — that sheared my legs at the knees and took off the left side of my face.

I spent four months in a VA hospital, pretending to get along much better on the prosthetics than the other amputees although the legs were uncomfortable as hell and made my sensitive stumps bleed and ache intolerably. I hid the fact during physical therapy because I needed to get out.

It took months of searching and following leads before I finally found Philly a few blocks out of Haight-Ashbury, flashing on LSD in an unfurnished apartment with a cluster of other kids, including Jenny. The hippie phenomenon had already begun to grow corrupted, social outrage and communion giving way to the serious drug dealers and pimps. I lifted Jenny and searched her collapsed face for shimmers of shyness, but now she only looked like a toad.

I waited it out. I thought he might be a guru of some type, a nexus around which others orbited, but everyone who came into the room asked about Jenny instead. Apparently she was the supplier. I fed both of them and bathed them and kept them alive. It took Philly four days to recognize me. Jenny never did, and still hasn't.

Philly managed his grin, searching both sides of my face, scanning the scar tissue. He said, "Hey."

"How are you feeling?"

"Christ," he murmured, "they got your goddamn legs too, huh?"

"How do you feel?"

"Pretty good. Man, you don't know what it's..."

"I'm glad."

I used my crutches on him until he vomited blood, his kidneys bruised nearly green, a couple of ribs cracked, then hauled him to his feet.

My voice was full of whispery hiss.

"You set Thomas Martin up," I said. "You told Judge George that he was screwing Jenny, didn't you?" I slapped him and shoved his head into the wall, clunking it over and over the way he had that day in the hospital, his flesh even colder than mine. "You murdered him. You were willing to kill her, as well. Just because you were jealous."

"She fell in love with him," he grunted. He'd bitten part of his bottom lip off and the blood flowed free in pulsing gobs, that quiet wrath still showing through the agony. "She loved him. In her way." He wept, his arms spread as if wanting to hug me. If I hugged him his ribs would pierce his heart. "I loved her," he groaned, using the past tense though she sat near his knees with the whites of her eyes showing, busted nose dipping at the same inelegant angle as mine. "I loved her."

I left them there.

Once a season I get sentimental. Every time I'm about to go back to Summerfell my landlady Mrs Grantham sees the urge in my eyes and hides my legs; it takes a while of crawling around but I eventually find them.

Claire, married with two kids, lives out beyond McCleerey's Hollow, presumably happy. I never see her.

Instead, I return and beat the hell out of Judge George, making sure his shrieks hit a certain pitch, and he waits for me with the crystal realization that he deserves his fate no more or less than the rest of us. He seems to take more pleasure from it than me. Then I hobble down to creek's path and watch the flicking trails of water wearing the stones, shaping and shoving them along. I listen to the 1AM freight rumble out of Rude Bridge Hills and imagine that if I could run as fast as I had that afternoon on the ridge I would take the chance and jump the train no matter the consequences. There must be a sequel to my life. ∎

Being Vice President is not nearly as time consuming as people seem to think.

Oh sure, I have to defend freedom and democracy, but not that many people die around the world. Not important ones. So I get time to try to be interested in things and to go places and to meet people. Geo thinks its very important to get a feel for the common people so I do whenever I can.

And they appreciate it. Just last night, for instance, Wayne — he's one of our numerous body guards and very common — he said, "Excuse me, sir, but Mrs Quayle asked me to remind you about going to *Swan Lake* tonight."

"Gosh," I said, "it's a little on the cold side for swimming."

Wayne laughed and said, "Hey, you're grooved in there a lot more than people think, sir."

And I laughed along and said, "I do my best, Wayne."

We go out a lot of nights, Maddy and me. In fact, there are a lot of misconceptions about the Vice Presidency. The time thing is only one of them.

Of course I had a lot of things going for me when I ascended to my high office. For one thing, Geo had already done a lot of Vice Presidenting so he could explain all the stuff he wanted me to do.

For another I already knew my way around Washington. I was a Senator for eight years, remember, like Jack Kennedy.

Washington is not nearly as hard to learn your way around as a lot of people think. Of course I had an advantage there too. Way back years ago they hired the same guy to build Washington as built Indianapolis and he used the same plans. So I'll tell you a little trick I use. Whenever I have someplace to go in Washington, I just think of the name of the street it would be in Indianapolis and that way I know where it is.

But what you really want to know about is that murder I solved, isn't it?

Well, it was just one of the things that results from the fact that being Veep doesn't take all the hours that God sends, bless Him.

I mentioned the trip to *Swan Lake* already because I wanted to show that Maddy and I do a lot of social engagements. Although I don't have official duties at most of them, often as not people ask me to comment on one thing or another and because I am important they take a lot of notice of what I say. So even when I'm not being VP, I can't get away from it, if you know what I mean. So it's a full time job all right. I may get a lot of spare time but it's not as spare as other people's.

Of course I do have a lot of specific jobs and not just to go to funerals or to generals in South America. I am in charge of the Senate and that helps me keep in touch with a lot of my old friends and use my influence. And I am Head of the National Space Council. That takes some time.

Not that I know everything there is to know about space. Well, nobody does, do they? Space is a huge area. There's a lot of uncharted waters in space and one of our jobs is to draw a map of them. But I read about space when I get a chance and I get a lot of experts to read even more about it. Nobody expects me to know where all the streets are out there and I'm sure they weren't designed by that great guy who did Indianapolis and Washington. I mean, they were designed by God, of course. Now there is a great guy.

But I mentioned space because it's an example of how when I have to do something I don't know all about I get to have experts. In fact I have a lot of experts.

In fact I even have an expert on being Vice President. That's Pete. He's a real talented young lawyer and he's a great guy and a friend of Geo's and of Jim Baker's. That's one of the things about being in this team. Everybody cares. Important guys like Geo and Jim take time from their busy schedules to show an interest in just about everything I say and do. Not that they're more important than me. Well, they are, but not in the fundamental kind of way because everybody is equal really, and that's one of the things that made this country great.

But they do care and that helps me care about them. Especially Geo, of course, because he's the one who took me out of Indiana and put me into the world. I really love the guy. Well, you know what I mean. It's okay for a guy to love a guy that way. I mean, I would really miss him if he was gone. I mean, for instance, if Geo died or something, well I just don't know what I'd do.

But the murder I solved, you want to know about that.

It began, I think I'd have to say, when Maddy and I went to this dinner at the Fortesques in Georgetown. I remember it because I had just been to track meet at Tucker's school and all the arrangements went wrong. First the camera crews got there late. Then my limousine, VP-1, wouldn't start so I had to catch a cab from the kids' school.

And I remember the taxi driver, a fully equal person of color, and I talked to him, because it was a chance to talk to a common person and there also wasn't much else to do.

So I said to him, "Hey, how about that deep doodoo Marion Barry's in?"

The driver didn't say anything at first, so I waited. He might have been a little confused — which often happens when I speak to common people. Or maybe he even hadn't heard about it, because not everyone watches television, you know.

But at the next red light he turned to me and he said, "Did you hear the latest Dan Quayle joke?"

I was a little surprised, but I said, "Hey, you know, I *am* Dan Quayle."

"That's okay," he said. "I'll tell it slowly."

But then the light turned green and I guess he can't drive and talk at the same time. Before long we arrived at the Fortesques.

Marilyn — that's Maddy, my better half, well, not better but equal but different half — she was already there. And as soon as Pete and I walked in the door Maddy and Wayne — he was guarding Maddy's body that day — they came over to me. And with them was another woman. Well, Maddy said, "Oh Danny! The most terrible thing has happened."

"What is it?"

"Robin Fortesque has had another stroke. He's dead."

"He was in a wheel chair anyway, wasn't he?"

"Honey," Maddy said, "I'd like you to meet his daughter, Janine." And she nodded to this other woman.

"How do you do, Mr Vice President?" the woman said, and she was a pretty cute lady for her age. Not that I would look at another woman than Marilyn, except when I was being introduced or something.

"I'm fine. How are you? Oh, sad I bet because of your dad."

"Yes," she said.

"We first met Mr Fortesque last month," Maddy said.

"That's right," I said. I knew it was right, because Maddy's got a heck of a head for stuff like that.

"He told me," Janine said. "You made quite an impression."

"Janine. That's an unusual name," I said. "Is it foreign? Not that there's anything wrong with that, of course. Some of the best names are foreign. Or at least they were."

Geo taught me that: talk about them instead of yourself when you meet them. It's one of the little tricks that's good to do as Veep. He's one great guy, Geo and I'd really really miss him.

"We met in Milwaukee," Maddy said. "There was a convention for stroke victims that Danny was invited to."

Mike Lewin is from Indianapolis, where most of his many award-winning novels are set, but for not far off 30 years he has had the good taste to live in Somerset. He is something of a crime writer's crime writer, admired by his peers for his stylistic economy, clever plotting and glorious wit. He's a successful short story writer and radio playwright, as well as novelist. Out in the USA this autumn are *Family Planning* (St Martins), second in a series set in Bath, Somerset, about the Lunghi family of private eyes, and Mike's Young Adult debut *Cutting Loose* (Holt). He reads his own *Rover's Tales* on an audio book available now from Blackstone Audio in America. We're delighted that he has allowed us to use here one of his infamous stories about 'Danny', with whom he shares a home state.

Photo: Elsie

And then I remembered, there had been this big party with all these people in wheel chairs. I'd talked about wheel chair basketball and the technological advances that had been made and how good for the game it would be when they made wheel chairs that could jump.

"I remember," I said. "Your dad was the one whose wife kept giving him licorice, wasn't he? That's your mom, right?"

"He certainly seemed to like his licorice," Maddy said, not without a certain pride in her spouse's memory.

But this lady Janine looked at me in the strangest way. In fact it was so strange I turned to Pete and whispered, "Do I have a pimple on my nose or something?"

But before he could say "No sir, Mr Vice President, sir," or "Yes sir, Mr Vice President, sir," Janine grabbed me by the lapels.

Now Wayne was about to kill her when I said, "It's all right, Wayne."

You see, I didn't think that Janine meant it personally. And two deaths in one family on the same day would be a real shame.

Anyway she said to me, this Janine — and she was shouting — "Did you say that my father's wife gave Daddy licorice?"

"Yeah. Lots of it. In fact, he didn't eat anything else at this party, did he, Maddy? Even though it was a buffet and all the food was free and it was on a

...he turned to me and he said, "Did you hear the latest Dan Quayle joke?"

I was a little surprised, but I said, "Hey, you know, I *am* Dan Quayle."

"That's okay," he said. "I'll tell it slowly."

low table so guys like him could get at it. Isn't that right, Maddy?"

"Yes," Maddy said. "He ate a lot of licorice."

Then I said, "I like licorice all right even though it's black, but I wonder whether eating so much is good for a person."

Well, at that, this woman Janine screamed. She did! A real scream. And she ran away.

"Boy," I said, "her daddy ought to teach her some manners."

Of course people of foreign origination have different ideas of manners. That's one of the things you have to learn real fast when you're Vice President. I remember Geo told me, almost first thing, "Danny," he said, "you're going to have to get used to the fact that not everybody is like you."

And it's true. You do have to get used to it.

Well this Janine had no sooner run away screaming than she came back leading this old guy by the arm. "Tell him," she said to me. "Tell him."

"Please don't shout at me, lady," I said. "You may be an orphan but that's no excuse to shout because I'm not deaf. In fact I don't allow anyone to shout at me unless they're my superior officers in the National Guard or members of the Cabinet. And," I added stingingly, "you aren't either one of those."

"Tell him about Daddy and the licorice!"

Pete whispered, "That's the Surgeon General, sir."

"Oh," I said. I turned to the old guy. "Sorry sir," and I saluted. "What was it I can do for you?"

"Janine has just told me that you saw her father being fed a lot of licorice last month."

"That's right."

"Well spotted, Mr Vice President. I congratulate you."

"Uh, thank you sir."

Another thing Geo taught me was when someone congratulates you, thank them. You don't get congratulated that often in life that you can afford to turn one down.

Then the General and Janine went away again.

I took Maddy to one side and I whispered to her, "I know I am supposed to be friendly to everybody, but that Janine is really a pain in the neck, don't you think?"

But just about then I was introduced to the Botswana Ambassador, so I had to concentrate. In fact he looked like a chauffeur my Uncle Gene use to have. The chauffeur was pretty prickly so I said to this guy, "I don't want to offend you, so maybe the best thing is for you to tell me up front just what kind of ambassador a Botswana Ambassador is."

And that was the last I heard about Janine until I got the letter.

'Dear Mr Vice President', it began. 'My stepmother got sentenced to Life Imprisonment this morning and I wanted to thank you'.

And then there was a lot of technical stuff. In fact, I was busy reading up on space and I thought about just sending a standard 'You're Welcome' letter but then Maddy came in and I showed it to her.

"Oh my," she said.

That kind of annoyed me. Not in any significant way, because a love like ours is too strong for anything significant, but anybody can get annoyed sometimes. "Your what?"

"Do you remember Janine Fortesque?"

Well, of course I did.

"She's written to thank you for telling her about the licorice."

"Oh," I said. "What about it?"

"Well Janine is a doctor."

I hadn't realized that, but of course we are getting more and more foreign doctors over here these days.

"It turns out that what you said about her father being fed licorice proved that his wife murdered him."

"Murdered him? How?"

"With the licorice."

"They were only little pieces."

"Being a doctor," Maddy said, "Janine knew that licorice raises the blood pressure."

"It does?"

"It's all here. Glycerrhizinic acid in the licorice affects the adrenal gland and stimulates aldosterone production which promotes sodium absorption, hence fluid retention and elevated blood pressure."

"Oh," I said.

"Janine's stepmother was feeding Mr Fortesque licorice in order to keep his blood pressure up so that he would have another stroke and die. And he did. And so the stepmother just got convicted of murder so Janine will inherit seventy-five million dollars."

"Wow!"

"So Janine's written to thank you. Without you, her stepmother would never have been convicted."

"Those stepmothers can really do it to you sometimes, can't they?"

"Danny," Maddy said, "you ought to let the world know about your part in bringing this murderer to justice."

"Do you think so?"

"Definitely."

So, world, that was the story. And boy, I'll tell you this: am I glad I never really liked licorice all that much anyway! ∎

PARKER by

When he was fifteen, Londoner Alan Austin started selling comics for a living – he was the first person in the UK to do so full-time. Many of the best-known names in the British comics boom of the 1980s came into the scene through Alan's famous duplicated fanzines (this was back in the days, mind you, when 'fanzine' didn't refer to a glossy, full-colour photojournal with a straight spine). Nowadays, Alan sells second-hand books instead of comics. He's been writing since 1990. Parker is part of a series, featuring one of the most unusual protagonists we've encountered in a while. Alan asks us to stress that the photograph above is of Parker, not Austin – though, frankly, we're not convinced.

Filthy grey trainers and ancient boots shuffled along the gravelled path under a slate sky, as old voices rustled and blew away on the November wind. Gravestones poked through the untended grass on both sides of the pathway to the stone chapel. No funereal black for this shambling assortment, other than the occasional armband. Trenchcoats held together with string, stained anoraks and body warmers, fingerless gloves and torn trousers. Standing either side of the chapel doors were two policemen, buttons shining. Behind the chapel in the road, an unmarked car with a plainclothes man smoking a cigarette. Coughs and snuffles echoed inside the chapel as the tramps took their places in the pews. A scuffle for positioning broke out momentarily, but was soon quashed by a voice harsher than the rest. Parker removed his rancid cap and grinned apologetically at the master of ceremonies.

The Catholic priest, who thought he'd seen everything in his long tenure at St Mary's, pretended everything was as it should have been. He managed to fool most of the assembled, who were intoxicated. The atmosphere was one of vague irritability rather than subdued merriment, these being habitual drinkers. The one note of sobriety stood at the back, a man in a black suit. Parker turned to him and, on seeing the man's face illuminated in a shaft of light from a high window, clutched his heart in superstitious fear — until he remembered that O'Brien had a brother, a man of means. He'd not believed it, until then. The resemblance was uncanny.

The priest said as little and as much as he dared about this man he knew nothing of, but whom he had judged by the calibre of his mourners. Music played, the doors opened and the ceremony was over. Parker waited until the rest had filed out, all except the man in black. Together, they took up position at the rear of the procession as it made its way to the open grave.

"You must be Parker," said the man in the suit.

"Uh-huh," said Parker. "And you'd go by the same name as the one in the coffin."

"We weren't twins, but the resemblance was close when we took to wearing beards and glasses. I'm sorry if I startled you."

As they spoke, several of the men in front were turning their heads, nudging each other and pointing.

"So it was you that laid all this on," said Parker. "I expected the pauper's grave for O'Brien."

"We hadn't spoken for fifteen years. He had his ways. But he was my brother."

"He was a friend of mine. How is it that you know me?"

"Ryland, back there in the car. CID. He drove me here. Said I should speak to you."

"I don't know who did it. I've already told them that."

"All right, so tell me all you know about Michael O'Brien."

The two men stood at the back of the crowd surrounding the grave as the priest sent O'Brien on his way. The coffin was lowered, the handful of earth thrown in, and the crowd edged away uncertainly, as if expecting more. Parker and Gerald O'Brien walked away to stand under a tree, as a light rain moistened the air. Back in the road on the far side of the cemetery, almost out of sight, a small group of men watched in silence.

ALAN AUSTIN

The man in black lit a cigarette, put it in his mouth, lit another from that and handed it to Parker. Parker told his story, in this way.

O'Brien was already there when I showed up. Must be seven, eight years ago. I'd moved around a lot, never more than a year in one place. Maybe London suited me, but O'Brien might have had something to do with it. I'm still here. Still hanging around the Embankment. It's a prestige address, you know.

The first time I saw him, he was drinking from a bottle inside a brown paper bag, like a Bowery bum. Only reason for the bag was the sherry was fifteen quid a bottle and he didn't want everyone to know. He always covered his drink in a paper bag, because it was always the best. Took me a while to find out, but when I get curious about something I don't let it go like most of these wet brains. Most of them can't remember their mothers' faces. O'Brien was different.

Like me in some ways, and he picked that up soon enough.

For three years I watched him, and he didn't know how closely. But I sleep sometimes. I wake up and back he comes with the goods. Always had a drink. Never shared it. Even seen him sell it when he had spare, and next thing you know his shoes are shiny new. Sometimes he'd trade it for fags or a bunk up. It was driving me crazy.

Where did the fucker get it?

One day I lose my rag. "O'Brien," I says, "are you for real or what?"

He looks at me askance and says I'm not makin' sense. "You got a big house with a servant and a mistress, or is it the television you're doin' this for?" I says. He laughs like a lunatic, like what I said was really funny. I felt like thumping him, but I once saw him throw Fat Mary into the Thames just for the fun of it. Good-natured, like — he soon pulled her out. But no one buggered him about more than the once.

"Parker," he says, when he's finished his laugh, "maybe it's just that I've got my own personal guardian angel lookin' over me."

"More like the devil," I says, and he laughs even louder.

With that rusty hair and beard and those thick specs you couldn't tell what was on his mind from his eyes or a twitch of the jaw. But he wasn't disliked. Not by anybody. Not even by the coppers that knew him. There was no malice in him. I've seen him fight, but he never put anyone in hospital, least not for long. I once saw him pull some Jap tourist's kid from the path of a lorry. Did it quick, jumped off the bench before the rest of us even heard the brakes squealing, and saved the brat from a severe crushing. The daddy comes along and, not knowing what's happened, drags the kid from O'Brien's arms, babbling in his own tongue but pissed off all the same and O'Brien just shrugs it off. Me, I'd have put in for the reward.

Life was hunky dory at No.1 Bench, The Embankment, until Louise arrived. I'd seen her before, and I knew that she meant trouble. I'd seen her sitting with this unsavoury bunch in Leicester Square. A right pickle of degenerates, muggers and perverts. Filthy lot, I'd cross the street to avoid them. There she was, flirting with these dirty buggers twenty and thirty years older than she was, lewd gestures and the dirtiest language. A fine-looking girl, too. Good body, nice legs. Not one of those flabby bints with legs like saveloys.

Long green punk hair she had, too, but each to his own. And she always drank cider.

One night around the middle of July couple of years back, she walks past us. About two in the morning, and the roads were quiet. O'Brien was drinking wine and kept on saying how pleasantly pissed he was and just in the mood for it and so Louise walks past and gives him a look. He smiles at her but she keeps on walking, under the bridge, and I see O'Brien's eyes follow her arse. Into the shadows she goes and we lose her. Can't see her at all in the dark under the bridge. Then out she comes the other side and she's standing under a street lamp, bending over with her skirt hitched up and her bare backside pointing in our direction. Beautiful white and shining, it was, in the reflected light, like Greek sculpture in a museum. Only the girl's head is turned back and smiling at us from under all that green hair.

I make to stand up, but O'Brien pushes me down with his left arm and pockets his booze inside his overcoat with the other, and heads towards the bridge. The girl has rearranged her clothes and she's walking on, but not very fast. O'Brien caught her up before the next bridge and that was the last I saw of them for a couple of days.

"What are you looking at?" he said, next time I saw him, striding through the tube station just after dark. Maybe I was jealous. Louise didn't hang around with us, but every now and then she'd stand outside the tube until O'Brien saw her. Sometimes he'd go off with her, sometimes he'd put his feet up and go to sleep. He didn't want her to get the wrong idea.

One day I was going through Leicester Square and there was some heavy conversation going on with Louise and a few of her friends. I got the gist of it from the other side of the fence. The girl had sussed that O'Brien had some way of getting drink whenever he wanted it and the others were onto her to find out what the source was. I was curious myself, of course, but the thought of that filthy lot taking an interest in O'Brien really got my bile up. I went back to warn him.

He was in the Gents down from the tube having a fag. I told him someone wasn't minding their own business far as he was concerned. Told him what I'd heard. I half expected him to laugh it off, but he swore like a nutter, grabbed me by the throat and asked me to describe the scum I'd seen Louise with. He knew them, but only vaguely. It came into my head as the right time to ask him right out where he got the booze.

I came to, I don't know how much later, with a sore jaw and a bruise on my head where I'd hit the porcelain on the way down.

I was angry with him, but I saw his point. It was a dumb thing to ask. O'Brien made himself scarce for a few days. Louise came by and asked for him, so I told her he'd joined the navy. But he wasn't one for running away. He rolled back one evening, pissed as a newt but determined to stay his ground.

He gave me a bottle of whiskey because he felt bad about knocking me down. Then, over the next few months, I got to know him better than anyone, often walking along the Embankment in the small hours just talking. He talked about Louise a lot. She may have been a slut but she had a hold on him. I'd try to talk him out of it, but he said he saw something in her that nobody else even imagined. She was still a pain from any angle. Never gave up asking him where the booze came from. He even gave her whatever she wanted in that way, but she didn't shut up. Maybe she was under some pressure from her pals in the Square.

One day she must have gone too far — or it just got to him at a bad time. I didn't recognise her at first. She was begging outside a Chinese in the Charing Cross Road. I thought it was Sinead O'Connor. Head shaved down to a grey stubble, flecked with green. I said something about the radical haircut. O'Brien took a dislike to her hair, was all she'd let on.

That night was the last time I saw O'Brien in one piece. He thought he'd managed to shut her up. Apparently she'd fallen asleep, dead drunk, when he was playing with his cut-throat razor, half-a-bottle less pissed than the girl herself. She had a few nicks, but he did a nice job under the circumstances. Maybe he wanted to be free of her and somehow he'd worked out that if he cut her hair off she'd lose her appeal, lose her power over him. But it was a mistake. She went straight back to the Square — and there was more than one of them sweet on her in their own warped ways.

O'Brien wasn't around the next night. It was pissing down at about one o'clock in the morning, and I was under the bridge making the most of a cheap sherry. A copper I'd seen off in the distance, asking questions of some people I knew by the tube, walked up to me and asked if I'm called Parker. They must have fingered me. I'd done nothing, so I told him. He asks me to come with him, friend of mine's in hospital, hurt bad and asking for me.

He was fitted up with tubes to his arms and nose and looking cleaner than I'd ever seen him. He was barely conscious. Nurse told me he'd been stabbed twenty-seven times. Copper tells me to find out who did it. They left me alone with him.

"You're looking well," I said.

"Don't talk shit, you thick fuck. I'm done for." He could barely speak.

I asked him if there was anything he wanted to tell me.

"Find yourself a nice girl and settle down somewhere," he said. I told him not to come the crap.

"Stay away from Leicester Square".

That was as much as I could get out of him. He nodded off. The nurse came in, called the doctor and he said O'Brien was in a coma.

He died at half past three in the morning.

Parker and Gerald O'Brien reached the other side of the cemetery as Parker finished his story. The Embankment drunks had disappeared, but the police presence remained. As O'Brien walked out of the cemetery gates, into the road, a shrill scream came from the other side, where a group of shabby men holding bottles and cans stood on the pavement. With them, a girl with shaven hair holding a bottle of gin.

"It's him! The bastard's come back!" She turned and tried to push through the crowd behind her, but they stood still in confused silence. The girl, unable to retreat, came across the road, weaving unsteadily. Standing on the white line, she took a drink and shouted across to the other side as the vehicles sped by.

"Look what you did to my hair, you shit! My hair! It was all I had that I was proud of! You knew that, didn't you?" She was looking at Gerald O'Brien, who remained silent. "Ghosts in daylight now, is it? You don't frighten me, you ginger bastard!"

Louise took a step backward and a car swerved to avoid her. Another sounded its horn and she turned to hurl abuse at the driver. The unmarked car with the CID man in front and the two uniformed men in back came slowly up to the kerb where the Leicester Square drunks were standing, and stopped. All three cops got out as Louise threw her bottle at O'Brien, who stepped aside. Parker took a few steps backward and stood the other side of the cemetery gate. One of the tramps called Louise back but she didn't seem to hear.

"Louise, come back and keep your trap shut!" he said. Parker recognised him as one he'd often seen with the girl in the Square, and in dark alleyways.

Louise raved on. "Do you think I liked being screwed by you? Not after the first time, I didn't. No matter how pissed I was, you stinking creep! Twenty-seven times I slept with you. Twenty-seven times you penetrated me, but you kept it all to yourself. Not even a hint, you selfish bastard."

The uniformed policemen stepped out into the road, following a nod from the CID man, who had heard enough. Louise struggled, but her strength was no match for the law.

Parker and O'Brien left the station together, having made their statements. O'Brien lit cigarettes for both of them as they walked along.

"That wasn't all of it, was it? Michael must have told you, before he died."

Parker grinned. "The nurse, she was a good girl. Not fond of the police, I reckon. I'm leaving the hospital, and she comes after me. Hands me a small bundle, wrapped up in a plastic bag and tied up with string."

"His personal effects?"

"All he had. He told her not to let the police see it, and only to let me have it when nobody was around. It was a bunch of keys, and a note. Your brother was a bright spark, all right. Never realised how bright, until I read that note. In it he tells a fairy story. About a man in need, desperate need, who finds the key to what he wants, or what he needs.

"One night, he's walking down some dark passage back of some warehouses off Covent Garden. A door opens and a man comes out, locks up. O'Brien watches him from the shadows. Man goes to put the keys in his back pocket, but drops them as a lorry goes by out in the street so he doesn't hear them drop. But O'Brien had seen them glint by the light of a street lamp. He picks them up, then dives back into the shadows. He waits until no one has passed the end of the alleyway for about half an hour. It's very late, dead quiet. He walks over to the door, keys in hand. Sorts out which keys are most likely to fit which locks. There's three of them, and eight keys on the bunch. Couple of minutes and he's through the door. He sees an alarm on the wall just inside the door: old type, that needs a key. Finds a small one and turns it off. He reaches for a light switch and all of a sudden it's Christmas. The place is full of drink.

"He can't handle it, so he just sits down and has a quiet think. Then, calm as you like, he gets up, walks out of the place, locks up, without taking a single bottle or even a can of lager. He goes to Clerkenwell, knocks up someone he knew in a previous life who knows about keys. Gets casts made. Goes right back and drops the original set, right where the idiot dropped it. He waits a couple of days, then goes back in the middle of a Sunday night with his own set of keys. First key he tries goes in, turns. Nothing's been changed. Opens the door, alarm off same way as before, shuts the door behind him and he's in. Up and down the aisles he walks, like he's strolling in a supermarket. Takes half an hour savouring it all. Finally decides on a bottle of best brandy, and that's all he takes. Out again, alarm on, locks secured, gives the door a good shove to make sure it's solid, you never know who's about. You can see his mind working, and can't you just admire it? Never takes more than a few bottles at any one time. A place that size, they'll never miss it. Or if they do, they'll put it down to pilferage by staff and sack some innocent kid who humps the stuff about. Even more likely, it's just a shade over the pilfering that some bastard's been up to already."

"He always was better than me at school," said O'Brien. "They always told me to pull my socks up so I'd make something of myself one day, like my brother was sure to do. Didn't turn out that way." They stood on a busy junction by a set of traffic lights. O'Brien threw his cigarette into the road and looked at his watch. "It's late now. But I know a club. You look like you could do with a meal."

"If it's all the same to you, Mr O'Brien, I'll say no thanks and pass, on account of I've some late shopping to do."

Parker walked off into the night. O'Brien detected a spring in his step that belied the man's appearance. ∎

CRIMEWAVE
Issue 3 is published on 1st December, 1999. Various special offers will be listed here for *Crimewave* subscribers.
B5, colour pb, 132pp, £6 or £11 two issues
Europe £7/£13 • RoW £8/£15 • USA/Canada US$12/$22

THE THIRD ALTERNATIVE   *ISSUE 20 OUT NOW!*
Glossy, colour, 68-page A4 magazine of breathtaking new speculative fiction, interviews, profiles, cinema, travel, reviews, comment and artwork.
Only £3 or £11 four issues
Europe £3.50/£13 • RoW £4/£15 • USA/Canada US$6/$22

ZENE   *ISSUE 19 OUT NOW!*
The definitive writers' guide to the independent press, featuring magazines and books from around the world.
Only £12 six issues (subscription only)
Europe £15 • RoW £18 • USA/Canada US$24

✳ SPECIAL DUAL SUBSCRIPTION OFFER (1)
A further discount for subscribing to *Crimewave* plus *Zene*.
Only £22
Europe £27 • RoW £32 • USA/Canada US$44

✳ SPECIAL DUAL SUBSCRIPTION OFFER (2)
A further discount for subscribing to *Crimewave* plus *The Third Alternative*.
Only £21
Europe £25 • RoW £29 • USA/Canada US$42

✳ SPECIAL TRIPLE SUBSCRIPTION OFFER
A further discount for subscribing to all three magazines.
Only £32
Europe £39 • RoW £46 • USA/Canada US$64

THE PLANET SUITE by ALLEN ASHLEY
A *tour de force* of memory, mythology and astronomy, this audacious book can be read either as a novel or collection of linked short stories. 'This is the course for the future!' *Brian Aldiss* 'Highly recommended' *Starburst*
Massive discount for TTA readers: £3
Outside UK £4 • USA/Canada US$7

FROM OTHER PUBLISHERS:

TALEBONES
From the USA, #15 of the highly regarded sf/f/h magazine edited by Patrick J Swenson. Stories by Larry Tritten, Hugh Cook, David Wesley Hill, Mary Soon Lee, Mark Rich, Sue Storm and others, plus an interview with Jonathan Lethem, columns by Ed Bryant and Janna Silverstein, reviews and much more. Digest, colour cover, 76pp, £3 (Eur £3.50/RoW £4/US$6)

Postage and packing is absolutely FREE. All offers run until the publication of the next issue of CW, when they may be renewed, dropped or altered.

Last Rites & Resurrections has sold out.

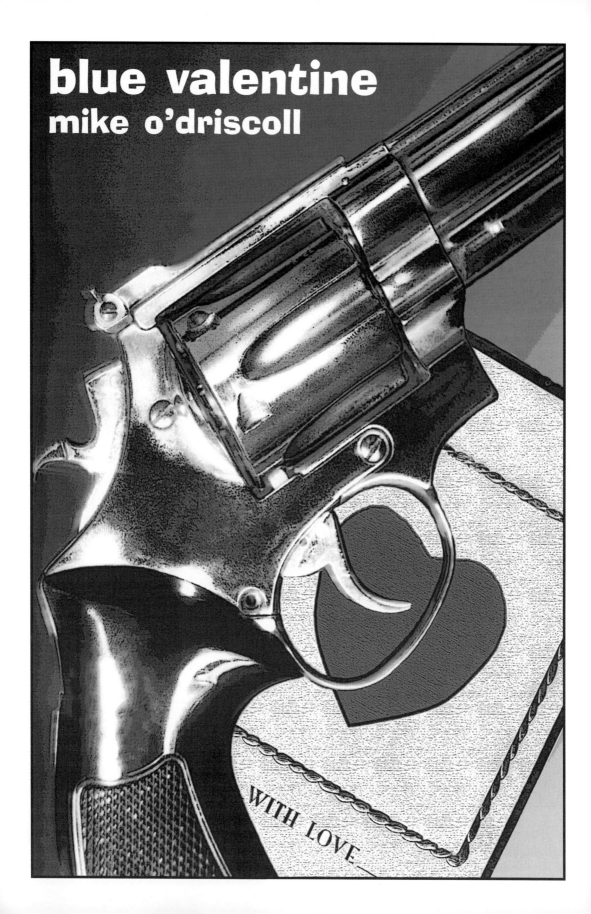

blue valentine
mike o'driscoll

Hope is a word that no longer makes sense to Cole Trenchon. There is one world of feelings and regularity and there is a separate, grey existence in which these things do not retain their conventional meaning. The old life is out beyond the window, represented by the migrant labourers heading back across the border and two old timers across the street jawing about matters he cannot comprehend and that young northern couple trying to get in touch with that fabled border ambience they've heard so much about but which Trenchon is sure does not exist.

He waits for death, not stoic or unafraid but wearied by hiding from the past. In truth, he has been dying for three years and such knowledge has made him old at thirty. He refills his glass with tequila, taking note of the others whose occupancy of the cantina seems preordained, as if here only to witness some ancient ritual. Though his connection to life feels tenuous and fleeting, it was not always so.

The call came that morning at the diner. He'd been working as a short order cook for six months, keeping to himself, not trying to build a new life, just not being who he really was. The manager called him out front and pointed to the phone. He picked it up, letting his eyes range over the fruit haulers and labourers who sat at the tables eating pork and beans, and for one moment he felt a terrible longing to unburden himself and in the process perhaps find some redemption. But the moment slipped by before he could flesh it out and when he spoke his voice betrayed the emptiness in the place where his heart used to be. "Yeah?"

"Hello Trenchon." The name was spoken hard and cold but even so, he detected some small measure of respect in it and for that he was grateful. It was a voice he had come to expect and recognising it he was almost relieved.

He tried to think of the right thing to say but in the end all he said was, "I'll be waiting," and even then the words fell but reluctantly from his lips. He hung up and went back to work, finishing his shift at midday, then walking the few blocks to the one-room apartment he rented on Arroyo Boulevard. It had a black and white TV set and a washbasin and was on the second floor above an adobe cantina called the *Lucky Star.* Once upon a time the irony of it would have meant something to him, but this was Nogales and he'd had his fill of such things.

The day had dragged on like an old blues song heavy with portent and pain. He'd felt the walls begin to close in, compressing the air around him, pushing him to the edge of panic where desperate thoughts crowded his head, whispering that it didn't have to finish this way. But he'd soon enough realised the treachery of such thoughts and it was this and the need to breathe for a little while longer which finally drove him downstairs to the cantina, not any desire for the company of strangers. He bought a bottle of tequila from Rafael, took note of the two Mexicans shooting pool at the rear and the pimp at the counter trying to flog his two jaded whores to a drunk, then made his way here, to this table by the window that looks out on the bustling street.

Dusk settles on him like a feverish chill, ushering ghosts to his table. In the past he'd kidded himself that he'd shaken them off, that he could get back to being a regular guy living some kind of regular life. He wrote those songs but all they ever amounted to was wishful thinking or maybe spells to ward off bad things. But no magic can change what he's done.

His head is tenanted with bad memories that caught him unawares. He wrote a song about that too but he cannot recall the words. When he first came to this border town, he'd allowed himself to think it was over, that what was done in the past would stay there and not dog him all these days. But he sees now that he was just lying to himself, trying to make things easier than they would otherwise have been. For when the past comes tonight, it will only be to put him in the ground.

After a week in Flagstaff the town's inertia was getting to Trenchon. He was down to his last twenty-nine dollars and Los Angeles was still over 500 miles away. The

If you've been reading in the science fiction or horror fields over the last few years you're sure to have seen at least one of the more than forty stories that Mike O'Driscoll has sold to various magazines and anthologies. Now he has diversified into cri-fi, bringing with him the attention to atmosphere and character which have made his reputation in the so-called 'dark fantasy' world. Mike, who lives in Swansea, owned a video shop for five years, which perhaps explains the cinematic nature of his writing.

Illustrations: Wendy Down

snow still lay thick on the San Francisco mountains to the north and the nights were still bitterly cold. Faced with the prospect of sleeping in his old Ford, Cedar City was beginning to seem like a fond memory. Then this morning he'd seen an ad in the local paper for a singer at a club out on route 40. He went and did three songs for the owner who told him his regular guy had fallen on the ice and broken his hip, a sign, Trenchon figured, that his luck was changing. Five songs into his set that evening and with the small crowd of bikers and truckers working hard to maintain their indifference, he realised he was right; it was changing for the worse. He started out with his usual covers, Kris Kristoffer-son, Johnny Cash and John Hiatt before playing two of his own songs. No one seemed to notice.

He launched into a Tex-Mex version of 'He'll Have to Go' and was rewarded with a few tapping feet, but when he finished forty minutes later with another of his own songs, a country blues ballad called 'Don't Paint Me Blue', their lack of appreciation had got to him. A waitress told him a lady wanted to buy him a drink. He walked down to the far end of the bar where a woman he thought too beautiful to be on her own, sat alone at a table. She wore a tight fitting black trouser suit with a white blouse beneath. Her raven hair was pinned up atop her head and her pale throat shone with a thin veil of sweat. Trenchon stood before her, taking in the sight while she looked him over in return, neither of them making any bones about it.

"You tried hard," she said. "You deserve better."

"Thanks," he said, figuring she was too smart to be coming on to him but hoping she was anyway.

"Sit down, have a drink," she said. "Martini okay with you?"

"Fine." He slid into the seat beside her. "What's your name?"

"You played here before?" she said, ignoring his question.

"First and probably last gig here. I'm moving on tomorrow."

"Shame," she said. "That song you finished with, that your own?"

Trenchon nodded. "Wrote it a month ago."

"It's beautiful."

Her closeness both excited and weakened him, but such confusion was a sweetness to be welcomed. He wondered if she knew the effect she was having on him or what demands she might make of him. He felt certain that there would indeed be some.

"Is that definite, you leaving town?" she said, after a while.

Trenchon shrugged. "Haven't had much luck round here. Maybe I'll do better someplace else."

She put a hand on his arm and what had been a suggestion of arousal in his mind became something solid in his jeans. "What would you say to staying on here awhile?"

"I'd say you're not serious then ask what you have in mind."

She laughed and removed her hand. "My husband has invested in a club. He's hired some musicians but he's still looking for a singer."

"You're offering me a job?"

She took a pen and piece of paper from her purse, wrote something down and gave it to him. "Come tomorrow," she said. "Eleven o'clock."

He looked at what she'd written, the name of a club on Izabel Street. "I don't think so," he lied. "I really should be moving on."

She stood up, leaned over and brushed his cheek with her lips. "Whatever," she said, moving out from behind the table. "It's your choice." And she walked away, not looking back but leaving him there, half-desolate and not even knowing her name.

The *Blue Lariat* was a long, single storey saloon with its name spelled out in an arc of neon letters over the entrance. Trenchon carried his guitar inside and saw a guy in a suit leaning on the counter. He turned to face Trenchon, brushed his light brown hair back over his head. "You're the singer?" he said.

"I don't see anyone else auditioning," Trenchon said.

"The trenchant Mr Trenchon," the man said. He was taller and heavier than Trenchon but he moved with surprising grace as he came out from behind the counter. "I'm Cable Jessop. Stage is up there." He went through a door off to the left and Trenchon stepped up on to the low stage and took his guitar out of its case. A Washburn semi-acoustic with a rosewood fingerboard and spruce front, it cost him $500 in a second-hand music store in Portland ten years ago. He plugged the jack into an amp and began to strum a few chords, feeling the tension fall away. Jessop returned, followed by the woman from last night and another man. "This is Mr Guddrew," Jessop said. "And his wife."

"Sheryl says you can sing, Mr Trenchon," Guddrew said, opening a bottle of beer. He was of medium height and his powder blue suit failed to conceal his spreading waist. "Let's hear what you can do."

Trenchon glanced at Sheryl Guddrew who lifted herself onto the counter. She wore red jeans and a loose-fitting blouse and she gazed back at him with an intensity that unnerved him. She laughed, as if sensing it. "Stage fright, all of a sudden?"

Trenchon did 'It Feels Like Rain', and followed it with 'Silver City'. Guddrew sipped his beer, while Jessop stood beside him mouthing the words. "You got some of your own stuff?" Guddrew said, when Trenchon stopped playing.

He nodded and sang 'Death Valley Oasis', and 'Gonna Take Yesterday With Me When I Go'. When he finished, Sheryl Guddrew clapped loudly and looked at her husband who said, "You think he'll fit in?"

"Get real, Mace," she said. "He's better'n them already."

Guddrew turned to Jessop. "Whaddya think, Cable?"

"He's got talent, Mace. Give him a shot."

"Looks like you got a residency, Trenchon," Guddrew said. "I'll leave Cable and you to work out the details."

Trenchon didn't know what to say; it had happened too fast. He watched in confusion, as Sheryl Guddrew followed her husband out of the building. "Come have a drink, Cowboy," he heard Jessop say.

He went down to the counter and said, "Mr Guddrew know anything about music?"

"No," Jessop said, passing him a bottle of Coors. "But I do."

"What kind?"

"The good kind."

"Like mine?"

"We'll see," Jessop said.

"What business is Guddrew in?"

"You familiar with inquisitive felines?"

"Not music?"

"Call it the entertainment industry."

"I've heard of that — it's a broad term."

"That's right. So, you want the gig?"

"I don't know," Trenchon said, stringing it out. "I got plans."

"Sure you have."

"Girl I used to know works for a music publisher in LA."

"Is that right? Well, see, I know the fella who books the acts for *Mr Luckys*."

"*Mr Luckys* down in Phoenix? I heard of it."

"He has agents and producers showing up there all the time."

"Is that right?" Trenchon was interested.

"Could be that this is a case of serendipity."

Trenchon allowed himself to smile. "So when do I meet the band?"

"They'll be here soon."

"So what do you do for Mr Guddrew?"

Jessop drained his bottle. "I assess people's strengths and weaknesses. Like yours is the ladies."

"Is that so bad?"

"Depends," Jessop went on. "Some fellas can walk away even when it's there on a plate, others can't. Are you the walking away type?"

"Depends who it is I'd have to walk away from."

"Mrs Guddrew. She is not for you, understand?"

Trenchon remembered the touch of her hand and the promise of her lips. "I understand," he said, believing that he did.

The band was made up of Hollis, the bass player, Tony the drummer and a slide guitarist named Joe, who claimed to have played with Gram Parsons. They played five nights a week at the *Blue Lariat* and Trenchon used the gigs to fine tune his songs. It was three weeks before he saw Sheryl Guddrew again. She came in alone one night and took a seat at the counter. Lester, the manager, poured her a drink.

Trenchon had been wondering when she would show up again, but even so, he kept his mind on the music, leading the band through John Hiatt, Joe Ely and John Prine. He played half a dozen of his own songs and finished as usual with 'Don't Paint Me Blue'. They were hot that night and played three encores. Afterwards, out back in the tiny dressing room, he felt like he could walk on water. He filled the sink with cold water and stuck his head in, thinking of Los Angeles and the big time. He wondered why Sheryl had come, and was pleased that she'd seen him at his best. He towelled his face dry and pulled a clean shirt over his head. "You do autographs?" he heard. Turning, he saw Sheryl standing in the doorway, holding out a pen. She wore a black sleeveless dress that reached to just above her knees and carried a white jacket across her arm.

"How did you get back here?" Trenchon said, thrilled that she had come but not wanting it to show.

"How do you think?"

"You gave Lester the evil eye or you just walk through walls or some other kind of miracle."

"You believe in miracles?"

"Only the human kind," he said, watching as she sat in the only chair.

"That's the kind I do."

"Where do you want me to sign."

She leaned back and put her legs up on the dressing table. "I can think of some places," she said. "But let's not rush things."

"Can I get you a drink, or something?" Trenchon said, reaching forward to brush a few loose strands of hair from her eyes.

She caught his hand and brought it to her lips and kissed his callused fingers. "Something, maybe," she said.

A weird humming reverberated in his head and expanded out into the room. He was surprised she didn't hear it, nor the pounding of his heart. He remembered Jessop's warning then and reluctantly drew his hand away.

"What's the matter? You don't like appreciation?"

"You ever serious?" he asked.

"I put serious effort into avoiding it."

"I can't afford any entanglements."

"Is that what you call this?"

"I don't call it anything but what it is."

"What if I put a spell on you?"

"I bet you could."

"How so?"

"You're too beautiful to be human."

"You're perceptive. Don't tell anyone else." She took his arm again and pulled him close. "I might get burned at the stake."

Trenchon kissed her and tasted vermouth on her lips. She prodded her tongue against his teeth and slipped it into the space he made for her. When she pulled away he said, "I was right."

She laughed and stood up. "I'll give you a lift home," she said. "I hear you have a room near the observatory."

"Fine," Trenchon said, telling himself he could handle her.

"Five minutes," she said, leaving. "Then meet me out front." Trenchon finished dressing then went out to the bar and bought a bottle of scotch from Lester.

"You were okay tonight," Lester said, his glazed eyes betraying no obvious sign of approval. But given his usual taciturnity, Trenchon took it as a high compliment. "Had a special audience."

Trenchon said, "She said Mr Guddrew appreciated what I was doing here."

"Yeah," Lester said and left it at that.

She was waiting outside in her Mercedes. Trenchon got in and she pulled out into the road, heading south on route 89 and then south again on the Interstate. "This the long way round to Mars Hill?" he said, lighting a cigarette.

"It's the scenic route." She put a hand on his thigh. "Enjoy it." Trenchon tried to think of ways to make what he knew was going to happen not happen, but he was fighting a losing battle.

She turned off the Interstate and drove along a single lane blacktop for ten miles or so. When she swung the car off the road, he saw moonlight on a lake stretching away to their right. "I live out here," she said.

"So where's your husband tonight," Trenchon said. He opened the scotch and drank from the neck before passing it to her.

"He and Jessop went to Phoenix on business," she said. She was about to say more but he reached out and snaked a hand round her head, pulled her close and kissed her face, her throat, her lips. She put down the bottle, rose out of her seat and straddled him, guiding his hands down from her head. He slid them beneath her jacket and squeezed her breasts through the material of the dress, feeling her press against his groin. "I feel a miracle coming on," she breathed.

Finding the zip at the back of her dress he slid it down and slipped his fingers beneath the waistband of her panties and felt the firmness of her buttocks while his other hand moved round to cup a breast. She pulled back from him and freed herself from the top half of her dress so that the moonlight silvered her upturned breasts and dark nipples which he licked tentatively, as if tasting some forbidden narcotic. Her touch, when she reached down and unzipped him, was sweet and cool, but as she pulled the gusset of her panties to one side and bore down on him, he felt her heat drive the chill from his flesh.

After they had made love, they passed the bottle back and forth. She began to talk about her past, of childhood in Casper, the suffocating small-town mentality that had finally driven her away and how she'd ended up waitressing at a nightclub in Phoenix where she'd met Guddrew. They went out together for three months before he asked her to be his wife. She stopped then, as if waiting for him to say something, and though he wanted to, he did not know where to begin. She seemed to sense this and prompted him, "What brought you to Flagstaff? I mean, I thought all you country singers graduated to Nashville."

Trenchon looked out the window at the stars. "Nashville would be fine, but the truth is I'm heading for LA. I know someone there works in the music business."

"You're hoping to get a break?"

"Doesn't every singer? I've been bumming round for four years, ever since I got..." Trenchon didn't finish the sentence.

"Since you what?"

He looked to see if he could gauge her reaction. "I did some time up in Oregon."

Her expression of affectionate curiosity didn't change but he felt he had missed some subtle shift in her thinking. "What did you do?"

"I beat up a guy," he said, the words coming out wrong even though they were the truth. "I was doing some small time dealing in Portland. Some shitheel felt I was moving in on his action and decided to make a thing of it. Turned out he was friendly with the cops and I ended up doing five years. I was nineteen."

"Poor baby," she said. "You didn't deserve that."

"I was married," Trenchon said, surprising himself. He never usually spoke about it but here, now, with Sheryl, it seemed right. "She was a local girl. I got her pregnant and her folks tried their best to turn her against me and not have the child but we married even so."

"Where is she now?"

"Three months after we got married was when I got fucked by Portland PD. Mary never came to see me in jail, never even wrote. When I came out, she was gone and her folks wouldn't tell me where or even what she'd had."

"You still don't know?"

Trenchon shook his head, feeling something close to absolution.

"I'm sorry, Cole, that must've been hard to take."

"Forget it," he said. "I almost have."

"But not quite," she said, sliding into his lap. "Maybe I can help make it total amnesia."

Later, when she drove back into town, Trenchon made her stop at an all night store. He went inside alone and asked the guy behind the counter where the cards were at. He couldn't find what he wanted, it being well past the date, but he found a card with a picture of a blue heart on the front and no message inside. He paid for it and borrowed a pen and wrote her a simple message, then went back outside where the first grey light was showing in the east. He got in beside her and gave her the card.

She tore open the envelope and stared at the picture, a smile breaking across her face. "Valentine's Day was a month ago," she said.

He shrugged. "Read it."

She opened it out. "'Don't Ever Paint Me Blue'. That's your song, right?"

"I wrote if for you."

She laughed softly. "You wrote it before you ever met me."

"But even so," he said, "I had you in mind," and he really felt that he had.

Guddrew held a party out at his place near Mormon Lake to celebrate his fiftieth birthday. Nearly two hundred guests took advantage of the warm Spring afternoon to indulge themselves in his hospitality. The band played a set on the stage in the marquee erected on the lawns that swept down towards the shore. Afterwards, they sat around drinking beer and talking music but Trenchon only half-listened to an argument about whether Nancy Griffiths wrote better songs than Mary Chapin Carpenter, and he merely nodded when they asked for his assent that Garth Brooks was a major league asshole.

After two months in town, Trenchon was feeling restless. He had enough songs now for an album but he was still waiting for Jessop to come through with his contact in Phoenix. Every time he mentioned it, Jessop told him to be patient. Well, his patience was almost all used up. Consequently, his thoughts had turned back to LA and the break that was maybe waiting for him there. Only for Sheryl, he'd be long gone. They saw each other twice a week at a motel in Williams, and spent long afternoons fucking and making plans for a future which didn't seem to be getting any closer. He had money now, only a couple of grand to be sure, but enough to get them both to LA, if only she'd leave Guddrew. But for the moment she showed no inclination to make the move. Sometimes it was hard not to imagine that her feelings for him were superficial, that it was just the sex that bound them. He'd picture her doing with Guddrew the things she did with him and this nebulous masochism would make him resolve to give her up. But such was his feverish desire it made dust of his resolution. Whenever he brought up the subject of leaving she'd tell him LA wasn't going no place and he should have faith in Jessop. He would come through, she'd say, and laying beside her, holding her in his arms, he'd feel powerless to disbelieve anything she said to him.

Jessop came up and joined them. "So what about Lyle Lovett?" he said. "He did some acting?"

"He got his pecker out on screen," Joe said. "If you call that acting."

"That was Huey Lewis. Lyle was the baker."

"It was a shit movie anyways," Hollis said.

"Hey, Cowboy," Jessop said, turning to Trenchon. "What do you think, the Stones to do an album of country?"

"The fucking Stones?" Hollis cut in. "Jesus, man, I don't see that."

"No man, he's right," said Joe. "Listen to 'Far Away Eyes' or 'Country Honk' on *Let it Bleed*. Keith got the ear for it."

"That's pastiche, man," Hollis argued. "They're just pissing on the genre."

Jessop leaned close to Trenchon. "You got a moment?"

"Sure."

Jessop grabbed two beers from the table and led Trenchon through the guests milling about over the lawn and on down to the lakeside. "You're getting restless, Cowboy," he said. "Am I right?"

"I got plans, Cable," Trenchon said. "You know that."

"You're pissed I keep putting you off about my friend down at *Mr Luckys*, right?"

Trenchon said nothing.

"I was in Phoenix a week ago, ran into the guy. Introduced me to a fella called Frankie Carroll. You heard of him?"

"The record producer?"

"That's the guy," Jessop said, lowering his voice. "Only keep this to yourself. He tells me he's on the lookout for new talent, so naturally I mention you're playing for Guddrew and you play and write your own songs. So he says it could be he's interested."

Trenchon tried and failed to hide his excitement. "You mean he wants to come see me play?"

"He said you should put some stuff on tape. Like a demo."

"He wants to listen to my songs, is what you're saying?"

"Like I said, make a tape and I'll see he gets it."

"Goddam Cable," Trenchon said. "I won't forget this."

"Yeah, I know," Jessop said and wandered back up towards the party.

Trenchon lit a cigarette, his mind already mulling over what songs to put on tape. All originals or maybe include some covers for easy reference?

He saw Sheryl approaching and was eager to share his news. "I'm gonna make a demo," he told her as they walked together along the water's edge. "For Frankie Carroll."

"Hey, that's great," she said, kissing his cheek.

"Yeah, Jessop came through just like you said."

She put an arm around his waist and said, "I'm happy for you, Cole."

"If this works out, I want you to come with me."

"What are you saying, baby?"

"I want you to leave Mace."

Sheryl stopped walking and turned to face him. "It isn't that simple, Cole."

"Why not? You don't love him and you said yourself that all that fat fuck is interested in is money."

She leaned into his arms and kissed him. He felt himself getting aroused. More so when she reached down and squeezed him through his trousers. "We have to wait till the time is right," she said. She backed away from him suddenly and let out a small cry.

"What is it?" he said.

"Mace, I think he saw us."

"Where?" Trenchon said, looking up the slope towards the marquee.

"Over there." She pointed to the trees off to the left.

Trenchon looked towards the copse but saw nobody there. "You sure?"

"No, but Jesus, Cole, if he finds out."

Trenchon felt a surge of anger. "Look honey, he's gotta know some time."

"I know that," she snapped. "But not yet."

"Maybe I should talk to him, tell him it's — "

"What? Over? Are you out of your mind? You do not understand that man, what he's capable of."

"It's what we want," he said, stepping towards her.

She held up a hand to ward him off. "What you want, is to get us dead."

"For chrissakes let me help."

"I'll handle this. It'll be our time soon enough."

"When?" Trenchon said. "Or do you think I'm going to wait forever?" He turned his back on her and walked off along the water's edge.

When she arrived at the motel Sheryl seemed preoccupied and aloof and gave him no clue as to what was on her mind. She refused a drink and seemed little inclined to talk, undressing quickly and climbing in to bed as though in a rush to get it over with. Trenchon pulled off his clothes, worried at her distance, uncertain as to what it meant. She made love like she was going through the motions, as if all her passion was spent. Afterwards he began to fear that he might be losing her and that fear was a small sliver of pain in his heart.

"What's wrong, honey?" Her back was to him, her face turned towards the window. "Talk to me."

"It's Mace," she sobbed, turning to him. "He knows something."

"How?"

"I don't fucking know how. I just know he's watching me."

"All right, take it easy." He held her close. "Has he said anything?"

"You don't know him like I do," she murmured. "He doesn't work that way."

Trenchon sighed and sat up, irritated at her un-willingness to trust him. He reached for the bottle of scotch on the floor. "Maybe you're imagining it all."

He tipped the bottle to his mouth but she knocked it from his grasp. It fell without smashing and spilled scotch over the carpet. "You are such a fucking dreamer," she said.

The accusation stung him; she knew he liked to see himself as pragmatic, even if it wasn't always true. "Okay, so maybe he does suspect something. What's he going to do?"

She laughed but there was no humour in it. "You really don't know, do you?"

"So tell me."

"You don't see it, Cole, 'cos you're so caught up in your Goddam dreams."

He hit her hard across the face, bloodying her lips. He regretted it right away and felt like a heel. "Jesus, honey, I didn't mean — "

She got out of bed, her face livid with rage. "Don't ever apologise, Cole. You wanna be a man, that's fine, just accept the consequences when the time comes."

"Look, I'll talk to him, I'll make it okay."

"You're talking like a crazy man," Sheryl said. "He'll kill me is what he'll do if he finds out."

Her words were like stone. Maybe it was that or the fierce certainty in her eyes but, for the first time since he'd known her, he saw that she was deadly serious. It was a few seconds before he could speak. When he did, he told her that he would never let that happen. She held his gaze a moment longer, then nodded and began to pull on her clothes.

Hungover, it took him a few moments to recognise that the noise didn't originate inside his head. He got up and stumbled to the door. Opening it, he saw Sheryl, wearing a scarf and dark glasses. She hurried into the room and he closed the door behind her.

"What happened?" he asked, hoping he didn't already knew.

"He found out," she said, sitting on the bed. "He found out and he did this."

Trenchon sat beside her, gently removed the glasses and saw the discoloured flesh about her eyes and upper face. "Oh baby," he said, putting his arms around her. "How could he do this to you?"

"He found the Valentine card," she said, dabbing at her eyes with the sheet.

"Jesus!" He turned away in an effort to contain his anger. "He didn't have — "

"It doesn't matter," she cut him off. "You have to get out of here, now."

"I'll talk to the fucker, tell him you're through with him."

"Listen to me, Cole, you don't know Mace. He'll be sending Jessop and the others for you."

"Let them fucking come." Rage made him stupid, like some hot-wired punk.

"They'll kill you," she said, clutching his arms, pleading with him.

"Kill me?" He found it hard to believe that any of this was real. "You're saying Mace would do that?"

"Yes, and if he finds out I've come to you, then I'm dead too."

The truth of what she was saying finally sank in and brought with it a cold calm certainty. He would not run, he would not abandon Sheryl. "I can't let him get away with this," he said, the rightness of it like a fire in his brain.

"What you said before," she said, putting a hand on each side of his face as if to drive her meaning into his head. "About not letting him hurt me?"

"I meant it."

"Go to the motel and wait for me there."

"What will you do?"

"A gun," she said. "I'll get a gun."

"Yeah," he said. "Then I can make things right."

"I know that, baby."

"I love you."

"I know that too. Now go."

He pulled on yesterday's clothes and threw the rest in a shoulder-bag. It was just past eight, but the five hours sleep he'd already had felt like five hours too many. He ran down the two flights of stairs to the street and got in his car. He lit a cigarette and headed west out of Flagstaff, a slow fire smouldering inside his belly.

He was halfway to Williams before he remembered his guitar. He turned the car round and headed back towards Flagstaff, knowing that it was a mistake but doing it anyway. He'd owned the Washburn for ten years and to abandon it now would be like running out on a friend. He wasn't made that way.

He followed the Interstate around to the south and came on Mars Hill Road from the east. He parked in an alley a couple of blocks from the apartment building and walked the rest of the way to the entrance. His room was two flights up. Sheryl was gone and no one had been since she left. He found the guitar-case under the bed. He opened it up and ran his fingers over the rosewood neck, its smoothness calming him. He caught sight of something on the bedside table and as he reached for it his heart missed a beat as he recognised the cover.

It was the card he'd given Sheryl, the one she'd said Guddrew had found. There was a line through the words he'd written and below them, a new message in her hand.

He sat down heavily on the bed, his mind reeling as it tried to find a meaningful purchase on feelings that suddenly made no sense. Guddrew had found the card, that's why he'd beaten the shit out of Sheryl. He had to pay for that; that was something solid, a thought he could hold on to like a drowning man clinging to a piece of flotsam.

The squeal of brakes broke through his numbness. He ran to the window and saw Jessop and three others get out of two Sedans. He put the card in his pocket, grabbed the guitar and fled the room. He climbed up to the third and top floor and pressed himself against the wall, knowing what it was to feel real fear. Heavy footsteps came up the stairwell and stopped one floor below. "Try it." That was Jessop. The door opened and they entered his room. He moved closer to the stair-well, peered through the metal rails, saw his open door and heard them tearing the place apart as they searched.

"Nothing," another voice, then Jessop again, telling them to wait outside.

Trenchon pulled back from the stairwell and heard their footsteps come back out to the hall, then the door closing. "What's he looking for?"

"Some kinda card. Waste a fucking time 'cos Trenchon's long gone."

"You would be too if'n you done what he done to her."

"You saying you wouldn't fuck her?"

"If it was on a plate, mebbe, but he went too far."

"Maybe she was asking for it."

"Well that's a risk he took and look where it got him."

"Nothing's worth the risk where Guddrew's concerned." Trenchon recognised Lester's voice. "Especially not that bitch."

The door opened and Jessop said, "Have you assholes done debating the morality or otherwise of fucking and beating up another man's wife?"

"We done here?"

"Seeing as you asked, Lester, you can stay in case he shows up."

Trenchon waited till he heard the cars pull away, then went down and stopped outside his door. Sounds came from inside the room, scraping his nerves. His own voice, singing a ballad about drinking. He grabbed hold of the slim end of the guitar case, hefted it, then gave the door a gentle kick and took a step back.

"Who is that?" Lester called from inside. Trenchon heard something else, the metallic click of a clip sliding home.

"That you, Lester?" Trenchon called, trying to sound nonchalant. "Open up will ya, I got my hands full with breakfast."

"Sure." The door opened and Trenchon swung the case as hard as he could, catching Lester solidly just beneath the jaw and knocking him back into the room. He shut the door and kicked Lester half a dozen times in the head till he was still. His lower jaw was smashed and a bloody lump of flesh hung from his lips. Trenchon crouched over him, saw it was his tongue, half-severed. There was no movement from Lester, not even from his eyes which, strangely, no longer seemed so reticent. Sickened, he grabbed Lester's gun and left the building. Instead of returning to his car he took the bus out to Williams. Sitting in the rear he took out the card and re-read her words, rubbing salt into the raw wound of his heart.

It seemed impossible that the world could change so much in so short a space of time, making lies of all that he'd believed. Watching the hills to the north, he thought about the past and his wife, imagining his child, whatever it was, making new memories because, painful as they were, they made more sense than what was left to him now.

The curtains were drawn and the television was tuned to a country show on MTV; Johnny Cash in Folsom, his granite face proof against the vicissitudes of time. It was a hollow lie that left a bitter taste in Trenchon's mouth. His mood fluctuated between despair and elation, sometimes both at the same time. He tried not to think about the card fearing it might lead him to a truth he didn't want to acknowledge. It was easier just to keep focused on Guddrew.

It worked for a little while, until he remembered the things Jessop and his men had said and what they implied. It became harder then, not to think about Sheryl and what she'd done. By the time she rang in the late afternoon, his feelings for her had coalesced into numb resignation. "You're okay," she said, her voice a whisper. "You got away."

"You saw me leave," he reminded her.

"Yes." Something wrong, some uncertainty in her voice that pained him. "I'm not thinking straight, baby. I'm so scared."

"You're right to be."

"He's gone to see Jessop now," she said. "See why they haven't found you."

"I want you to come to me now," Trenchon said, desperate for her to mean something to him once more.

"I want to, Cole, but it isn't that easy."

Her voice sounded real; it was only the words that hurt. "Please," he said.

"He won't give up. I know him, he'll have Jessop hound us into our graves."

"Jessop is my friend," he said, blankly.

"Jessop is nobody's friend," she said. "The only thing we can do is kill Mace. Tonight. I have a gun."

"Kill him?" he asked, trying to come to terms with the real meaning embedded in her words.

"If we want to be together, baby," she said, "we don't have a choice."

"You want me to do it, is what you're saying?"

"It's the only way."

"And you'll wait for me," he spoke the lie for her, weighing Lester's gun in the palm of his hand.

"Yes, baby, then we'll be free."

"Yeah, free."

"Is everything all right, Cole, you sound…"

"No," he said, trying to make the words sound real. "Everything's cool."

"Wait for me," she said, then she was gone and it was as if he'd spoken to some other person, someone he'd never known and he figured that was the truth.

He waited, watching the red minutes tick by on the clock's LED display. Outside thunder rumbled in the north, somewhere over the Canyon. He flipped channels, looking for distraction, finding none. He thought about all that she'd meant to him and how little he'd meant to her. And Guddrew out there, gunning for him and the worst of it was, not knowing why. If he knew that, he could accept the way things had turned out. Cable would know; he was a shrewd operator, his friend. What would be simplest would be to go now, before she came. Walk away from it all, forget he'd ever met her. That's what Cable would do.

At the window he opened the curtains a crack and watched the darkening sky. Rain was falling and lightning flashed in the north. Thunder followed, nine seconds later. There was never enough time. He returned to the bed and picked up his guitar, strummed it gently and began to play 'Don't Paint Me Blue', silently mouthing the words. In the quiet gloom he played all his originals, putting a gloss on a world that had lost its sheen. He lit a cigarette and read the card once more in the brief flare of the match, trying to recapture what he had felt when he'd written his message. The match died and he saw another light streaming through the crack in the curtains and moving across the back wall. He put away the Washburn as he heard the car pull up and its engine shut down in the angry hissing rain.

A listless wind drifts down Arroyo Boulevard, carrying the sound of an engine and whispers of escape to his ears, but the stink of desperation exposes the lie. Nogales slumbers on unaware. Trenchon stubs a butt out in the crowded ashtray and glances through the window to see the dark sedan pull up beside the pimp's Toyota. Jessop gets out; he's hardly changed at all, maybe just a little thicker round the waist.

He stares through the window of the *Lucky Star*, his gaze falling on Trenchon who is wondering how long he'll take to die. He drinks the last dregs of tequila, wanting it to wash away his fear. It doesn't. It hangs off him like an invisible shroud. The worst thing about death is the anticipation of it but this is not a new insight, nor one that offers relief. Jessop steps through the door and comes to his table. There is neither hate nor anger in his eyes, perhaps only a little regret. "How've you been, Cowboy?" he asks.

Trenchon's gaze wanders the room, spies Rafael and the others watching the newcomer, scenting excitement, maybe even blood. "What took you so long?"

Jessop shrugs then says, "Time to go." He turns and walks back out to the car. A moment later, Trenchon follows and gets in the passenger side. Jessop pulls out into the road, heading south. "How come you stopped here?"

Meaning, why hadn't Trenchon gone south of the border? It's a question he's often asked himself and the only answer he ever came up with was that he hadn't wanted to draw it out any longer. "You'd have followed me down there."

"True enough," says Jessop.

He drives in silence to the border post where two weary cops wave them through. Mexican Nogales is drab and lifeless and soon behind them. Out in the desert on the highway to Magdalena, the cloudless sky is full of stars. Trenchon watches them for the first time since he became aware of his dying and remembers the fascination they had held when he was a kid.

Jessop gives him a cigarette and says, "I never wanted to kill you, Cowboy."

Trenchon wonders if he's playing games but then he realises that Jessop too might be in need of absolution. "You don't have a choice."

"No, not after what you did. Tell me why?"

It doesn't matter now, Trenchon realises. The truth can no longer hurt. "It was supposed to be Guddrew," he says, then takes a drag from the cigarette and holds the smoke in his lungs as if it were something precious. "After what he did to her. After what she said he did. I would have too, it was in me to do it but I went back to my room after she'd gone."

Jessop nods but says nothing.

"I found a card I gave her. After all we'd been through, after what I was going to do for her. I figured Guddrew made her write that and that it was a case she didn't have the guts to tell me it was over. But I was wrong."

"How do you figure?"

"I was there when you came looking for me, hiding upstairs and I heard what you said, that I was the one who hurt her. It made no sense till I realised she put the card there for you to find and take back to Guddrew."

"Meaning," says Jessop, slowly, "he'd never seen it."

"Meaning none of it was real, not the bruises, nor Guddrew's finding out."

"Not until you made it real," Jessop agrees. He takes the next turn off the highway on to a dirt road, drives a mile or so, then pulls over. "Let's take a walk."

They get out and head east into the desert, Trenchon a little in front. They walk two hundred yards or so when he stops, his mind weary but still wanting answers. "Why did she do that to me?"

"It wasn't just her, Cowboy."

"What do you mean?"

"I told you she wasn't for you, right from the start."

"What are you saying?" Even as he asks the question, the truth infects him like poison.

"What she wrote," Jessop says. "About you leaving her alone; I told her to write that." He takes a gun from his jacket and points it at Trenchon. "You should have listened to me, Cowboy. You should never have fucked her."

He was right, Trenchon knew, but it had never been in his blood to do what others did. He was a dreamer after all, hard as it was to admit. "I thought I was going places," he says.

"If you'd killed Mace that night, I'd have let you live."

Trenchon stares at the ground. "I believe you."

"If you'd just been gone before she came, me and her would have worked out some other way to get rid of him. I wouldn't have held it against you."

"I can believe that too, Cable."

"You shouldn't have killed her. You took away my reason for killing Mace and left him with no reason to let you live."

Trenchon accepts the truth of this and doing so, he finds the strength to look up and meet Jessop's gaze and let him know he's right.

"What else can I do?" Jessop says. "What else am I cut out for?"

The question is rhetorical, not requiring any answers but Trenchon gives him one anyway. "Nothing."

"Same as you." Jessop puts the barrel of the gun against Trenchon's head.

"I guess so," says Trenchon, and afterwards nothing else. ■

Michelle
SPRING

'The best book yet in this amazing series' IAN RANKIN

Michelle
SPRING

NIGHTS IN
WHITE SATIN

A LAURA PRINCIPAL INVESTIGATION

Out in August in hardback

'The best book yet in this amazing series:
Cambridge dons, college skeletons, sex scandals,
and a night of madness... If you're not intrigued,
go check your pulse'

Ian Rankin

ORION

Out now in paperback and available through all good bookshops

'Laura Principal is Britain's coolest woman private eye … well crafted, well written and well worth a read'
Val McDermid

Laura
PRINCIPAL

ORION

Martin Edwards

PENALTY

"Football isn't a matter of life and death," said the old man. **"It's more** important than that."

Alan Wardle smiled dutifully. It was one of his grandfather's favourite lines, but lack of originality did not rob it of truth. Tom Jepson had devoted the best part of seventy years to the game he loved and, above all, to his home town team. Mossborough Athletic could not have had a better or more faithful servant, even in those distant days when Britannia Park had echoed to the roar of thousands of supporters rather than to the present day rumble of the dual carriageway which passed close to the site of the old dressing rooms.

They were making a final pilgrimage to the place which Alan, as a boy, had looked on as his second home. By that time, of course, the glory days had long gone. The Latics had been relegated from the Fourth Division in the early sixties. Succeeding years had seen them sink through the lower leagues to their current resting place in an amateur competition for sides from the small towns and villages which dotted the west side of the Pennines. Alan remembered a crowd of two thousand gathering here fifteen years ago to watch the final qualifying match before the first round proper of the Football Association Cup. He could still recall the excited talk of that time and the reminiscences on everyone's lips of the famous fourth round replay here against Manchester City — the never-to-be-forgotten occasion of Peterkin's penalty kick. But the qualifier, like the City game, had ended in defeat and disappointed hopes, and the following week only a handful of people had turned up to witness a goalless draw against a team of no-hopers from Saddleworth.

Now soccer was not even played at Britannia Park. The ground was owned by the local council — the directors had sold it twenty years back in return for having the ratepayers bale them out of one of their periodic financial crises — and a decade ago the site had been earmarked for retail development. The council had offered an alternative ground a mile away, which formed part of a sports complex providing all year round facilities and excellent parking. Of course, the directors had accepted, although the cars that cruised in each week belonged to people wishing to take advantage of the squash courts, bowling alley and bar/cafeteria rather than to the handful of diehards who came to watch the keen but hapless lads who wore the once famous red and white quartered shirts of Mossborough Athletic.

Alan reached the highest point of the couch grass covered knoll which had once comprised the terracing at the Gasworks End of the ground, and looked about him. Every football club formed during the nineteenth century had, it seemed to Alan, been based within sight of a gasometer, but the huge grey cylinder which had dominated the Mossborough skyline for generations had been demolished shortly after the team had played its last game here. At around the same time, vandals had burned down the grandstand. In recent years, the rows of small houses which had lined the streets leading to Britannia Park had also been levelled to make way for buildings more suited to the modern age: DIY stores, petrol stations and a drive-in hamburger restaurant. A mock Art Deco sign marked the britannia complex now stood in the place previously occupied by turnstiles leading to the Popular Side, but planning hitches had stalled progress for the past couple of years.

In the meantime, nature had sought to reclaim the old football pitch. The River Dalam — not much more than a stream really — ran close by and drainage had always been a problem, as Tom Jepson, groundsman for upwards of forty years knew well. Now that there was no one to care for the place, it had become wild again, with nettles and brambles which made any attempt to traverse the pitch a hazard to personal safety. The white lines marking out the pitch boundaries had long gone, but the flaking concrete steps of the terracing were still visible here and there. Alan sat on his haunches and watched his grandfather making painful, stick-aided progress up them to the top of the mound.

"You've seen some battles here, Grandad."

"Aye." The old man was wheezing, partly from the effort of his climb, partly as a result of too many Woodbines chain-smoked through nail-biting cup ties of the past. "I have that. And I wanted to take one last look at the place seeing as how tomorrow they start digging it up."

"Sacrilege, eh? I can almost hear the ghosts of the people who cheered the lads on in the City game, bellowing their protest. How many came that day, wasn't it a twenty thousand gate?"

"Summat like that. Capacity were only fourteen, officially, but the police turned a blind eye. Not like these days of all-seater stands — stadia, do they call 'em? I can see the kids now, hanging off the rafters they were, to say nothing of clambering up on to the corrugated sheeting over the far end of the Popular Side, to get a better view."

"Might all have been different, if Peterkin hadn't missed that penalty."

Tom Jepson sighed heavily. "Aye, I've often thought…"

"What, Grandad?"

The old man seemed to be talking to himself as much as to Alan. "I've often thought…it were like a judgement on the club."

A broken iron upright, part of an old crowd barrier, rose from one of the moss-covered steps. Tom Jepson grasped it for support and looked down on to the jungle of weeds that had once meant so much to him.

"There was murder done, you know."

"I don't understand."

"You're a reporter, Alan, and I've never had much time for the local press. They never gave the Latics their due, even in the club's heyday. Besides, my guess is you'll be moving on before you're much older. There's not much here for someone of your age. I can see you heading for Manchester or Leeds, mebbe even London if the right job comes along. But at least you've always cared for this town and that's more than I can say of some. Anyway, you're not a bad lad, though I say it myself, and I'd as soon you hear the story from me than anyone else."

A dedicated, lifelong crime fiction fan as well as a novelist, anthology editor, CWA activist, critic and short story writer, Martin Edwards is a Liverpool solicitor – as is his best-known character, Harry Devlin. The latest Devlin book is *The Devil in Disguise* published by Hodder & Stoughton. Martin's love of the genre makes him one of British crime fiction's most valuable properties; his love of football (he says he spent his 'formative years watching Northwich Victoria', and his father wrote the club's history) shows in this non-series piece.

Illustrations: David Checkley

"What story?" Alan asked, unable to conceal his bewilderment. His grandfather was a taciturn man, not much given to speechifying.

"It were nigh on forty years back," said the old man, "and yet I remember it better than yesterday."

A woman was at the root of the trouble, the old man said, adding that they usually were. But this wasn't just any woman.

Betty Stubbs would have made heads turn in Mayfair, let alone in Mossborough. Even as a young girl, she always had a posse of admirers. She was not beautiful, strictly speaking, and to describe her as merely pretty would also miss the mark. Betty was *striking*, that was the word. She had a voluptuous figure which she revealed, with as much imagination and daring as dress conventions of the day allowed, endless legs and a mass of untamed chestnut hair that shook in the Pennine wind whenever she laughed. Which was often, since Betty loved life and laughed a lot.

Even in the years immediately after the war, when entertainments were few and a match between two of the dullest teams in the Football League could be guaranteed to draw spectators from far and wide, few people were better known at Britannia Park than the Stubbs family. Betty soon became a pin-up with the Latics players. There was a bit of bother concerning a muscle-bound left back who fancied his chances with her, but after a mysterious late night altercation with two of the brothers in the car park of The Eagle And Child, cracked ribs kept him out of the side for a month and he was soon transferred to Port Vale, with whom he never recaptured his previous form.

By the time of her twenty-first birthday people reckoned that she had broken the hearts of a dozen young bloods through her readiness to play the field and she showed no sign of wanting to settle down. Yet Betty took everyone by surprise.

By Mossborough custom, each May an end of season dinner dance was held at which prizes were awarded to the footballers most esteemed by the fans. Invariably the manager of the day assured those gathered that next year would see the recruitment of new star signings, a decent Cup run and promotion to the Second Division. The promises were part of an essential ritual, for football supporters have always been sustained by hope for the future as well as nostalgia for the past as means of coping with the disappointments of the present. In this particular year, however, many of the locals reckoned that the following season might just see the achievement of those long-harboured ambitions, as a result of the arrival of a new club chairman, Roy Drinkwater.

Roy was a local businessman who — to the disbelieving disgust of many — had managed to escape the call-up during the War on health grounds. He had proceeded to cash in on the black market and a series of shrewd speculations after VE Day rapidly increased his fortune. Before long he bought up Mossborough Hall, when the previous owner died of a stroke. Roy relished the role of local squire and in the time-honoured fashion of moneyed men with no previous interest in the game, decided that the time had come for him to join the Latics' board. He described it as 'giving something back to the community', but sceptics reckoned that he aimed to take out as much in terms of social status as he put back in by way of hard cash.

He presented the awards at the dinner dance, but disappeared shortly afterwards. Those few observers who were sober enough to notice realised that Betty had vanished at much the same time. Within forty-eight hours, it was an open secret that the couple were courting and a week later their engagement was announced.

"It'll never last," said Tom Jepson, comforting his friend Len Pope. Len was a local lad, son of the town's best butcher, and a reserve team winger. He had been seeing Betty for a few weeks prior to the dance, which he had missed on account of chicken pox. He had delegated to his young and pimply brother Alf the task of escorting Betty to the dance and instructed him to keep a close eye on her. But Alf proved no match for the man people in Mossborough called Mister Moneybags. Len clenched his fists, barely able to suppress his rage. "Mebbe not, Tom, but that feller Drinkwater will have spoiled her for the rest of us. Now that she's tasted steak and smoked salmon, she won't be content with pie and chips again."

Roy and Betty married at the local church on the last Saturday in July. Laughingly, they told the reporters who joined the huge crowd of well-wishers that they had fixed the date so as to be sure that the honeymoon was over before the next season began.

A year later, the honeymoon was also over so far as Roy and the Latics were concerned. Results in the league were inconsistent and the team made an early exit from the FA. Cup. Adhering to the time-honoured strategy of all football club chairmen, Roy adopted the expedient of sacking his manager. The replacement he chose was Sandy Mulkerrin, a canny Scot who had guided his last two clubs to promotion. Mulkerrin quickly signed Eddie Le Roux, a hard-tackling South African ball-winner who had moved restlessly from club to club over the past six seasons and then persuaded Roy to fund the acquisition of a one-time international whom form had deserted over the past couple of years. Danny Peterkin was his name and in the last few matches before the close season, playing up front alongside the recently elevated Len Pope and feeding off Le Roux's shrewdly timed through balls, he gave enough hints of his pedigree to become a favourite with the critics from the Popular Side.

Everyone in Mossborough looked forward to another new season with hopes higher than ever. Except, that was, for Tom Jepson. His duties as groundsman, both necessary and voluntary, took him to Britannia Park seven days a week and no one was closer to dressing room gossip. That was what prompted him to have a quiet word with Len one night in the social club after time had been called.

"I hear you've been seeing a bit of Betty Drinkwater lately."

"More than a bit," said Len with a smirk, "if you catch my meaning. I did that lass an injustice. She's not forgotten how good pie and chips can taste."

"The two of you are taking a hell of a risk, you know."

Len put down his pint pot. "Betty's like me, Tom — partial to playing away from home. Remember that header of mine at Bradford on Good Friday?"

And that was as far as the conversation went. But stories continued to reach Tom's ears, stories about what Betty got up to when Roy was wheeler-dealing down in London during the summer months, leaving his wife to enjoy herself as well as to play Lady Muck in the big house they shared. Len was not the only one with whom she dallied. Roy had been persuaded to offer Le Roux a summer job assisting the head gardener in the grounds of Mossborough Hall and according to rumour the South African knew more about Betty's silk sheets than his master's herbaceous beds. The affair had seemed doomed when Le Roux drifted off to Joburg in July, but shortly after he returned for pre-season training, he was seen in a not-quite-discreet-enough corner of a pub in a village ten miles away canoodling with Betty.

How much Roy knew, or guessed, became a fertile source of speculation. Some reckoned that he was ignorant of Betty's wandering, that if he found out there would be hell to pay. Roy was a rich man and no one had more influence in Mossborough. If he set out to ruin a man, the chances were that he could achieve his aim. But if Len realised the risk, he discounted it. For his part, Tom sided with those who reckoned that Roy was more than willing to turn a blind eye to his wife's adulteries. Just as the man had bought control of the Latics without caring a jot for soccer, so he had married Betty as a means of proving that he could have anything he wanted. Tom guessed that there were plenty of women in London who were only too willing to give Mister Moneybags a good time and that Roy had found a way of living that suited him well.

The new season began with a whimper: a knee injury kept Peterkin out of the early games and a goalless draw at home was followed by a heavy defeat over at Barnsley. But Len snatched a late winner in the third match and by the time Peterkin was fit again the Latics had secured the berth in the middle of the league table that was all to which they customarily aspired.

Peterkin's return, however, sparked a dramatic improvement. Although he was not a big man, he had the strength as well as the pace to shrug off the attentions of clumsy defenders and his partnership with Le Roux soon became feared. By Christmas the Latics were challenging for promotion and there was an added bonus in that two goals from Peterkin had taken them into the third round of the FA Cup for a crack against one of the more illustrious sides which entered the competition at that stage. One of Peterkin's goals had been a penalty and his accuracy with a dead ball was the most notable of his many gifts. Throughout his career, he had only ever missed one penalty, in a friendly match during the war — and on that occasion a subsequent measure check proved that the penalty spot had been marked ten inches off centre.

In retrospect, Tom saw it as inevitable that Betty should fall for Peterkin. Like attracts like and they both, in their different ways, were stars. Moreover, Peterkin was pally with Le Roux, and Tom gathered that the South African had actually been instrumental in bringing them together. Le Roux was a hard-living character, whose only regret about the war seemed to be that its ending deprived him of a chance of excitement. He was as indiscriminate with women as in his choice of ale and more than willing to share his good fortune with his mate.

From the start, though, it was clear that this was not just another casual dalliance. Peterkin was a handsome man with a relaxed sense of humour and Betty found him irresistible. For the footballer, the lady of the manor had obvious attractions, but Tom sensed that her appeal to Peterkin lay in more than her looks and availability alone. In those days, soccer clubs paid their staff a pittance and a career in the game usually came to an end by the time a man was thirty-five or so. After that — what? A lifetime of looking back? Only a few made it into club management and for the rest, lacking any sort of training for jobs in the wider world, there was the grim prospect of a succession of unsatisfactory, poorly paid jobs followed by arthritic and impoverished old age.

Unless, of course, one married well.

Tom began to dread the thought that the lovers might decide to confront Roy Drinkwater with the truth — that Betty wanted a divorce. What would it do to the Latics? Peterkin would have to go, for a start, and there was every chance that Roy would withdraw his money and allow the team to slide back into the obscurity from which it was currently threatening to escape.

The third round tie came and went in a blur of excitement. Plymouth Argyle made the long trip up to Britannia Park and left in despair. Le Roux clattered into the opposition's leading scorer in the first minute and sent him hobbling to the dressing room, never to return. After that the outcome was never in doubt and Peterkin sealed the victory with a free kick from twenty-five yards soon after half-time. On the following Monday, half of Mossborough listened to the wireless to hear the draw for the next round — and in the social club Tom joined in the jubilant cheer when it was announced that the Latics would once more play at home, this time against their mighty near-neighbours, Manchester City.

It was going to be the biggest day in the club's history, no question. Every window in the streets around Britannia Park was festooned with the club's favours and suddenly there was not a person in the town who did not claim to be a lifelong supporter of the team. Tom had to smile when men who normally preferred to spend their Saturdays in the trivial occupation of shopping with their wives stopped him in the street to exchange a word about the prospects for the big match, to ask about the state of the pitch and to assure him that they would, of course, be there, rooting for the Latics from the top of their voices.

The pitch was a worry to him. The winter programme coupled with January's flooding from the Dalam had turned it into a sea of mud and the constant battering from twenty-two sets of studs gave the grass no chance to grow back. For all his efforts, the chances of being able to produce a good surface for the City game were nonexistent. That dismayed him, for he took a pride in his work, yet he was realistic enough to acknowledge to himself that the poor conditions might suit the Latics. City's skilful but lightweight defenders were likely to find Danny Peterkin and company a handful on a poor surface.

He was more bothered, frankly, by the goings-on between Betty and her new boyfriend. Yet there was even less that he could do there to influence the course of events. All he could think of was to keep as close an eye as possible on the affair and take any opportunity that arose to pour oil on troubled waters — at least until the season was over, preferably with promotion achieved and the club's finances strengthened by success in the cup.

To make matters worse, Len was in despair. He trudged about the place as though he expected Sandy Mulkerrin to tell him that he was dropped for the big game, although there was not a chance of that. In the club one night towards closing time, Tom bought the young man a pint and asked what ailed him.

"I'm all right," snapped Len. "Why d'you ask?"

"I've got eyes in my head." Tom sighed. "Is it Betty?"

"She's thrown me over. Permanent, like."

"Plenty of fish in the sea, lad."

Len glared at him. "There's only one fish I'm interested in. You know that."

Tom leaned towards the young man and spoke softly. "Listen here. This fling you had with Betty, forget it. It were never going to last. She's poison, Len, believe me."

"Oh aye?" Len stood up. Always a hot-tempered young man, he had begun to shout. "And what would you know about it, Tom? All you care about is the bloody Latics. I sometimes think you'd commit murder if only it would guarantee bloody promotion!"

And with that he smashed his glass of beer to the floor and strode out into the night.

Tom did not see him again until the night before the big match. That evening, the social club was packed as never before. The atmosphere was thick with smoke and excitement as stranger bought drinks for stranger and everyone speculated on what the following afternoon's result might be. Peterkin was there with Le Roux; they sat in a corner, joking with each other and every now and then a supporter would come over and wish them well for the City game. Neither player had to put his hand in his pocket to buy a drink; by ten o'clock Tom saw that they both had a bleary look and he began to worry about whether they would be at their fittest by three the following after-noon. No point in hoping that Mulkerrin would impose some sort of curfew: the manager was at the other end of the bar,

swaying in between a couple of barmaids who had joined a group of fans in raucous song. Len sat by himself, sullen and unapproachable. From time to time he shot Peterkin an angry glance.

At twenty past ten the door opened and Betty Drinkwater came in. She did not make a grand entrance; she did not need to, for heads began to turn as soon as she walked across the room. She had not been seen in the club since the end of season shindig at which she had met Roy. Tom watched as, bold as brass, she walked straight up to Peterkin and asked him to buy her a drink. Then she sat down at the table, crossed those long elegant legs and smiled at her boyfriend, daring everyone else to be shocked.

Out of the corner of his eye, Tom saw Len get to his feet and for a moment he feared there would be a confrontation. The young man's face was thunderous. But he headed straight for the door and although he knocked a chair to the floor in his clumsy haste to be away, and banged the exit door so hard it was a wonder it did not come off its hinges, he gave neither Betty nor Peterkin a second glance. At least, thought Tom with relief, someone would be getting an early night.

Time was called and Betty leaned over and whispered something in Peterkin's ear. He nodded and they drained their glasses before walking out of the room together. Their hands, their bodies did not touch and yet the intimacy between them was apparent to every person in the room. As the door closed behind them, Le Roux seemed to make up his mind. He put his pint pot down on the table and followed them out.

The room buzzed with excited speculation. Tom hesitated only for a moment. Trouble was brewing, he felt sure, and he feared that the Latics would suffer from it. He hurried out into the cold night air. The car park was quiet and there was no sign of anyone walking down Albion Street. Betty, Peterkin and Le Roux must have taken the cinder path which led from the back of the club round the Popular Side towards the railway viaduct.

The crunching of his shoes on the cinders seemed to him unnaturally loud. When he heard voices he halted and pressed himself against the back of the club building. In the dim light coming from the frosted glass of a small window he could just make out the vague shapes of Betty and the two players.

The South African's slurred voice said: "The three of us, Betty. What could be better?"

"Forget it, Hansie. You've had too much to drink. Go home and sleep it off. Can't you see the two of us want to be alone?"

"Listen, you bitch…"

"Who are you calling a bitch? Danny, are you going to let him speak to me like that?"

Peterkin sounded nervous. Tom didn't wonder: Le Roux was taller, heavier and famously violent if crossed. "Hansie. Look mate, why don't — "

"Shut it, Danny. Remember what we said. Share and share alike?"

"You're pathetic!" said the woman. "Have you forgotten what happened the last time you came up to the Hall? I told Danny about that, you know. We had a good laugh over it, I can promise you."

The South African roared with rage and Tom heard a sharp crack followed by a scream. Someone — was it Peterkin? — gasped. Tom moved forward and saw a dark figure detach itself from the shadows.

"You bastard!" Len shouted.

The moon peeped out for a moment from behind a cloud. Tom saw the burly shape of Le Roux, bending down to look at a huddle on the ground. The South African turned at the sound of Len's voice, but too late. A fierce blow knocked him down and Tom watched with horror as Len raised his arm. There was a glint of steel in the darkness. "No!" Tom cried.

Too late. Len plunged the butcher's blade into the prostrate man's chest. Le Roux grunted: it seemed a meek noise for such a big man.

"You bloody fool," Peterkin said hoarsely. "You stabbed him, Len. You stabbed Le Roux."

Len was panting. "You ought to be counting your blessings, Danny. I meant the knife for you, I've been waiting for my moment. But never mind that now — how's Betty?"

Peterkin said, "She hit her head on that pipe as she fell."

Tom knelt by the woman's side. She was very still. "I can't feel a pulse."

"He killed her," muttered Len. "The bastard killed her."

"And so you knifed him," said Peterkin. "Oh God, I can't believe it."

"Shut up!" said Tom. Someone had to take charge of the situation. "No one can help Betty. Let's see to Le Roux."

They bent over the South African's body. But he too was dead.

"It wasn't me," said Peterkin. His hands were shaking uncontrollably, his voice was little more than a squeak. "I wasn't involved. I'm an innocent bystander."

"Forget it," said Tom. "We're all involved."

Len glared at the corpse of the man he had killed. "The murdering swine. He deserved to die."

"For God's sake," said Peterkin. "What are we going to do?"

Tom gave the two footballers a long hard stare. "Use your heads, for once. There's only one thing we can do."

Alan Wardle stared at his grandfather. "There was another option. You needn't have concealed the crimes. You could have told the police, made a clean breast of things."

The old man shook his head. "Think what it would have done to the club, lad. The chairman's wife killed in a fracas with a member of the team. One player knifing another to death. And all on the night before the biggest match in the Latics' history."

"It's only a game!" Alan did not try to hide his horror. "Nothing more, a game!"

"But it's bigger than any individual," said the old man calmly. "Bigger than young Betty, bigger than that South African thug. No, Alan, don't expect me to apologise. I'm too old for that, I've survived too much. Not a day's gone by in the past forty-odd years without I've thought back to that dreadful night, when the three of us, Len, Peterkin and me, buried those two bodies so that no one would realise the truth."

"And no one did?"

"Not a soul. It worked like a dream. I always knew it would. We gave out that Betty had run off with Le Roux. The feller was a rolling stone, people willingly believed him capable of anything. Caused a nine days wonder, like, but nobody guessed what had happened. Least of all Roy Drinkwater."

"I feel," said Alan, closing his eyes, "as if I don't know you at all."

"You know how much the Latics mean to me."

"Why did you have to tell me now?" the young man demanded bitterly.

"Disappointed you, have I?" Tom sighed. "Ah well, I had no choice, lad, if I'm honest. The diggers are coming here tomorrow, aren't they? I reckon they'll find what's left of the skeletons."

"You mean...?"

Tom nodded. "We buried them under the pitch. I was the groundsman, remember? I reckoned it was the safest place, provided the graves were deep. And I was right."

Alan swore. Words were beyond him.

Tom gazed out towards the overgrown graveyard of Britannia Park. "Betty, you know, we put her under the penalty spot at the Gasworks End. But in the end, it didn't do us much good, did it? No wonder Peterkin missed that penalty kick." ■

DIAMOND PASS

JOHN MORALEE

Death and guilt brought Cal back to Diamond Pass. He could have driven faster, but he wanted to delay his arrival, and prepare his mind for what was ahead, by staying well below the speed limit on these rough, unpredictable mountain roads. Ten miles from the town, the black BMW passed over a precarious bridge of rust-red girders and wooden planks, the vehicle shaking as though frightened. His wife Heather woke up and looked around, blinking in the flickering sunlight. She gasped as she saw the river far below. The river was burgeoning with melted snow from the dark peaks of the Catskill Mountains, the water roaring over the engine noise.

Born in 1973, John Moralee of Washington, Tyne and Wear, is a pure mathematician by training, but admits to being 'more interested in pursuing a career in writing'. His stories have been published in a number of magazines (including CW1 with 'An English Rose, With Thorns'), and he has twice been shortlisted for the Ian St James Short Story Award.

Illustrations: Wendy Down

"Cal?" she said.

"Nearly there," he promised.

When the car reached the other bank, it seemed to sigh with relief, though it was just the air-conditioning changing pace. Ahead, the road disappeared into the forest of spruce and balsam firs. Cal still did not recognise the scenery, but after another couple of miles a feeling of familiarity crept up, slowly, until he felt as if he had never left. Suddenly, the road plunged into a green valley filled with bright light and a river as shiny as spun glass. They were there: his childhood home, Diamond Pass.

Not much had changed in fourteen years. Pushed to one side of Diamond Pass like the unwanted bastard child of a rich man, the Bradley and Sons trailer park where he had grown up sprawled alongside the riverbank for two depressing miles. It was hard to look at, so he looked instead at the town itself, which was much more appealing to the eye, the stores and hotels looked like an old frontier town prettified by a Norman Rockwell fan.

Cal was coming back *officially* for his mother's funeral. He had feared and hated her just as much as loved her while she was alive, and he felt pretty much the same about her now. Yet here he was. He did not even know why; it was as though a long and invisible umbilical cord had reeled him back against his will into the darkness of her womb.

"Are you all right?"

"I'm fine," he lied.

Heather knew he was lying but said nothing. They had been married seven years now, and she knew his moods better than he did. He felt ashamed. He felt like a criminal returning to the scene of a crime.

Diamond Pass, the official town, was a small but affluent tourist town where many bright, young New Yorkers kept their second homes and spent their vacations. There were three large hotels, the best of which was the Grange Hotel at over two hundred dollars per night. Cal and Heather booked in at the Grange Hotel. Their suite was large and looked out on a perfect view: the Catskill Mountains, the peaks still heavy with snow, the huge blue sky hazed with heat.

"It's beautiful," Heather said, hugging Cal from behind.

He nodded, but inside he felt sick. He was still delaying his arrival. Heather sensed his tension and pulled away.

"Do you want to see your family today or do you want to leave it until tomorrow?"

"To—" He changed his mind mid-sentence. "—morrow."

For the rest of the day they did the usual tourist things, assiduously avoiding the trailer park for the sumptuous sights up among the mountains and reservoirs. In the Catskill Forest Preserve they stood beside lakes and waterfalls and ancient trees just enjoying the pure, sweet air. Then, that night, they made love as if for the first time. It would have been perfect — if Cal had not let his own thoughts wander to another time and another woman, Nadine.

Nadine. She had been his first love, the girl he wished he'd married fourteen years ago. The last time he'd seen her she had been sixteen. Today Nadine would be thirty, he realised with shock. The big 3-0. In fact, it had been her birthday last week. He had forgotten until that moment. Since their last time together, Cal had been around the world as a soldier in the US Marines, gained a college education, achieved a degree in psychology, and married a brilliant woman. His life was good. Better than good — perfect. He wanted Nadine's life to have been the same; she had been the only ray of light in his dark past. *She* had encouraged him to leave Diamond Pass even though he'd not wanted to leave her. *She* had understood that living there would have been the death of him. *She* had recognised something within him that he, as a teenager with little ambition and no dreams, had not. *She* had saved his soul by insisting he signed up for the Army, the hardest decision either of them had ever made. The Army had educated him, given him a sense of freedom that had opened his mind to new possibilities, new interests. It was his time to thank her in any way he could.

As Heather slept, Cal lay awake, wondering if Nadine still lived in Diamond Pass. He had no illusions about them getting back together (he was very happily married to Heather) but he did need to know what had happened to her.

Tomorrow, he promised himself, he would find out.

"I really think I should do this alone," he told Heather, in the morning, as they ate eggs-benedict in the king size bed, taking turns to feed each other with the toasted muffins and ham dripping with fresh butter. He hoped to catch her with her mouth full, so she would not put up much of an argument. Unfortunately, she held up a hand to her mouth, stopping him.

"Cal, I want to meet your relatives."

"I don't want you to meet my relatives," he said. Seeing her expression, he needed to explain, "They're crazy, some of them. Jimmy-Ray is about the best of them; he sent me the letter. The others never liked me. God knows what they'll make of me for leaving here, never mind you coming back with me. If they hear your accent they are likely to spit in your face."

"They have something against New Yorkers?"

"And anyone else. For your own sake, please stay out of it, okay? At least until I've made the funeral arrangements and tested the water."

"Anyone suspicious would think you didn't want me with you. Like you're embarrassed."

"That's not it," he said. "Well, a little — my family is embarrassing, not you. Look, why don't you enjoy yourself at the mall or do some sightseeing? Just a couple of hours? I know your mother would like a gift from the pottery store we saw."

Heather nodded, albeit reluctantly. "This doesn't mean I don't want to meet your relatives, Cal. You can't hide them forever."

Dreading what he would discover, Cal drove to the trailer park. As soon as it was within sight he could almost taste the poverty, and it made him ashamed to be an American. The hundred or so mobile homes looked as if they had been dropped from a great height and left broken and flattened. They were not going anywhere in a hurry. There were recreational vehicles up on cinder blocks, rats crawling around underneath. Huge satellite dishes poked up from dark niches like mushrooms. Garbage was everywhere, of all kinds, as if a tornado had ripped through the valley rearranging the furniture. It looked like a disaster zone. But it was always like this. The townspeople had tried their best to hide the trailer park behind a white picket fence and some recently planted firs, but it would take fifty years for the trees to thicken enough to block the view from the road. He passed dozens of parked cars not fit for scrap, then turned right, going a hundred yards to where an evil-looking trailer hid between two junk heaps of damp mattresses.

Its owner was his half-brother, Jimmy-Ray.

Cal paused for a few seconds, opening the envelope Jimmy-Ray had sent him, reading the letter again. He had only found out about his mother's death because of the barely legible letter. Jimmy-Ray wrote like a three-year old in big, wobbly letters, which was somehow endearing at the same time as being sad, but he'd made it clear someone had to pay for the funeral and it sure wasn't going to be *him*. Cal was the oldest son; therefore he had to pay. Until he paid, his mother's body would remain in the Diamond Pass Hospital morgue. Cal carefully folded the letter back into the envelope, put it on the dashboard, then stepped out of the truck. The smells worsened outside. Was someone keeping pigs? Possibly.

He trudged across mud and brackish water until he reached the trailer's door. He knocked and announced himself. He heard some grunts and groans and swearing, then the door opened and a big man squinted down at him. Jimmy-Ray was dressed in grease-stained jeans, a string vest and a baseball cap that advertised a brand of beer no longer manufactured. His red hair was long and wild, just how Cal remembered it. Jimmy-Ray had a ginger goatee beard these days, and though he was slim his stomach bulged like a large fish trapped in a net. "Hey, Cal! You looking good, man. All that time in the Army done you good, I reckons." Jimmy-Ray noticed the BMW. "You leave a car like that around here you're asking for trouble, but I guess it'll be safe long as we look out the window. Come in, get yourself a cold one."

Bachelor clutter filled the small space. A shotgun rested against the refrigerator beside a fishing rod and a baseball bat that looked as if it had been dented by more than a ball. Cal was probably stereotyping Jimmy-Ray, but he knew what he had been like when he lived in Diamond Pass: violence clung to him like stale sweat.

Jimmy-Ray hurled a beer can at Cal, which he just caught. He popped it open and drank the beer that didn't foam all over his hands. Then Jimmy-Ray began talking, getting him up to date on family business.

For over three hundred years this part of the Catskills had been the home to a poverty-stricken underclass. You could call them white trash, if you didn't know them. Some people call them hillbillies…but no name adequately described them. They were as misunderstood as the Native Americans, and just as isolated. Unlike the Native Americans, no big Hollywood directors wanted to make movies about them. Cal was one of them, and though he'd gained a New York accent long ago, he found himself soon talking just like Jimmy-Ray. It was as if no time had passed, as if he had stepped back through a doorway into his old life, the life he had tried so hard to leave behind. Jimmy-Ray was everything he would have been if he had not left.

"Your mama wanted a proper burial," Jimmy-Ray said. "Said you'd pay for a real wood coffin, not one of them cardboard things."

"How long did she know she was dying?"

"Six months," Jimmy-Ray told him. "Didn't want you to know until after she died, though. Never could figure her out, you don't mind me saying."

Cal did not mind. His mother had always been a strange woman, sometimes as nice and loving as a Disney Mom, but sometimes a psychotic rage had possessed her that had turned her into something ugly and witchlike. Many were the times she would hit him for eating too loud or leaving the toilet seat up. Cal was one of her three so-called 'mistakes'. His half-brother and half-sister were her other 'mistakes', but they'd been adopted by relatives, so maybe in his mother's mind *he* had been her favourite, the one she'd kept. Who knew?

"I'll pay for it all," he said. Jimmy-Ray grinned at that.

"You can stay here if you like. Just fifty bucks."

Fifty dollars to stay in a trailer. A bargain. "I've already booked a hotel. The Grange."

"The Grange? Wow. You've sure done all right for yourself, Cal. Nice fancy suit you're wearing must've cost a hundred bucks." There was desperation in his eyes. "You ain't got a few bucks to help out an old buddy?"

There was a pause you could have filled by reading *War and Peace*. Cal suspected any money he gave to Jimmy-Ray would be wasted on drink, but he was in too awkward a position to say no.

"Sure," he said. He handed over what he had in his wallet — a pathetic thirty dollars. It disappeared into Jimmy-Ray's back pocket. Cal headed for the door, but stopped. He had not asked any questions about Nadine.

"What's up, bro?"

"I…" He could not ask. He was afraid of the answer. "Nothing."

He intended to return to the hotel, but somehow he ended up driving to what used to be Nadine's home where she'd lived with her mother and four sisters deep in the woods. The house was made of corrugated iron and a tin roof. Nadine had called it the Tin Box. How six people could have fitted inside was a mystery. Today, the Tin Box looked deserted. He was glad in a way because it meant Nadine lived somewhere better. But to be certain, he went up to the dusty windows and peered inside. It was too dark to make out anything. He tested the door. There was a padlock on it that was at least five years old. It would not move. He walked around the house, disturbing a rat's nest. Rats crawled over his shoes, trying to climb up his legs. He kicked them off and hurried to his car. It had been a bad idea coming here. What had he expected? Nadine running out of the Tin Box like a character in a romantic novel? Oh, Cal, you saved me! You're my hero!

Yes, he realised. That was what he had expected.

But things never worked out that way, of course.

He had to forget about Nadine. He had Heather now. He could not rewrite the past.

But the Tin Box stared at him, its windows glaring.

There was a general store nearby that looked closed except for a sign in the dirty window. He went in and asked the old man behind the counter if he knew anything about the people who had lived in the woods. Yes, he said. The man told him they'd moved out a long time ago; he didn't know where. Cal thanked him and bought a Dr Pepper and drank it as he walked back to his BMW. He saw some boys running off, and when he reached the car he saw that they'd scratched the paint on the door where they'd tried to open it. He was lucky they had not had time to steal the CD player.

As the week progressed, he soon discovered, as he had feared, that Jimmy-Ray was the only person who would be friendly towards him. When he visited his Aunt Jenny and Uncle Avery, Avery would not even open the screen door while he talked. Avery said, "You reckoned you was better than us poor folk, Calhoun. You come back like some kind of hero in your fancy BMW and Italian shoes, you think everybody wants to shine your shoes. You done wrong, now you want forgiveness?"

"Forgiveness for what?"

"You know. Well, it's too late. I ain't talking to you no more. I'll be at the funeral, but don't expect us to stand near you. Go on — get." And he locked the main door and would not reply to another word.

The same happened with his old friends — Frank and Steve and Mitch and Zeke. He knew they had the right to feel the way they did — he had avoided them for over a decade — but the hostility was surprising. He felt as if there was something else behind their anger. It made him decide that if he wanted more than a handful of people at the funeral on Friday then he would have to use Jimmy-Ray as an intermediary. Jimmy-Ray agreed. Jimmy-Ray said he would invite everyone who knew or worked with his mother, but he needed gas money. Cal paid him a hundred dollars and ignored the whiskey on his breath.

By then Heather had grown weary of his excuses.

"Cal, what exactly happened when you left? Why does no one want to see you?"

"I wish I knew. I only joined the US Army, not the Iraqis."

It cost a few thousand dollars for the coffin and the headstone and burial plot; more money than many people living nearby earned in a whole year. Boom or recession, the funeral business always survived.

He viewed his mother's body a single time. He half expected to see some signs of the cancer, but all he saw was the pale and shrunken corpse of a middle-aged woman that had lived a hard and unrewarding life. Tears welled up as he touched her icy cheek. It was strange how he felt sentimental towards someone who'd shown him so little love. It was strange.

Friday was a cold and wet day for a funeral. Cal held an umbrella over Heather as the rain began again. She squeezed his hand, her touch comforting. Cal could not wait for the ceremony to be over. He planned to leave Diamond Pass as soon as the ceremony was finished. A week in Diamond Pass had reminded him of all the reasons why he had fled and stayed away. Diamond Pass was like a scab waiting to be scratched off; you just had to ignore it.

The priest delivering the eulogy sounded bored as he read out a list of his mother's achievements. There were few dozen people gathered, women mostly. Aunt Jenny and Uncle Avery were there. Uncle Avery glared at Cal. Cal wondered what he had done to so offend him. Nobody cried. Everyone who had stayed in Diamond Pass seemed to have aged faster than he had. The priest finished quickly; then did not stay long before excusing himself. The coffin was lowered into the coffee-dark earth.

"Do you want to go now?" Heather asked.

He surprised himself by saying, "Not just yet. I want to find out why everyone hates me"

"I'll be in the car."

"Okay."

He walked over to Jimmy-Ray. "Well, that's that then."

"Yeah," Jimmy-Ray said, sounding tired, which summed up how he was feeling.

"I've been meaning to ask you something."

"Yeah? Like what?"

"What's going on with everyone? Uncle Avery looks like he wants to take me out into the woods and shoot me."

"It's the Nadine thing, Cal."

"What about her? Is she doing okay?"

Jimmy-Ray looked down at the ground. "Ah, Cal, I thought you knew."

"Knew what?"

He did not answer.

"Knew what?" he repeated.

"She's dead."

"No."

"I'm afraid so."

"God. When? How?"

"I thought you knew, Cal. I didn't want to bring it up — figuring you was sensitive about it. But — Jesus! — you don't know nothing, do you?"

"No."

"Nadine died a few years after you joined the Army. I sent you a letter about it. When you didn't reply I thought you didn't want to come back because of what people was saying. I guess you never heard she married that dead-beat Whit Wilson, huh?"

"She married someone too? Jesus. I never knew."

"It was all in my letter."

"I didn't receive it. I was moving around a lot." He shook his head as if trying to shake out the unwanted knowledge. "I can't believe it. She's really dead? You're not kidding with me?"

"Would I kid about death, man? Her grave is just over there. The little black headstone. Check it out for yourself. But — "

Cal interrupted, "Hold on, tell me in a sec."

He located Nadine's grave. The cheap headstone was already weathered, the words faded to a ghost of the original. Rainwater trickled down the epitaph. He read the words once, twice, before he pulled up straight as though he had been electrocuted. The words were engraved on his mind like an angry wound, throbbing.

Nadine Marie Wilson,
Loving Wife and Mother.
Rest In Peace.
Born 1969 – Died 1986

"Loving wife and mother?" he said. She'd had a *baby* as well as a husband?

Jimmy-Ray appeared beside him, touching him gently on the shoulder. "Cal, come away. You don't want to get into it."

"Nobody told me Nadine had a kid."

"Nadine didn't want you to know."

"Why not?" he said, but he already suspected his answer.

"Cal...the baby was yours."

"She was pregnant when I left?"

Jimmy-Ray nodded.

"God, you mean people think I abandoned her?"

"That's about the size of it."

"Tell me everything," Cal said.

"It's a sad story, Cal. You don't want to know it."

"I do. I do. And don't leave anything out."

"Can you drive?" Cal asked, leaning down to the passenger window. He could feel his pulses throb all of the way up his arms. Heather looked up from reading a travel book and flicked a long strand of hair out of her eyes, frowning. He never asked her to drive because he knew she hated it.

"Is something wrong?"

He did not want to explain yet. He was too weary. "Can you drive?"

"Uh, yes. I *can* drive, but you — "

"Thanks, I appreciate it."

Heather changed seats. Cal got in and buckled up and stared at the cemetery. "Let's get back to the hotel. We're leaving."

"Now?" Heather said. "What's wrong? Are you thinking about your mom?"

"No, it's not her."

She started up the engine. She did not say anything until they were almost to the hotel. She looked at him with concern. "You're not having an affair, are you?"

"God, no."

"But it's about a woman, though."

He nodded.

"Then what is it?"

"It's Nadine."

"Who?"

"She was an ex-girlfriend. My first girlfriend. We were deeply in love a long time ago."

Heather almost kept the jealousy out of her voice. "You never mentioned *her* before."

"No, and it was a mistake. I've got to tell you something that could change how you feel about me, something that might make you want a divorce."

"Cal…"

"I think the only way I can do this is if I start at the beginning and tell it all and you don't ask questions until I'm finished."

Heather stopped the car. She closed her eyes and rubbed them with one hand. She looked as if she had toothache and was preparing for an unanaesthetized extraction. "I'm listening."

"Before I enlisted I had a girlfriend called Nadine Bell. I didn't want to leave her, but we were young and it seemed the best thing. She broke up with me to make it easier for me, though I didn't know that at the time. So I left, and I never wanted to come back. She didn't tell me she was having my baby." Heather took an intake of air as though surfacing from a deep dive. "Anyway, she had the baby. Nadine's mother convinced her to marry Whit Wilson, a guy who'd had a crush on her for a long time. Whit had a job and some money coming in, so it was a practical solution. Whit agreed to keep the baby girl as long as everyone pretended it was his. They pretended. Wilson loved Nadine, but I don't think she really loved him. It must have eaten at him for two years. He would get drunk or high and beat her up, then beg her forgiveness afterwards. Nadine was so scared of his temper that she decided to take the baby and leave. This was 1986. But…he caught her. He was drunk at the time and he wanted to teach her a lesson so he hit her with a hammer. He hit her over fifty times. He killed her, and then kept hitting her. He turned her face into a pulp, smashing all of her teeth. He would have killed the baby, too, but Nadine had left the baby with her sisters while she was packing. After he had killed her, he felt such remorse that he took his rifle into the woods and shot himself in the head. His body wasn't found for months. Just about everybody blamed the whole thing on me for leaving Nadine pregnant, which is why Uncle Avery could kill me. It's like I've been leading a double life. It's all my fault Nadine died, Heather. If Nadine had been married to me instead of Whit then none of it would ever have happened. I'm responsible for ruining three people's lives. Me and my stupid selfishness. I should've never have joined the Army. I should've stayed *here*. Maybe then nobody would've died. God, I'm so sorry for dragging you into this mess."

Heather opened her eyes. "W-what happened to the baby?"

"Custody was given to Nadine's sister Darlene. Jimmy-Ray's given me her new address. The baby — Christine — she'll be fourteen now."

"What do you want to do?"

"I want to make sure she's in a happy home. I think she has a right to know her real father."

"Let's swap seats," Heather said.

"Why?"

"We'll do it now, that's why."

"You don't have a problem with this?"

"It's not your fault, is it? Nobody's to blame except this Whit Wilson man. I can tell you want to see how your daughter is living, so let's do it. Drive there." There was tiredness in her voice, but also determination.

"I love only you," he said. "You know that, don't you?"

"I know it," she said.

They swapped positions, and Cal turned the car around. The address wasn't marked on the AAA map at all, but Jimmy-Ray had given him some rough directions. It was high in the mountains, approximately an hour's drive. Most of the drive was through a grey wall of low clouds that dissipated only after he'd driven above them. Down in the valleys the clouds lingered like wet cotton-wool. There was some snow still at the sides of the road packed feet thick. He drove into a small nameless town and asked directions at the gas station. The attendant said the house he wanted was just a couple of miles south.

They reached Nadine's sister's house a little after two. It was an improvement on the Tin Box, but not much — it was part of a converted motel complex where several families on welfare lived in close proximity. He parked nearby and turned off the engine. For a minute there was just the slow ticking of the engine cooling down and the soft sighing of breathing.

"Here it is," he said.

"I'll come with you."

"Thanks."

They walked up to the door. Cal thought that perhaps nobody was in, but then he heard a television inside and the excited shouts of children playing. He knocked. When no one answered, he knocked again, louder. A chain rattled. The door opened ever so slightly.

"Yes?" said a little blue-eyed girl.

For an instant he thought it was his daughter, but the girl was too young, only five or six. Her face was smeared with chocolate. "Is your mom there?"

"Yes."

"Can I see her?"

"No."

"Is she really there?"

The girl nodded, but it was clear she was lying and did not feel comfortable about it.

"It's all right," Heather said. "We're friends. Is there an adult looking after you?"

"Grandma is sleeping."

"Can you wake her?"

"She don't like waking. She got a hangover."

"Please wake her," Heather said.

"Uh — okay." The girl closed the door.

After a minute an old woman unlocked the door screaming, "Get me some Excedrin, Wayne!" She was dressed in a blue bathrobe that smelled of cigarettes. Her face was half hidden by straggling black hair bleached blonde at the tips. Even from a distance Cal could smell the whiskey on her breath. She groaned and complained the light was too bright.

Cal could see five small children in the darkness of the apartment. He could see dark purple bruises on them fading to yellow. When one boy tried to crawl between the woman's legs she slapped the child on the head as loud as a gunshot, making the child cry and run back into the dark. The action seemed to be an automatic response, no more than a reflex. She reminded Cal of his own mother. Another child tugged her gown and held up a glass of water and an Excedrin capsule. She swallowed it, grunting. "I need two, stupid." Wayne hurried to get a second. The woman's eyes were like black pits fiery with suspicion. "Well, what do you two folks want?"

"We're looking for Darlene Bell."

"That's me," the woman said.

Cal could not believe the woman was in her mid-thirties; she looked so worn out. "I'm looking for my daughter," he said, the words clogging his throat. "I'm Cal, remember me? I used to go out with Nadine."

"You ain't from welfare?" Darlene Bell said.

"No."

"So what you here for?"

"I'm Cal. Calhoun Andersen."

"Cal? Why didn't you say so? I remember you. But what you doing here? Don't you know Nadine's dead?"

"Yes, I'm here to see *Christine*," he said. It seemed to register with Darlene this time. He waited while she took a second Excedrin from her son.

"You looking for Chrissy?"

"Yes, that's right. Chrissy."

"You're way too late, hon."

"What do you mean?"

"Little bitch ran away."

"You don't know where she is?"

"No. And you don't want to go looking for her." She laughed. It was a wicked, dry laugh.

"I don't believe you," he said. "I think you know where but won't say. If you don't tell me where she is I'll get a social worker to take away your kids."

"You wouldn't."

"Try me," he said. "You might even get some jail-time for child abuse."

"Child abuse? What you talking about?"

"You can't slap kids, Darlene. That's breaking the law."

Darlene Bell regarded him with pure hatred. She started to say something, a lie, but he warned her with his eyes.

"She lives at 54 Sycamore Street. I tell you what, Cal Andersen, you go there you'll ruin that girl's life."

"We'll see about that," he said.

54 Sycamore Street was a white-painted house on a quiet street corner in the suburbs. There were lace curtains in the windows that he was sure he saw move as he parked. The lawn looked recently cut, the hedge trimmed. A Cherokee pickup truck was parked in the half-open garage.

"This is where she lives?" Heather said. "It's lovely."

"Darlene must have lied to us. This is far too nice."

"Check it out anyway."

He stepped out onto the sidewalk and jogged up the drive. He rapped on the screen door. He waited. Nobody came to the door. "Look, I know there's someone in there. I saw you at the window." He saw a ghostly shape come towards the door and heard the main door unlock with the snap of a bolt. A woman opened the screen door. She had dark hair cut to shoulder length curled up in bangs and vivid green eyes, but he recognised her through her new look. She recognised him and her eyes widened. She held on to the door until her knuckles turned white.

"Nadine," he said. "Nadine — that is you?"

She nodded sadly. "Cal, my God, how did you find me?"

"Purely by accident, it seems. I was looking for my daughter. The daughter you never told me about."

"Cal, this is so hard to explain." She looked up and down the street, then back to him. She was just as beautiful as he remembered. "You had better come in. Is that your wife in the car?"

"Yes."

"Bring her, too. I think I owe the both of you an explanation."

He agreed. He beckoned to Heather and introduced the two women, and Heather followed him dazed by the revelation. The hallway was bright and airy and smelled of pine needles. Nadine directed them into the living room. He could not help but notice the framed photographs on the television of Nadine and a pretty girl, Nadine and a brown-haired man, the three together in a wedding photograph, the girl in soft pink satin, Nadine in intense white, joyful, radiant, her cheeks flushed, her eyes shiny. The groom looked so proud of his new family. That man could have been me, he thought. But he also knew that it could not have been. Certainly not at that confused time of his life, when he had not known what he wanted.

"Darlene told me Christine lived here. Now I understand why she was reluctant. You've been hiding all of these years."

Over coffees, Nadine explained.

"Cal, I had no choice. I was in a bad marriage to Whit that just got worse. Whit started hitting me just about every day in places where no bruises would show in public — my back and ribs were black and blue. I wanted to leave, but he threatened to hurt Christine if I ever told the police. I was scared, but I didn't know what to do. So I stayed with him. I stayed with him hoping he would stop, but he liked hurting me, he liked to make me suffer. One night, he beat me up until I was unconscious. When I woke up it was dark and I heard noises in my bedroom. I opened the door and saw Whit with another woman, a prostitute he had picked up for the night. He saw me standing there and she just laughed. *Laughed.* At that moment something just clicked in my head and I went into a black rage. I grabbed his rifle and shot him, and when the woman tried to escape I hit her with the butt of it. I hit her once — but it killed her.

"So there I was with two murders on my hands. I couldn't explain it to the police. I called Darlene. It was my sister's idea to dress the woman up as me and ruin her face. Then we dumped Whit's body in the woods. She knew where to put the body where he would be found, but not for weeks. Meanwhile, she identified the dead woman as me, and the police assumed Whit was responsible. His body just verified it.

"After the investigation was over I came back as a different women: Abby Smith. I've been Abby Smith for twelve years. Christine knows me by no other name. She thinks her name is Christine Smith. I have fake birth certificates for the both of us thanks to one of Darlene's friends. For the last seven years I've been married to a good man, a man who doesn't abuse Christine or me. For his and Christine's sake, please don't tell the police. Keep my secret." She looked at both of them expectantly, a nerve in her neck twitching, her feet unconsciously tapping. "Cal, Heather, that girl who killed two people died in 1986, just like it says on the grave. Don't bring her back to life." She glanced at the clock on the wall. "Please go before Christine comes back from school. She has a good father, don't spoil her life."

"Tell me," he said, "is Christine happy?"

"Very happy," Nadine said.

Heather coughed.

Cal said to Heather, "I think Nadine should stay dead. What do you say?"

"I say...we should return to the hotel before it gets dark. We have to pack. We should let 'Abby' live her life."

"That's what I think, too."

They stood up. Nadine kissed Cal for what he knew would be the last time, her lips cool on his cheek like a single drop of rain on a hot summer day. He hugged her, then released her.

"Bye, Nadine. Bye, Abby."

"Thank you, Cal."

She showed them to the door. It was a long walk to the car, but Cal felt as if he were lighter, younger, and freer. As he was pulling the BMW away from the kerb, he looked back a single time. He saw Abby waving not at him but at a girl coming down the block, a girl who looked so like her mother that for a crazy moment he thought he had slid into the past, an alternative past, a past that was fair and good and happy, a past with loving parents and with promising futures; then he turned away and looked at Heather and smiled and reached across to touch her hand. She smiled back at him.

The BMW turned at the corner, leaving the past behind. ■

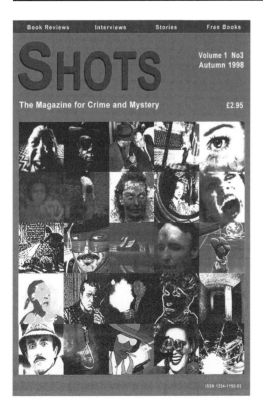

in his image

steve rasnic tem

Something iffy had slipped into his face. Of course it was probably just a matter of looking too closely. An occupational hazard — KT was always looking at things a little too closely. Couldn't see the forest — actually hadn't seen a forest in years. Couldn't see a face for all its pixels. He stared into the mirror, ran one finger down his skin from right eye to lower cheek, fascinated by the way the skin tones changed, the crinkles vanishing then reforming, new lines appearing, and everything just taking a few seconds too long to spring back into shape. A loss of elasticity, a decrease in flexibility. Signs of age as sure as the whitening of his scraggly beard hair and the bluing of the flesh under the eyes. A mask, wasn't it? KT's old-man mask. Sometimes he considered shaving the beard and getting some sort of tribal tattoo across the lips and around the chin to replace it, maybe make the dark under the eyes a permanent, deeper mark. Something bold to mask his age. But he suspected that much tattoo on facial skin would be a painful process, and he didn't have the time anyway.

Instead he threw cold water on his face and turned away from the mirror. He didn't think many people liked what they saw in the mirror. Always this discrepancy between the face they imagined and what appeared on the screen. Like listening to your voice on tape: the words and the particular pattern of speech might be yours, but the voice wasn't yours at all. You sounded better, you looked better, in your head.

Except media types — actors, announcers. They spent their lives making the face and the voice match what they imagined, what someone else imagined, what they read in the script. KT figured he of all people should envy such control, but he didn't. There was comfort in the discrepancy between image and substance. Rightly or wrongly it suggested depth of character.

In any case, *Nothing to have an anxiety attack over*. His favorite saying of late, he'd posted it at the top of his web site. Of course people who were compelled to remind you there was nothing to be anxious about often suffered from raging anxieties. He could feel the nerves playing with the muscles of his face like spider hairs. Damn, but he was a mess. Nothing to worry about. No big deal. The face was a mask and the mask was just a few cells deep, nothing more than a thin layer of electrons.

He made his way back to the screen, fatigue causing him to bump into things, sending stacks of old magazines tumbling onto discarded pizza boxes, stray clothing, unopened mail. He hardly noticed. He owed a new client a picture by midnight, and one of his few prides was that he never missed a deadline.

The assignment was another creepy one — he seemed to be getting a lot of those lately. A drawback of advertising on, doing most of your business through the web. Photo Manipulations Inc. There was always some fool wanting him to graft a young starlet's head onto a naked body, but that was more idiotic than creepy. He'd accept their credit card, though — who was he to say? They were just images, after all. They couldn't really hurt anybody.

But fellows like this new client — and they were almost always male, very few women appearing to need his services — what they wanted

Steve Rasnic Tem has
stories forthcoming in
F&SF, *Best New Horror*,
White of the Moon and
a Sideshow Press
anthology concerning
animal rights. His most
important piece of
writing of the last
several years, however,
was the welcoming
speech delivered
recently at his
daughter's wedding
reception (23 years in
the making). Steve and
his wife Melanie are two
of the guests of honour
at World Horror 2000,
to be held in Denver. If
you want to know more
about the Tems, you can
visit their website at
<www.m-s-tem.com>.

couldn't exactly be called pornographic, he supposed, but pondering the whys and wherefores of their requests to any degree always filled him with unease. The best he could do was lose himself in the technical aspects, leave the philosophizing to the alternative news groups. Wet images, dry images, women covered head to toe in a stew of nameless food items. Everyone seemed to have a special interest.

But it was all just a shim of electrons, a thin peel of a mask. Nobody died, they just got older, more set in their ways.

The new client had sent him a snapshot of a young boy, six, maybe seven, a little stocky, reddish hair, his back turned to the camera but his face twisted around to see who was behind him. Smart kid. It pays to know who's behind you. Only a hint of anxiety in the kid's expression but still plainly there, especially at the higher magnifications. The other photo the client sent was that of a fat sow suckling her young on a bed of straw and gray, lumpy mud. KT's assignment was to replace the sow's head with that of the young boy.

What KT was being paid for, of course, was to make it look good. It wasn't supposed to look as if someone had grafted a boy's head onto a hog's body. Skin tones and textures had to match, color blends had to be seamless. There had to be some hog in the boy and some boy in the hog. Despite your good sense, you had to believe your eyes. You had to believe that a creature such as this in fact existed.

He was almost done with the project, and even though he'd been staring at the image constantly over the last day or so, seen it even in his dreams, he still couldn't stand to look at it. So he looked at the picture and yet he didn't look at the picture. He looked at pixels, he manipulated bits and bits of bits, but he could not bring himself to look at this picture.

He had performed one additional manipulation, unasked-for, but which he knew from experience the client would want, even though he might not have the right words to ask for it. KT had tweaked the areas around the eyes and the mouth to make the boy's anxiety more pronounced. No additional charge. A boy sow down in the mud, suckling his young. Completed. He didn't know what the client would do with such an image. He didn't want to know. He emailed a low-resolution sample, let the guy know how to download the higher quality version from KT's site.

The rest of the evening KT worked on his web site, scanning images from magazines and newspapers, adding elements to aspects of his own face already in electronic storage. His web pages contained samples and descriptions of his business, price lists and submission information, but the deeper you went into the site the more personal it became, until finally you arrived at KT's personal newsletter, *Mews*, and a gallery of images he'd created, including many self-portraits. He'd tried to explain in several different ways in the newsletter that the multitude of self-portraits on the site was not evidence of some runaway narcissism, but simply to avoid the emotional and legal complications inherent when you manipulated the faces of other people without their permission.

The title *Mews* had been a spur-of-the-moment invention, risking silliness in its multiple meanings. He lived in a complex called Dogwood Mews, meant to emulate an old English neighborhood with its facing townhouses and cobbled courtyard, the dogwood at its center in fact a sculpture of a tree out of wire and fibrewood and plastic laminates, the woodgrain a photographic image bonded to melamine. There were also word plays: 'News' which he watched constantly but never seemed to believe or understand, the muse of inspiration of which he appeared to have very little these days, the musings of solitude which he had in plentiful supply, and finally the mews of complaint, the pitiful whining of a homeless or tortured cat, scratching and puking at the door. He'd originally included an image of a tortured cat as part of the masthead, which had outraged some so much he'd finally removed it. He kept explaining in his emails to these cat fanciers that the image had been manufactured, that he tortured images not animals, but many didn't seem to believe.

Most who bothered delving into these deep recesses of his site were more interested in his self-portraits than animal rights issues, however. Here his image suffered skinning, marring, evisceration, zombification, pixilation, posterizing, inversion, hue saturation, spherization, castration, immolation, all the tortures of the damned, and yet the only fallout for his physical being appeared to be intensifying fatigue.

Sometimes he recounted for his readers/viewers the steps involved in creating such personal disaster, but most of the time he was content to let them view the images without the technical background. People made assumptions about him on the basis of these images and sent him offers of aid both financial and psychological, long confessions, virulent diatribes, veiled threats, and more than one marriage proposal. He posted several commentaries suggesting that perhaps they interpreted too much, that an image took on a life all its own once manipulated, divorced from its original source, it's all just electrons, folks, charged particles and vapor-thin appearances and cosmic dust, but the outpouring had showed no signs of a decrease.

He had a second, larger monitor rigged up next to his first. After transferring some of his self-portraits to video he would display them here, now playing twenty-four hours a day. This permitted exact-size images of his distorted head he might observe while working, talk to, stare at eye-to-eye. Disconcerting sometimes, especially if any animation was involved. The mouth dissolving into a smile full of bone, eyes full of charged desperation in confrontation with the creator.

This, perhaps, was what had sparked his increased use of the bathroom mirror. Something to touch base with periodically, an anchor, even if KT didn't always like what he saw there.

Suddenly he could feel a razor-thin line of anxiety forming at the right corner of his mouth. It stretched across his chin and hooked into his jaw. He scrambled out of his chair and ran into the bathroom. Stacks of images flowing out over the rug, opened envelopes containing uncashed checks. A wicker basket full of unanswered bills on the floor next to the toilet. He wondered briefly if they might cancel each other out. A sour strain of body odor and spoiled food, but buried too far under glossy magazine layouts to do anything about. No one knew where all the bodies were buried, despite their claims. Children were killed everyday over the internet and no one lifted more than a mouse-clicking finger. Children's faces stolen and peeled away, leaving their bodies awash in a sea of red electrons.

In the mirror: his face soaked in cold sweat, fluorescent highlights in the whites of his eyes. He pushed closer to the glass and examined his face for rips: a nervous twitch by the mouth, a deep crease, but no trace of blood. He breathed a trembling sigh of relief. He looked terrible, but it was just an image, and he of all people knew that images could be edited.

A thunder of surround sound. The walls appeared to shake around him, his fingers twitching in accompaniment as if typing in changes. A couple of deep breaths to calm himself — he figured it was all a problem of sleep deprivation, he got obsessed with the work sometimes and simply couldn't be bothered with sleep — but his breath tasted of dank places and bad food and would not heal him.

A beating at the door. The infrequent visitor. He slipped back into the living room, performing a rapid survey of cleaning and straightening possibilities, and finding none elected to open the door anyway, not wanting the beating to continue a second longer. A pregnant woman stood in his doorway, weaving and drunk. He vaguely recognized her as a neighbor from across the way, despite the fact that a purple half-mask with plumes of ascending feathers covered the upper part of her face.

"So I heard you typing. Most nights I walk by I can hear you typing. Are you an all night typer or something?"

The mouth that said these words was unmasked, but outlined in a bright red lipstick that made it much more disconcerting than the half-mask above. The lipstick had an aging effect. Even with the mask he could tell the woman could be no older than thirty. The lipstick mouth added decades. It waited patiently for an answer.

"Well…I work with computers," he said. "I hit the keys pretty hard sometimes."

"I wouldn't know much about that stuff. But the thing is…my boyfriend's gone out again, and I'm scared being all by myself. Can I just wait here till he gets home?"

KT heard the words, but he really had no idea what she was saying. It might as well have been a foreign language. He couldn't remember the last time he'd spoken in person to a woman other than a checkout clerk. He wasn't sure he'd ever spoken to a pregnant woman. So he did what he always did when someone spoke to him in a foreign language. He tried to be the polite American. He nodded his head a great deal and smiled, even when she walked into the room. He didn't ask why she was wearing a Halloween mask in the middle of July; it would seem seriously rude to show any curiosity at all.

"Oh, look here. All these books and magazines and things to read. You must be a smart guy. I like to read, especially comic books. You like comic books?"

KT was pleased to hear a question he could answer. "Oh, yeah. I really love comic books."

"Do you have any Silver Surfer I could read?"

"Well, sure. Grab yourself a chair. I'll find you a Silver Surfer." He said it as if he were offering her a drink, and wondered if he should offer her a drink. But he wasn't sure what he had. He made his way into the kitchen, pausing now and then to lift up a stack of magazines as if looking for the comic, but knowing very well where the comics were. He felt so inordinately pleased to have the exact comic she wanted to read — what were the odds of that? — that he'd forgotten there were no empty chairs in the room — with the exception of his computer chair they were all piled high with boxes of clippings, and magazines waiting to be clipped.

He glanced over nervously to see her sitting on the edge of his bed, which he kept pretty much near the center of the room so that he might drop onto it periodically if he needed a computer break. He hadn't made it up or changed the sheets in a very long time, and seeing it now — and when you saw things through a veil of anxiety sometimes it was like seeing them for the very first time — he could see the yellow-brown pattern his body had etched into the bottom sheet. He could detect where his arms and legs had been, and his head, lighter patterns there like a facial topography. A clear spot like a mouth open in a faded mask. Instantly thought *Shroud of Turin*, and with that detected a small trace of blood near one corner of the image — he remembered a cut foot — but of course it looked like something more deliberate now. This gave him the idea for a sequence of images he might construct for his web site: portraits of people but with the people peeled away, only their shadows, and the shadows of their shadows, remaining. He would play with these remaining shadows, emphasizing and distorting them, perhaps distorting the objects they fell on, creating transformations wherever they touched. It would be a hopeful sequence in its way, advancing the idea that we could be effectual, even when fading into obscurity and oblivion.

There was orange juice in the refrigerator that smelled relatively fresh. He thought that would be the safest thing he could offer her.

From the other room: "Hope you don't mind my sitting on your bed?"

What was he supposed to say to a question like that? Was she coming on to him? "Oh...fine. Wherever you feel comfortable."

He gave her the juice when he came back in, feeling just a little alarmed that she hadn't yet bothered to remove the mask. As if reading his mind she said, "Tommy gave me this mask last week. He says I have to wear it all the time when he's not there. I don't mind it too much, but it makes it a little hard to see my TV programs with it on. I have to tilt my head some, make sure the eyeholes line up, but sometimes it slips. I tried putting a big old rubber band around my head to hold it in place, but it gave me a headache."

KT found a copy of the Silver Surfer and handed it to her with the juice. He didn't like the way she was leaning back into the bed, her skirt riding up. And her belly looked even larger in this posture, rising up off her spine like an explosion. "Maybe you could take it off for a few minutes, at least until you're done with your juice."

"Oh, I couldn't do that. He'd have himself a fit. And he doesn't even look like himself when he's mad."

"Most of us don't, I guess. I mean, the skin on our faces is so thin, really. Any strong emotion is going to move the features around in some significant way."

"You're a smart man," she said, as if just deciding. "I bet you wouldn't make your girl friend wear a mask even after Halloween. That's just ignorant."

"Well, it is a little unusual."

"I bet you treat your girl friend right, don't you?" Her voice lightly slurred the words. "I bet you appreciate her for what she is." Before he could confirm or deny she flipped open the comic. "I really like the Silver Surfer. His face is like he's got a mask on, but it isn't a mask, not really."

"His face is like what they call a 'neutral mask'," KT replied, eager to offer some obscurity now that his intelligence had been established. "It's a mask without any details, molded to the face like a hardened layer of skin."

She looked up then. Even with the mask on she appeared slightly dazed by the concept. "Well, I don't think it's a mask," she finally said. "I think he's kind of a good looking man." She picked up the comic and started reading. "You know you can go back to your work. I'll just sit here reading quiet until Tommy gets home."

The polite thing would have been to tell her he was done for the evening, then try to entertain her, ask her about her life, somehow ask her about what kind of man this Tommy was to make her wear the silly mask, but KT didn't know how to do polite. Besides, he *was* anxious to get back into his work — this was the most he'd talked to a live person in weeks and he had no idea if he was doing it correctly or not — and she'd just given him the easy out.

A distorted image of himself stared out from his second monitor. In some ways it looked better than him, a retouch job with straighter nose, stronger chin, and firmer eyes. His eyes looked so watery and unsure, as if always on the verge of tears. He couldn't remember having made this particular self-portrait, but then again he had made so many.

He logged on, picked up his email (the client was *more* than pleased with the sow child), then went over to his web site.

At first he thought a hacker had gotten in. There appeared to be alterations in all of the images in his gallery. Some fleshtones had deteriorated, leaving faces with a green or grayish cast. Pixels had floated out of place, outlines blurred. But not really enough damage, he thought, for it to be actual sabotage. Maybe a problem with his graphics card. Or maybe a problem with his own eyes. Fatigue can distort the curvature of the lens and…

Something iffy had crept into the eyes of his self-portraits. Or crept out of. The flatness, the deadness was gone. The eyes, even in heads of pain, watched him.

"So you think I'm pretty?"

He'd been so zoned he'd forgotten she was there. He looked up at her, the young pregnant lady stretched out on her back on his bed full of signs and indications, mask obscuring the upper part of her face, bright red lipstick alerting him to where her mouth would be if he wanted to come over and try it out. "Excuse me?"

"I *said*, do you think I'm pretty?"

Definitely someone else's life. But he could play along — he'd watched enough television, gone to enough movies. "Well, yes. Of course," he said, delivering his line.

"Why, *thank* you." She cozied back into one of his hair oil-spotted pillows. "I don't get too many compliments anymore."

Her pleasure saddened him. For the first time he noticed how faded her simple cotton dress appeared. The spots, the worn places. "Everyone needs a compliment now and then." His eyes went back to the monitor. One by one his images were slipping off the sides of the screen, leaving video noise in their wake.

"Well, ain't that the truth. Even if you know you're ugly, and you know the other person is lying through his teeth just to get into your panties, well, you still like to hear that sweet stuff."

He could feel his face flush, tried to will it another color, perhaps just a hint of Caribbean tan. "I don't even think I believe in ugly anymore," he said. "It's all just one image set up against another. Some looks get marketed better, that's all. Sometimes you can change your marketing, and sometimes you can't. That's the scary part, I think. You feel so damn helpless about it all. All these damn images of beauty and success and happiness that'll fit inside a frame and stay there while you look at it, admire it, covet it. And if you aren't careful, it all becomes this minefield that nobody ever gets out of alive. That image is a killer — it's got all our need and fear balled up in one place — it's a terrible thing and yet even the smartest of us think that's all we are."

Her head was bobbing, but it was because she was looking around at the clutter of his living room. He wasn't sure at what point he must have lost her, he hadn't been paying that close attention. But lost her he had.

Suddenly he felt acutely embarrassed for the way he lived. The place was like some skid-row trash heap and he was just the fly that landed there. He looked down at his stained T-shirt and shorts. He hadn't even been aware what he'd been wearing when she came to his door. He could've taken a bathroom break and washed and changed his clothes before coming back out but it seemed too late for that now. She could see how he lived and what he'd become.

"That's a real nice sports jacket," she said, oblivious to his musings. "Did it cost a lot? I bet it did and I bet you make good money doing this typing thing."

He tried to follow her line of sight, saw the sports jacket sprawled across an end-table where he'd thrown it after the last disastrous job interview. He could have done the job, of course — he never applied for any job he couldn't do — but the thing was trying to convince an employer that someone who looked like him could do the job. And acted like him. He wanted a job outside these walls, thinking it might save him from this continued craziness of solitary existence — a solitude that just had to kill him one day, he was sure — but he'd been like this so long it was difficult for anyone he met to picture him any other way. When he got back from that last interview he'd taken this long look at himself in the mirror and realized he hadn't a clue how he appeared to other people. He'd gone into that interview with dirt under his nails and white stuff at the corners of his mouth, and he hadn't even seen those things even though he'd made a studied self-examination before entering their building.

So they weren't about to give him a second look. They could not imagine anyone who looked like him working for them.

"It *is* a nice coat," he said. "I don't get many chances to wear it."

"Well, you should wear it more often," she replied. "Hey, maybe you could take me to the movies sometime. You could put that nice-looking jacket on and take me to the movies."

"I bet Tommy wouldn't be too happy with that." KT felt as if he had said something quite bold, but she didn't appear to react.

"Hey, you got a TV? Maybe there's a movie on now. You got your jacket and I got..." She held up her glass half full of juice. "Refreshments."

KT stood up, giddy with an odd sort of excitement. He hadn't felt so playful with a woman since before his older sister left home. She lived in Florida now, three kids, and they hadn't spoken in years. He went to the foot of the bed and started peeling away items from a pile of dirty clothes. "Ta da!" he said, revealing a dusty TV screen.

"Turn it on and come sit by me," she said, holding up her juice glass again. With a flourish KT slapped the 'on' button, grabbed the sports jacket and slipped it on. It bunched at the shoulders, spoiling the gesture, and he had to pull and tug to make it feel right. Then he threw himself onto the bed beside her, thinking she would either run or laugh and in fact he didn't really care which, as long as she reacted to what he'd done in some way.

The TV came on in the middle of an old war picture. KT recognized some of the actors — he was pretty sure they were all dead. More and more this seemed to be the case for him: watching movies full of dead actors. What was worse, he suspected anyone younger than he wouldn't even know these actors were all dead — the notion would never cross their minds. The way they were in the movie would be the way these actors would be forever.

"I bet Silver Surfer would make a good movie-type hero," she said, close to his ear, almost whispering, slurring her words. "They should make a movie about him. Mr No-face."

For just a brief moment he thought she was referring to him, that in his playful rush his face had slipped off and was now lost within the anxious clutter of the room. He pulled sweaty hands up to his mouth and nose and felt around, then jerked them away in embarrassment. "Oh, yeah." He laughed. "He'd make a great one all right."

She held the juice glass up to his lips. He was so close to her now he could see inside the eyeholes of her mask. Her eyes looked red, heavy and drugged. They would not fix on him. "Wait." She pulled the glass away. She took a small liquor bottle out of a big pocket in her dress, unscrewed it, and poured some into the juice. "Just to freshen it," she said, pressing it again to his lips. The glass was hard and cold and the liquor made his own eyes burn — -she'd obviously been adding stuff from the bottle to the juice the whole time she'd been here. He closed his eyes and let her pour it into him. The edge of the glass bit like a hard cold kiss and then the warm fluid tongue inside his mouth and her hard swollen belly pressed up against him, nose filling with the perfume and the stench of her, and with his eyes closed he was seeing the both of them inside his monitor, trapped inside the tube, falling out of their clothes and then falling out of their faces until they were just this liquid descent of electrons down the screen and off the edge into nothing.

"Oh, sweet Jesus," he murmured into her neck as he moved up to kiss her, and feeling the fullness of her beneath him he couldn't help thinking of the sow with the frightened boy's head and the babies sucking and feeding and there's nothing the little boy can do to escape. "Jesus," he said again, more softly now as if to pray that terrible image out of his head, and wondered not for the first time if now and again he brushed against monsters.

She clung to him with a desperate strength that frightened him, and when he finally opened his eyes to tell her that they should be more careful about the baby, because he really was worried about the baby, frightened for her baby, he could see that her mask had slipped, more of her face was exposed, and the rows of circular cigarette burns like tiny ruined mouths all around both of her eyes.

"Tommy says I've got to wear my mask," she whispered huskily, and refitted it to her face, and tried to draw him back into her, into her smell and lips and eyes, into skin thin as desire, brief as a flash of phosphors on a smoked screen, but all he could think about was how was she ever going to market this, how was she going to sell this, how was she going to put the best face on this, and, at least for the moment, this was no longer a place he was prepared to go.

Hours later he could hear them across the courtyard of the mews arguing, and if there had been screams he would have gone over there and stopped them. He would have played the Silver Surfer in his mask that is no mask, and he would have stopped whatever was going on.

But there weren't any screams that night. Perhaps there had never been any screams.

Instead he stood and waited in his doorway, listening to the rhythmic rise and fall of their argument that might not be an argument, studying the tree that had never been a tree, admiring the way the cool halogen of the streetlights washed the rounded stones of cast concrete.

When he finally went back inside he went first to the bathroom where he washed his face a very long time, then shaved away at the rough stubble of his beard until blood had welled in numerous nicks. The face that stared out at him was both terrible and new, one he had never seen before, and most likely would change to fit the given situation. It was the kind of face he had always wanted, it was the kind of face that might win him jobs and women, but he knew that at least for a few nights he would sleep with one eye open, a knife ready in hand for peeling the image away at the first sign of rebellion.

On his web site the self-portraits had apparently disappeared for good, broken and scattered into the ether. Just before dawn there was email, and an attachment: a picture of a fattened, battered cat with his face, so professionally done as to be seamless, so much of the cat in the line of his jaw and the tilt of his head, so much of his own terror as the feline head shifts to see the thing in fast pursuit. ■

Frank Hewitt was no ordinary celebrity. For one thing, he had talent. For another, he had that indefinable quality which meant it didn't matter that he didn't have *a lot of* talent. He was a star. The camera loved him just as he loved it, so that the public, who always wanted so badly to love what the camera saw, could love him too, and feel as though he loved them back. Not only that, he had a rare cross-media appeal. His voice was average and comforting enough that his interpretations of show tunes and middle-of-the-road classics would always be big sellers, but down the years he had also appeared in a number of very successful second-rate films. He was charming, and lovable, yet with an intriguingly sordid past. He did beer adverts, too.

The only trouble with Frank Hewitt was that he was still alive, and had been for some time. It was a growing disappointment to a lot of people who mattered in the entertainment industry. Somehow, despite his hard-boozing, chain-smoking, orgiastic journey through the world of showbiz, he had managed to avoid cancer, heart failure or a stroke and arrive at the age of seventy-three looking determined to make it to eighty and beyond.

His agent (and mine), Harry Schmeltzmann, spelled it out for me on the phone.

"The trouble is," Harry was saying, "I've got the people from CBC on my back about the tribute show. Then there's the biopics. Two telemovies and a feature. *The Hewitt Story*, *Frank Hewitt: The Story*, and *The Story of Frankie Hewitt*. It's a contractual thing. They can't go into full production until Frank actually kicks it.

.....TAKING CARE OF FRANK........

There are the exposés, too. Six unofficial biographies and two docufiction character assassinations for TV. Plus the arthouse revivals and video releases of his old movies. Not to mention the tapes and CDs of the recent Vegas shows, and the boxed sets and compilations. And guess what? There's an interactive CD-Rom lined up. Archive material and some stupid computer game and a Frank Hewitt quiz. That's without factoring in the hundred or so 'Frankie Hewitt Was A Fucking Genius' articles that the broadsheets and glossies can't run until he croaks. You know what it's about. All this crap is going to sell better when Hewitt is dead."

"But Hewitt is already old," I said. "Can't it wait until natural causes?"

"Wait? Why should it wait? A lot of people have put a lot of money into Frank's career down the years. They didn't know he was going to live this long, otherwise they might not have invested so much in the first place. Don't you think they deserve a decent return now, while *they* can enjoy it? Don't forget, Bendick, you'll be on a percentage of gross yield after Hewitt's death. If you knock him off."

"That percentage is microscopic, Harry, and you know it."

"The *percentage* might be miniscule, but the total yield adds up to quite a slice, Stan. And I'm on a percentage of *you*. So don't let me think any more that you're discouraging me from finding you gainful employment."

Not only that, but Harry must have been getting his own very special kickback from somewhere to be happy to sacrifice his ten percent of the fortune that Frank Hewitt pulled in every year.

"Hewitt's big, Harry," I said. "Very big. Won't there be more heat than usual from outside?"

"Possibly. But the dirt stays inside the industry, no matter who, no matter what. It has to. You know that. Stop looking for excuses."

"But I *like* Frank Hewitt," I said. "My dad liked Frank Hewitt. My grandfather *raved* about him."

"Jesus, Bendick, everyone likes Frank Hewitt, that's the point. Everybody *loves* him. Why do you think he's so huge? But the industry needs a boost. There hasn't been an elder statesman or Grand Dame of the entertainment world drop out of the firmament for some time now. Look, take it or leave it. I worked hard to get you this gig. I can always offer it to Grebb or Zabowski…"

"No, no," I said, with some reluctance. "I'll do it. Better that he gets it from a fan, eh?"

"That's the spirit, Bendick," said Schmeltzmann. "And make it look like murder. We'll get bigger press that way."

Leo Zabowski rang an hour later. I knew his ugly voice at once.

"Bendick? It's Zabowski."

"I know who it is," I said. "So you got the Frank Hewitt job."

"How did you find out?"

"Bad news travels fast, I guess." Zabowski didn't sound jealous at all, which

ANTONY MANN

was all wrong for him. "You know you only got it because Schmeltzmann is your agent *and* Frank Hewitt's, don't you?"

"Perhaps so, Zabowski, but ask yourself this: *why* is Schmeltzmann one of the biggest agents in Hollywood? Because he wouldn't touch second-raters like you with a barge-pole."

Zabowski laughed. It was one of my least favourite noises.

"Are you okay, Zabowski? You sound like you're choking on your own phlegm."

"That's hilarious, Bendick. Just remember. You might have worked with the big stars for the last few years, but your time is coming to an end. This business is crying out for some new blood."

"Keep dreaming, Zabowski. The world always needs dreamers, like Frank Hewitt sings."

"Yeah, well, anyway," said Zabowski flatly, his vitriol expended.

We waited then the both of us for the other to hang up. Eventually he got bored and softly put down the phone.

Hewitt's mansion, Cedar Grove, was out in The Hills beyond The Valley. Someone — possibly Hewitt — had cut some of the cedars down a long time ago to make way for the nine-hole golf course and the tennis courts. The two-storey white house, too big for your average family but perfect for a living Hollywood legend, sat snugly against a backdrop of evergreens.

105

Hewitt's fourth wife Clarissa met me at the front door. I had seen her photo in the gossip sheets. She was slim and blonde, perhaps naturally. Her face was set into a careless, superior expression that reflected wealth and the boredom that went with it, but she had kept her teenage looks, possibly because she was not long in her twenties.

"Stan Bendick?"

"That's right."

"Do you have your own gun or would you like to borrow one?" She walked me through into the tiled reception hall and to the base of a wide staircase that curved up and around. We were surrounded by *objects d'art*: Monets, Epsteins, Picassos and what have you, all waiting patiently to be fought over by Clarissa and the rival ex-wives and the eight or ten children from the previous marriages.

I patted my shoulder holster through my jacket. "As it happens, I brought my own."

"Fine. Frank should be upstairs. Third door on the left. Could you make it quick? I've got a hair appointment in forty-five minutes."

"I think your hair looks fine the way it is," I said.

She smiled sourly. "Well, thanks anyway, but what would you know?" She headed off to be rude to somebody else, but stopped in the doorway which led through to the rest of the ground floor. "Remember, third door on the left. Not second. *Third.*"

"I can count to three," I replied.

"Congratulations."

The door was unlocked. Frank was in.

He sat facing away from me, dozing in a high-backed brown leather chair in front of wide clean windows that overlooked The Valley and the winding bitumen road that led from there to here. The room was clearly Frank Hewitt's space: the soothing blue carpet was plush, the dark relief wallpaper almost three-dimensional. Frames displayed movie posters behind polished glass, and antiquated gold and platinum records. There were video tapes, photo albums and hardbacks on shelves next to the TV and VCR. Opposite the windows, beside a connecting door that was shut, sat a telephone on a small three-legged table.

Even the back of his head looked famous. I might have shot him then and there, but this was the man whose songs my grandfather had slow-danced to while courting my grandmother, whose movies my dad had sat in the back row to watch as a kid. It had been my honour to permanently retire a lot of stars in the last few years, but never one as big as Frank Hewitt. I wanted to see his face. My shoes made no sound on the thick pile.

He sat in the chair in a lemon yellow terry towelling dressing gown and tartan slippers, the back of his skull at an angle against the headrest. His breathing was light. He had never been a handsome man and now, in his old age, his midriff was paunched and his round face wrinkled and worn. Yet even in repose he was larger than life. It's a pet theory of mine that people in the public eye are imbued with a residue of the abnormally great amount of attention that is paid them, a concentration of a kind of psychic energy if you like. This residual force is then radiated back to the public by the celebrity. It's a constant, unconscious process. It explains why, when you meet someone famous in the flesh, they always seem to be exaggerated in some way, operating in a different reality. It explains why we call them stars. I began to wish I'd brought a camera.

But there was no future in coming over all starstruck. It would only make things harder. I had to take care of Frank before he woke. I had drawn my revolver and was picking my spot when he opened his eyes and looked at me. He hadn't been asleep at all.

"Er, hello Mr Hewitt," I said, lowering the gun sights.

"Call me Frank."

"Frank."

"Stan Bendick, isn't it?"

"Ah, that's right."

"I've heard about you, Bendick."

"You have?" Frank Hewitt had heard of *me*? I was flattered.

"We all have. You and your kind. Just because we're stars doesn't mean we're stupid. We know what goes on. We know where you live, what you look

like. Who you've murdered."

"Wow," I said. "That's great, Mr Hewitt...I mean, Frank...I mean..."

"Did you meet Clarissa?"

"Who?"

"Clarissa. My wife."

"Yes, I did, she's a lovely young woman, Frank. You must be very much in love with her..."

"She's a bitch, even worse than the others. Don't tell her, but I've cut her out of the will. Sure, she'll contest it, maybe even win, but I like the idea of her loathsome face twisting with selfishness and anger when she hears that she doesn't get a penny." He laughed, then pointed a stubby finger at me. "Let me tell you something about fame. It's only ever an accident, and it always ends in tears. I've had four loveless marriages, I've got nine children who either hate or fear me. All the money I've earned hasn't given me an ounce of joy or contentment. Any happiness I've had — and there hasn't been much — has come from the things that I could have had anyway, *without* being a star."

I hefted the gun in my hand. "Maybe you could look at it this way. You'll be making a lot of *other* people happy when you die."

"You mean the rich moguls?" he said bitterly. "The studio and TV bosses and the soulless parasites who buzz around them like flies on shit? The people who pollute this filthy industry more and more with every passing year?"

"Yes, them, of course, but what I meant was the ordinary people in the street, the people who look up to you without knowing what really goes on behind the scenes. Your fans will love you a lot more when you're dead."

He raised an eyebrow. "You think so?"

"Of course. Just look at Elvis. John Lennon. Look at Princess Di. After *she* croaked, there were millions of people who suddenly realised how much they loved her who didn't know more than the first thing about her!"

"That's a good point, Bendick. Not good enough to make me think that I *deserve* to die, but a good point nonetheless."

"Thanks, Mr Hewitt...Frank..."

I could hear the chutter-chutter of a helicopter in the distance, rising up out of The Valley. All else was still. I raised the gun again.

"Before you do that, you might want to take a look at the news on television," said Frank.

"If it's all the same with you, I'll buy a newspaper on the way back to town."

"It's for your sake, not mine," he shrugged. He reached down and picked up the remote from the floor, then swivelled in his chair. He pressed 'on' and flicked through the channels until he found Cable News. A generic modern-style female cue-card reader with small eyes was half way through reciting some lies about the economy, when either a mosquito got stuck in her ear or she was fed a line by the producer. She jiggled her ear piece and mustered a

concerned frown, then stared into the camera.

"This just in," she said. "We're getting unconfirmed reports that singer and movie star Frank Hewitt is dead. Repeating, reports are coming in that Frank Hewitt has been shot." Then, ruining my morning, a recent photo of me flashed up on screen behind her. The newsreader continued, "Police are hunting for escaped lunatic Stan Bendick, who is wanted in connection with the shooting. Police are warning the public that Bendick is likely to be armed and dangerous, and a lunatic, and to only approach him if they can get away a clear shot with no risk to themselves. Cable News will be running a five-day Frank Hewitt retrospective, including concerts, interviews with family, friends, acquaintances and people who never knew him, and panels of experts discussing every nuance of his incredible career, as well as phone-ins, competitions and whatever else we can think of. But now let's cross to Ned Denverson in our Mobile Aerial Unit, which just happens to be in the general vicinity of Frank Hewitt's mansion in The Hills, Cedar Grove...can you hear me, Ned?"

"I can hear you," came Ned's voice. On screen now was an aerial view of the nine-hole golf course and the big white house. "We're approaching Cedar Grove right at this moment, Elise. All looks peaceful. Hard to imagine that only minutes ago, crazed gunman Stan Bendick allegedly shot Frank Hewitt five times in the head and left him lying in a pool of his own blood. We'll see if we can get a look at the room where we suspect Hewitt was mercilessly slain."

It was getting weird. I looked out the windows. The helicopter that I had heard was closer now. I could see it banking in towards the house. I looked at the gun in my hand. I looked at Frank. Had I *really* killed him? It didn't appear so, but then, hadn't they said so on TV?

"How did you know…?"

"I heard the news crew setting up in the next room a couple of hours ago," said Frank. "Clarissa must have let them in. Just because I'm a star, doesn't make me deaf."

"There's a news crew in the *next room*?"

"You've been stitched up, Bendick. You and me both."

He was right. As he used the remote to switch off the television, the connecting door opened and Leo Zabowski walked in holding a gun. The news crew followed behind. It was a location unit comprising a female presenter, a soundman and a hand-held camera operator. There was a production assistant, too, a young man with a clipboard, and a pencil stuck behind an ear.

Zabowski was looking particularly repulsive today, I thought. Beads of sweat ran down his large bald head, adding their little bit to the stains on his shirt collar. His trousers were too baggy and, frankly, he could have done with cleaning his shoes. He was nervy and still overweight, although I'd heard he'd been trying to lose a few kilos.

"Zabowski, you're a disgrace," I said.

The presenter was a plasticky-looking brunette in her late twenties. I vaguely recognised her from the box. She glanced at Frank Hewitt sitting impassive in his leather swivel chair, then turned questioningly to Zabowski. "He's not dead," she said.

"I'm sorry, Ms Paxton," he said meekly. But with me, Zabowski was in a snarly mood, "You see, Bendick? You see? I was right! You can't do your job properly any more! Why isn't Hewitt dead, eh? Tell me that!"

"We…er…got to chatting," I said.

"Chatting? *Chatting*? Well come on, Bendick! Shoot him!" Zabowski gestured wildly at the window behind. "The news 'copter is almost here! It's a live feed! Do you want them to see that Hewitt is still alive? It'll ruin the broadcast!"

As far as moments in my life go, it was an odd one. I knew I'd been set up by Harry Schmeltzmann to take the fall, and also that Leo Zabowski was there to gun me down after I'd immortalised Frank Hewitt. But Zabowski could have simply shot me while he had the chance, and then finished off Frank afterwards. He made no move to. I noticed his body language. His stance indicated that he felt completely at ease. He saw no threat at all. And why should he? It was him standing next to the news crew, not me. He was on the side of the networks, caught in the illusion that the players in the world of TV and film are governed by a different set of rules from ordinary folk. I'm not saying that I didn't feel the temptation to go along with the plot, to play the part that had been written for me and slot unquestioning into prime time. I even felt the gun twitch in my hand and begin to slide across to where Frank Hewitt sat. Then I had a better idea. I shot Zabowski in the head.

The report was loud, but not surprising. It was a glancing blow that took a chunk of bone out of the top right hand side of his skull. It all but knocked poor dumb Zabowski off his feet. With perplexed curiosity, he poked at the wound with a finger, marvelling at the blood that ran down his hand, the sudden absence of cranium which over the years he had come to take for granted.

"Bendick?" he said. "What have you done?"

"Looks like I shot you, Zabowski."

"Fucking idiot! Don't you know that you've wrecked the programme?"

"Sorry," I said. I meant it. I shot him again. This time he went down. Not even Zabowski's head was thick enough to sustain two bullets.

Now there was news, and the news crew jolted into motion reflexively. The dark-haired presenter, Ms Paxton, took control with great efficiency, I thought. She whispered something in the ear of the production assistant, who nodded, then got on the phone. She stepped over Zabowski, strode to the windows and drew the curtains moments before the helicopter made its first pass. She instructed the crew: "Dick? Hal? Let's have one shot of the body and the gun, another of Bendick with *his* gun, then Frank in the chair. Then we'll start setting up sight and sound for interviews with both of them." Dick and Hal set to work as ordered.

Ms Paxton sized me up. "We'll do it this way," she said. "Turns out you're not

Antony Mann is an Australian writer living in Oxford with his wife Judy and young son Zachary. His recent stories have appeared in *The Third Alternative*, *Chapman*, *Staple*, CHESS and many others. Another story is due to appear in the upcoming *London Magazine* short fiction anthology. He has been writing on sport for *The Guardian* since 1997, and writes humour for the funniest chess periodical in the world, *Kingpin*. He can juggle five balls (count 'em!).

escaped whacko Stan Bendick after all. You're actually unassuming Frank Hewitt fan Stan Bendick, who happened to be here at Cedar Grove getting Frank to sign some teddy bears for a charity auction. Lucky you carry a gun, otherwise you wouldn't have been able to thwart crazed gunman Leo Zabowski, recent escapee from the loony bin, who had broken into the house to kill Frank Hewitt and thus deprive the world of one of its greatest stars." She nodded to where the young production assistant was still talking animatedly into the telephone. "Mick's sorting it out now. We'll be running the correction on Cable in a few minutes." She smiled at me, almost like she meant it. "You're a hero, Bendick. How do you feel?"

"Not bad, considering."

She turned to Frank. "Mr Hewitt? I expect we'll generate enough news and spinoffery from this incident to keep you viable. How do you feel?"

"I feel like I need a new agent," he said.

He wasn't the only one.

The door opened. Clarissa walked in. "I heard the shots," she said. "Did everything go all right?" She saw Frank. "Oh. Frank. You're alive. Thank. God."

"And maybe a new wife," said Frank.

"Mr Hewitt? Frank?" I said. "There was something I was meaning to ask you before, but I never got the chance."

"What's that, Bendick?"

"Can I have your autograph?" ■

THE BACK OF BEYOND

MARGARET WALKER

Yarrabalong is one of those remote and forgotten colonial towns that exists primarily for wheat and sheep. It is preloved — its paint work is peeling, its population is inbred and within its long, quiet streets a house may still be found whose interior has not changed in a century. Nevertheless, it is sufficiently pretty to captivate the odd tourist lost on his way to Melbourne, a thousand kilometres to the south, or Brisbane, six hundred kilometres to the north and is home to farmers, various itinerant professionals, shop keepers, government employees and the odd cash-strapped pensioner or two. Lastly, several self-funded retirees flourish there because, as if it were a faded virgin, they catch a dim memory of its former allure and they find living in hope an interesting concept.

On a dinted and dusky evening in the late harvest, Francis Gibbs, known as Frank, a seventy-something bilateral amputee tarnished by the stigma of half a dozen apprehended violence orders, dialled triple zero on his telephone. Shortly afterwards a young police constable, Trevor McDonald, broke in at the kitchen door noting that both it and the front door, the only other exit from the dwelling, were locked from the inside.

The old man was sitting on a commode chair, quite bloodied, with his pants down to his stumps and an agonized expression on his face. In one corner was a wheelchair. The commode was lined with blood, perhaps fifty to one hundred millilitres and otherwise contained two constipated turds. The floor beneath was streaked brown to the door and, lying languidly upon it, a blue cattle dog sniffed without interest at a grisly, offal-like bowl of food also drenched red.

"Thanks," croaked the old man.

"Is that all you wanted me for?" replied the constable. He prodded the bowl gingerly with his boot. "What's that?"

Gibbs grimaced. "Me balls," he groaned.

"Get you to hospital?"

"Not likely! Them places'll kill you."

"Where's your wife?"

"Gorn," belched Gibbs. "Left me."

About bloody time, thought McDonald. And now she'd finally gelded the blighted old bugger. Well, it was a standard joke that the relevant appendages had shrivelled due to alcohol abuse anyway. "No medical treatment?" The constable eyed him sourly before leaving. "Please yourself. Suits me."

The dog burped farewell and as he could no longer stand, Gibbs belted him with the back of his hand.

There was a term they used in Yarrabalong: not real bright. In the language of medicine this referred to an isolated population so lacking in breeding stock that

Margaret Walker has a
Bachelor of Science
degree in Anatomy and
Physiology and has
worked in Australian
and British hospitals.
She has studied the
human body, dissected
the upper limb and
visited the Sydney
Morgue, witnessing
there several autopsies
and unclaimed bodies
which were being held
for the police. She is
interested in forensic
medicine and her
published work has
been a series of articles
for the *Forbes
Advocate* concerning
nutrition. 'The Back of
Beyond' is dedicated to
Margaret's friend
Elizabeth.

Illustrations:
David Checkley

low intelligence, lack of initiative, depression, morbid obesity, alcoholism and domestic violence were considered normal. For the chronically over worked Sergeant Bill Kingsford, normal was a brand of black humour, and for Constable McDonald, born and bred in Yarrabalong, black humour was normal.

He was half way back to the station, wondering, as she had no relatives, where Mrs Gibbs could have gone, when he recalled the doors and realized that, as they had been locked from the inside, she couldn't have gone anywhere. Then he remembered the well-fed dog. He turned around and retraced his steps, calling first at the neighbours.

"Anything unusual going on next door tonight?"

"Wife screaming," they replied. "Nothing unusual."

"Gibbs has been castrated," announced the constable.

They smiled. "Good on her."

McDonald called Kingsford and together they returned to Gibbs' house.

"Where's your wife?" they repeated.

"I told you," said Gibbs.

The policemen searched the house. They prized open the floorboards. They searched the shed and roamed with torches as far as the river bank. In the pitch blackness, they went over the yard with a fine tooth comb wondering how an elderly bilateral amputee could have disposed of anyone in the few moments McDonald had been absent, and then locked the door after him.

Kingsford returned to the kitchen where Gibbs sat and gloated at them. He examined the dog's bowl, discovering its contents to be nothing but commercial dog food swamped with blood. Beneath this, apparently buried with the aim of being undetectable, was a small Swiss Army knife too fouled to yield anything imaginably like a fingerprint.

Kingsford heaved the old man up by his collar. "Where is she, you miserable little shit?" he shouted.

"Can't hear you with that ear," replied Gibbs peevishly. "Get me hearing aid. It's in the bedroom."

"What have you done with her?" roared Kingsford in his other ear.

"You deaf or what? I told *him* she's left me."

Kingsford waved the knife in his face. "What's this then?"

Gibbs leered at them with a mouth of rotting tombstones. "Me dog's got fleas," he cackled.

Kingsford and McDonald took him to the police station, a picturesque Federation structure cloaked gloriously in late autumn ivy, and grilled him solidly for an hour during which he rehashed his previous statement half a dozen times with the monotony of dementia.

"We're not going to get anything out of him," mumbled McDonald.

"You're not going to get anything out of me," replied Gibbs.

Then, despite his protests, they dumped him at the hospital for observation.

"He's been stripped and bathed," said the sister who admitted him to the eight bed establishment. "There's not a mark on him. And," she added. "Nothing's missing either."

"Obviously," yawned McDonald back at the station. "The blood belonged to his wife."

"But how do you know she was there at all, Trev?" replied Kingsford, finishing off the chips he had grabbed between the hospital and the phone. He'd read somewhere that dieting was impossible amongst the criminally insane and his obesity would have to wait until he could get a transfer. "We'll go and see Doctor Cameron. Check out the blood group. Make sure it was hers."

Doctor Cameron was old. Over the years he had cultivated a somewhat sardonic wit which owed a lot to his growing certainty that he would one day die on the job and spend eternity in Yarrabalong. He would have retired a decade ago but not a solitary city doctor had answered his desperate advertisements for a replacement. Not even citing the town's obvious if decaying charms could banish the streets of genetic misfits a general practitioner would be forced to see day in and day out.

"Gibbs, A-positive," he told the policemen. "Missus, O-positive. The blood tested A. It's his."

"Bullshit," said Kingsford.

"No, sergeant, it's medicine."

"How could the blood have been his?"

"You're the policeman, you tell me."

"But the hospital said…" interrupted McDonald.

"I know what the hospital said," replied Kingsford. "She does a runner, he locks her out so she can't get back in…"

"…And bleeds everywhere without leaving a mark on him? Surely the blood was hers. And how did he lock the door?"

"Stranger things have happened. Look, go back to his house, check for anything she might have taken with her. Purse, clothes, money, bankbook, jewellery. Look for signs that she might have left of her own volition. Particularly, fingerprint the dog's bowl. Find out which one of them fed it."

"Why?"

"Because we need to prove she was in the house." Kingsford spelt it out as if he was educating a kindergarten class.

"The neighbours heard her screaming," said McDonald.

"When?"

"I dunno."

Kingsford threw up his hands. "What kind of policeman are you? Go back and ask them *when*."

The doctor watched Trevor's retreating form reflectively. "Don't you think you're being a bit hard on him? I mean, he was born here."

"I am not responsible for his conception," pouted Kingsford irritably. "If I was I would have worn a condom. I suspect Marjorie was alive in the house when he broke in. Trevor takes everything on face value. Gibbs says she's gone, so he's halfway back into town before it occurs to him to check. We could be held responsible for her death."

"By whom?" asked Cameron.

Kingsford scratched his ear. "You're right," he said. "Thank God we live in Yarrabalong."

McDonald returned in ten minutes. "They dunno," he announced.

"Bloody hell," groaned Kingsford. "Okay. Let's get some fingerprints. The dog hadn't eaten his dinner. The floor was streaked with blood. Unless Gibbs got down on his hands and knees and licked the floor, it means the dog did it."

"Eat blood?"

"Haven't you ever had black pudding?" asked Doctor Cameron. "I used to be partial to it in my younger days."

"Someone hit me with one once, I think."

"But weren't you sleeping with his wife?" recalled Kingsford.

Doctor Cameron shook his head. He put away his two small test tubes and the litmus-like paper he had used to check the blood group. "How much was there?" he asked the policemen.

"There was blood all over the place," mumbled McDonald.

"Blood often looks worse than it is. You can lose a lot of blood and still walk through a door."

"But it's his, right? Hey!" exclaimed McDonald. "Maybe the dog was bleeding. Isn't that cannibalism?"

Doctor Cameron decided to put another advertisement in the morning's paper. Several lies, succinctly placed, he considered, might convince an overseas trained medico to sign up before he knew what he was in for. Then he could retire to the beach and kiss Yarrabalong goodbye.

The dog's bowl was smudged and bloodied beyond recognition. A slight half fingerprint on one side was unidentifiable, but several around the top of the can and on the can opener probably belonged to Mrs Gibbs.

"I'm not much good at this fingerprint stuff," slurred McDonald, unhappily comparing the powdered can opener with the smudged copy he had taken from Frank. "Probably not his. Could be hers."

"How do you open a can of dog food, Trevor?" enquired Kingsford.

"I've got a cat."

"Then how do you open a can of cat food?"

"I hold the can and squeeze the opener."

"And were there prints around this can?"

"Nope. Just a few at the top."

"And how does you mother feed the cat?"

"She's smaller than me and middle aged. She puts it on the bench, squeezes the opener and holds it down so the force doesn't spin it onto the floor."

"So Mrs Gibbs was there."

"How do you know?"

"You've just explained to me how an older woman uses a can opener."

"So you mean, stuff the finger prints?"

"Of course I don't mean that!"

Kingsford dusted the door. The deadlock was sparkling clean and had certainly been recently wiped, but at the base, above the smears of blood on the floor was a visible smudge in the shape of a half banana and about as tall. As if someone had closed the door with his foot.

"Gibbs has no feet."

"What about a nose? You broke the door open but was it closed by the dog?"

"What sort of dog would close a door?"

Kingsford swept a hand over the smears on the floor. They stopped at the door. "A hungry one," he said.

They returned to the station and contacted her husband's cousin, her only known relative, but she was not with him. They drove out of town along roads flanked by the brown long-pastures of drought time for five kilometres while insects, attracted by the high beam kamakazied themselves on the windscreen. They telephoned or door knocked the four hundred of Yarrabalong's eight hundred residents who lived within walking distance. They grilled its solitary taxi driver. They rang every women's refuge for two hundred kilometres, every cottage hospital west of the mountains, all the churches, fifteen other police stations, all without a whisper of her. They searched her house. Everything she might have needed, including her purse, was still in it.

Finally, at first light, they dragged the river and at midday Mrs Gibbs's lifeless body was discovered partially submerged a kilometre-and-a-half downstream from her home.

Both her wrists had been slit and, although it was initially supposed that her forearms were stiff from rigor mortis, it was discovered in the morgue that the arms had flexed because most of the tendons had been severed.

"Cause of death?" asked McDonald.

"Suicide," concluded Kingsford. "Get Doctor Cameron in about three, will you, to perform the autopsy but I don't think there's any doubt about it." He paused. "Did you see any blood anywhere along the bank? No? Neither did I."

"There was blood all over the kitchen."

"His blood." Kingsford shook his head. "It doesn't make sense."

"And how did he get her into the river?" said McDonald.

"The river's only fifty metres away. It's not impossible. Load her on the wheel-chair in the dark. Wheel down and roll her in. Wheel himself back."

"A bilateral amputee? Both doors were locked from the inside. He only rang us because he was shut in. The lock's up high. You can't reach it from his chair."

"So you opened the door and he disposed of the body…"

"I was only away five minutes and, in any case, why not tell the truth? Why not ring us and say, 'I found her, she did it'?"

Kingsford scratched his chin thoughtfully. "Was it murder?" he mused.

"Murder?" Trevor went white. "We ought to ring Sydney then."

"An elderly couple in the bush?" Kingsford raised his eyebrows. "They wouldn't give it a second thought. We'll get the same sweet bugger-all from the city we always do. CIB couldn't find Yarrabalong if you paid them overtime to read the map. We can handle this ourselves."

Mrs Gibbs's body lay in the sandstone mortuary wavering dimly beneath the single globe hanging from the ceiling. There was no refrigeration. There should have been in this climate, but it would be winter in a fortnight and no one had bothered in a small town for a single suicide victim who would shortly be transferred to the funeral director's in Forbes. That big town up the road had enough refriger-ation to prevent a corpse going black for anything up to three months, and they were mostly claimed before that.

The one exception was a businessman who had travelled to Yarrabalong apparently with the sole aim of shooting himself through the head. His corpse remained at eight degrees centigrade for four months by which time it had gone chocolate brown, swept with arcs of mauve. It began to bloat. The teeth drew back from the lips. Fluids of decomposition seeped into its body bag and the funeral director hit upon the novel idea of charging Yarrbalong's fascinated residents viewing fees. The fun stopped abruptly when a string of ex-wives each claimed the body in order to challenge the will. Needless to say, the disappointment was terrible.

Doctor Cameron inserted a new blade in his scalpel and drew a clean incision down the centre of the abdomen. He opened the fatty flesh and cut through the sternum with heavy clippers. Then he pulled the ribs apart to reveal the lungs. "Full of river water," he observed. "She drowned."

"You mean she was alive when he pushed her in?"

"That's what is normally assumed by the verb 'to drown'."

And though this might have been obvious, Cameron completed the autopsy, even to the weighing of heart, liver, and kidneys, stomach, bowel, uterus and ovaries. The brain would be fixed in spirits, weighed and examined at a later date. The body was full of blood. He sloshed it out with a soup ladle and Kingsford hosed it down the drains. In the tight room the air began to reek.

"They don't bleed right up until the moment of death you know," said Cameron. He handed around a packet of extra strong peppermints. "Squeamish, boys? Just until the blood pressure falls low enough to stop the bleeding. After that it takes perhaps two hours to die slowly of hypovolaemic shock. I don't think she's lost enough to get to that. And you see these slashes on her wrists. They've been done the wrong way. Across, you see. She cuts through the skin then you have tendon, vein, artery, nerve. She's cut the tendon." He burrowed into the violated wrist. The flesh squelched. "And, I think, half way through the vein only. You see how the wrist and the forearm have contracted. That's what happens when you cut the tendons and it effectively stops the bleeding. She probably fainted. That's all."

"And she did it herself?"

"If you do it yourself, you take the knife in one hand and cut it. The cut can only be lateral to medial because that's the way you hold the knife. So she cuts one side lateral to medial on her left wrist — he cuts the other — you see, because

115

the incision on the right wrist is medial to lateral — with the intention of finishing her off, she can't do the second side herself anyway, because she's sliced her flexor tendons and her hand won't work. But they both do it the wrong way. They should have done it down not across."

"A pair of idiots."

"Slitting your wrists, in any event, is an inefficient method of suicide and rarely successful because it's more often a cry for help. With these slashes, the tendons were cut, she couldn't have used her fingers to open the door — or close it."

Kingsford took a pair of electric shears and began to shave her head. The matted grey locks tumbled mournfully onto the floor and on the side of her temple above the hairline they saw a half emerging bruise.

"She didn't need to open the door," he replied over his shoulder. "Trevor did it for her. And look at that bruise."

"A corpse won't bruise if you hit it," added Cameron dryly. "She hit her head when she was alive. You see it's only recent. She may have fainted when her wrists were cut and woken up only after Trevor burst in and opened the door for her — made a lot a noise, did you constable? — hopefully, she was unconscious when she drowned. In any case, it couldn't have been Gibbs who threw her in the river, not in his condition. I imagine she hit her head in the dark, tumbled down the bank and fell in."

At that point the hospital phoned to say Mr Gibbs had passed a quantity of bloody diarrhoea.

"Food poisoning? Bowel cancer?" Kingsford asked the sister.

"A little less remarkable, I'm afraid," she answered. "He's got haemorrhoids."

"Which explains why the blood was A-positive," concluded Kingsford.

A sample from the dog food the following morning, however, was O-positive, and the vet, who mostly attended to farm animals, confirmed that the dog had ingested a large amount of the same blood group.

"How much? How much did she lose?"

"Impossible to say," answered the vet. "By this time a lot of it would have commenced digestion in the small bowel. But given the size of the dog, that is, the capacity of its stomach, I'd say, not more than half a litre."

"And less than a hundred mil in the bowel. So, between four and six hundred mil. Blood donors only give that much."

"Enough to faint if she was the fainting kind, but not enough to kill her."

Kingsford clonked the phone down upon the vet and turned on McDonald. "Why didn't you take the blood from the dog's bowl in the first place?"

"There was blood all over the room," complained the young man defensively.

"It never occurred to you that it might have come from two people?"

"It all looked red to me," said Trevor.

"Suicide, murder or accidental drowning?"

"But you opened the door for her, remember?" Kingsford accused his constable. "She faints, wakes up, remembers what's happened, staggers out looking for help, hits her head. Bingo! She drowns. She was alive somewhere in the house when he rang you. You didn't look past the nose on your face."

"It's not my fault," insisted McDonald.

"She's *dead,* you brainless idiot!" shouted Kingsford. "I don't know which is worse, Gibbs, Yarrabalong or *you.*"

Francis Gibbs was eventually charged with grievous bodily harm with intent to kill. He did not go to prison but instead, as there was no possibility of escape, he sat out his remaining days in a nursing home, dribbling saliva, cough sweets and whatever he'd consumed the previous meal. It was generally thought that he exhibited no contrition for the years of abuse and subsequent death of his wife, but from time to time he was heard to whimper, "I loved you, Marjorie, and look what you've done to me." ■

FEATHERS IN THE RAIN

S.J. GILPIN

I had stopped to take a breath up against the wall when the headlights from a limousine swung across the alley, picking out rain drops as they fell. For a second I could see a silhouette. Another duck, crouched over, stumbling to where the alley ends. I shot from the hip, three, maybe four, bullets out into the darkness. There was fire and smoke as the cracks hit back off the buildings. I ran on through the puddles and heard the quick squeal of tyres. When I got to the road the car was gone. There was no corpse on the floor. There was nothing. Just some blood and some feathers.

"This time we do it my way, McGrath," I quacked.

McGrath was the Chief of Police in Monterey. He had a big office on the fifth with a brass plaque on the door outside. There were letters from politicians in gilt frames along the walls, and pictures of what I took to be his family on the desk. The room breathed with the musty sweat of authority. McGrath was a fat man, forty, maybe fifty kilos over, and his eyes were squints. His hair was thin, like wagon lights on a slow exposure photograph. He had little affection for the private profession, but he knew his job.

"Talk, Delane."

McGrath got up from his desk. He walked slowly to the filing cabinet, unlocked it and pulled out a bottle of sour and two glasses. The glasses were cloudy with thick bottoms. "Do you take this?"

"Do I take it?"

He laughed and put the glasses down on the desk like he was smashing them. He poured us fat ones and clinked his down against his teeth. I wrapped a wing around mine and did the same. It was good stuff, probably black label proof. I felt better already. I looked up at the ceiling. It was low, patched with plastic tiles and ribbed by white tube lights. One was starting to flicker.

"So, Delane. You going to tell me something or you just come in here to screw my morning?" He smiled. Like he was pleased with a joke.

"Pour us another, McGrath, and I'll see what goes."

"Whatever the duck says."

Now it was my turn to smile. I drank the second whiskey slower. It was smoky and made my mind feel clearer. I wondered how a man like McGrath had got so high. There was mud on the carpet, and snow. "Okay, McGrath," I began, "but I've got to tell you, you're not going to like what I tell you."

His eyes squinted tighter. "Give it."

"I wasn't straight with you on the Ramires case."

"You what? You goddamn son of a bitch." His fist smashed down onto the desk like a buffalo dropped from the ceiling. He had stood up. His chair was knocked over behind him. His red face was redder. "You came in here to. Get out of here before I twist your neck."

I looked at him. He was angry. Sure, I knew he'd be angry, but he was angrier. He had lost it too fast. I reached into my coat pocket and felt for my Cubans and put them on the table. I pulled one out, flipped the cover and slipped it into my beak. There was a lighter on the desk to the side of the brown leather blotter. It was service issue. I took it in one wing and lit up my cigar. I faced the packet to McGrath. They were good smokes. I had got them off Alberti when I brought his daughter back. Alberti was a small time hood with a business off the east-side. His people took turns with the Cubans. Hence the cigars. His daughter had been making time with some Irish kid, name of O'Connor. There was drugs involved. Alberti is all sweet on his daughter. The kid winds up dead and Alberti gets the girl back. I took home the cigars.

"Pick up your chair and sit down, McGrath. You weren't level with me either. You knew about the Conchitas girl and kept stuck."

We know very little about Sam Gilpin, and most of what we do know his lawyers won't let us print. He reviews books for *The Guardian*, and for two of Rupert Murdoch's worst gutter-rags, the *Times Literary Supplement* and the *Sunday Times*. Uniquely amongst the contributors to this volume, he makes no claim to be the rightful heir to the throne of Macedonia.

Illustrations:
Roddy Williams

"The Conchitas girl. What're you?"

"Her brother comes into my office. He has a lot to say. Everything starts to make sense. You screwed up, McGrath, and it nearly cost me. This time we do it my way."

He picked out a cigar and looked at it, like he was checking treads.

"Cuban?"

"Bet the dollar."

His eyes asked it.

"Not at liberty."

He smiled wistfully and in one action passed it under his nose and into his fat mouth. His hand fell heavy on the lighter. His fingers clicked it and he took the fire. I could see that his hand was shaking a little. I had taken him off guard. He could go either way. He stayed standing up. He left the chair on the floor and looked out of the window. It was still snowing outside. When he spoke, the friendly tone was gone. "Okay, Delane, what you got?"

The first time I met Michael O'Connor, he was playing the tables at the Grand. He was on a roll. It was November. There were two dolls, blondes with big chests caught on his arms and he was piling up the chips like they were cookies. That night I was having it bad again. The lady had deserted me and I was burning up bills faster than I could open mine. O'Connor and me, we were playing the same deck. He saw how bad I was losing, and bought me some drinks. We talked. We got on. He even handed me a broad for the night. Not the prettiest one, sure, but it gives you a sense of the guy. Life was just the flick of a card for him, and you had to share it when the aces were high.

We took to meeting in bars before going off gaming. Soon we were spending more time with the beers than with the chips. And I started to do some business for him. Not at the casino, but my lines. O'Connor had a son, little Mikey, and he meant everything to his Dad. Mikey's mother had walked out. It turned out Mike Senior had been kind of drunk. She had made a bit of a scene, he hit her and she got scared. O'Connor wanted to get her back not for himself, see, but for Mikey, Mikey Junior. I kind of figured it was all in a good cause.

Anyway, this was all in the past, long before any of that business between Elaine and me. And I hadn't seen Mike for years. He had crossed state lines and that had been it. Then one night, it's fall and there is this man over my bed. I can't get to the 46 on my chair. It must be three, maybe four in the morning. My head is snaking. The light in the room is grey, silvery, cold. My legs are stiff and my beak tastes like an ashtray. I figure this is it. I figure my bill has come in. There is a pause. I hear a voice. "Delane. Shit. Wake up, man. It's me."

It's Mike. I look up. My head feels stretched. Except it's not Mike. He looks like Mike. Sure, he sounds like Mike. Just Mike must be older. Maybe I'm still asleep or something. "Who the fuck's 'me'? Make it good."

"It's Mike O'Connor, Michael's son. He said."

I figured. "I'm sure he said."

The kid didn't say nothing.

"How is he?"

"Look, you've got to help me."

"I don't got to do nothing."

"But he said." His voice was shaking, like a high note that can't hold.

"How the fuck d'you get in here?"

"I was in. I learnt some tricks. I can get in any place."

My mind felt cloudy, and I could see that my coat and my hat were on the floor. I took a cigarette out the packet on the side, lit it and sat upright in the bed. There was still some scotch left in the bottle. "Pour us a glass, and we'll see what does."

"But. There's a body." It burst out, like a pig's eyes under a truck.

I understood. Suddenly it all seemed clear. His agitated state. The time. Even the way my head was hurting.

I'm talking as I put on hat and coat, strap on my holster, check my piece. I'm giving instructions, taking the control. He tells me he's got a car. We have to drive. I tell him we'll go to third, park his car there and then take mine the rest of the way. I figure he'll be okay to drive a couple of blocks. I'll be following in the sedan. He looks relieved. He was glad he came to a professional.

"My dad, he called you the rubber dick."

"We talk on the way and we talk business."

Then we are both in the sedan doing fifty, coming up to the interstate. He gives me directions but that apart he doesn't seem in the mood for conversation. I am not sure if it's shock or fear or what, but he's muttering about an accident. I figure it's some girl. These things usually are. There's not a lot I haven't seen.

He gets me to pull up in the forecourt of some warehouse down on the docks. The plot is empty and fenced on three sides by a thick wire. It is in a part of the docks that I don't know well, on the side that gave up when the canal was built. The water looks quiet and cold and dark. It flickers orange under the industrial lights. I fire the lighter and start up a cigarette. It has started to rain. Mike is looking nervous, like he doesn't want to leave the car.

"Okay, let's go."

"I don't."

His voice swallowed itself like a tongue. He was shaking all over. His face had gone a white colour. I took the cigarette out of my beak, forced it into his mouth, and lit myself another one. He smiled. I smiled. We both started to laugh. So we just sat there, smoking the cigarettes, laughing like idiots, unable to say anything. By the time we had finished, Michael looked better. He got out of the sedan first and started walking over to a side door in the warehouse. It was on the wall facing the forecourt, at a right angle to the docks. It was not locked. I took the leather gloves from my coat pockets, put them on and flicked the handle.

Inside there was shelved stacking that went empty to the ceiling. It was a long way up and the lights had been left on. I helped myself to another cigarette, lit it and took it in. There were a few crates still around but they seemed forgotten, unimportant. I didn't wonder if I couldn't catch the musty smell of narcotics. Maybe that was the cut. The place was split up into aisles and Michael led me down one that was opposite the doors. I checked the luger in its holster. There was a lot of dirt on the floor and the air was dusty. The only noise was our footsteps. We took a left down some side aisle.

"His name's Steiner."

His. I looked at O'Connor. To myself. "His."

"Yeah. George Steiner."

"Not a Steiner Steiner?"

A ghost of relief drove across his eyes. He knew I knew my job. "A Steiner Steiner."

The Steiners were the biggest banking family in the state. They did business right across the count, legal and not so legal. The month before, old man Steiner had bought the Rialto off Donny Silver and the word was that the deal was less than medical.

We took another turning, this time to the right. There was a big cream door at the end of the aisle. We walked towards it. It had a metal pull on the front and was slid slightly open. A fan was hissing in a glass pane in the wall above and out of the gap between the door and the side wall white smoke was trying to make an escape. It was a freezer room. Michael collapsed onto the floor. He was crying.

"In the refrigeration?"

He nodded. The kid was a liability. I was angry with myself. The lack of profession-alism. I thought about taking him home. Not enough time. It was better to know.

I left him lying down and looked around for switches. No luck. I pulled my flash out of my coat pocket and flicked it on. The heavy door was well oiled. I slid it open some more and shone the light inside.

121

The sight made me giddy for a second. There was Steiner, or the man Mikey had said was Steiner, about fifty feet in but clear enough to make out. His body was somehow on a hook, hanging from a conveyor belt system attached to the roof of the freezer room. I could pick out dark patches on him that were probably blood. I checked the door for an inside lock, and then caught a glance at O'Connor. He was no longer crying. I stepped into the freezer.

My flash beam lit it up, but only in patches, like I was seeing through a telescope. There was nothing in the main hold, just a stiff whose dad couldn't help him this time. It was cold. I was grateful for the hat and the coat and the gloves. My feathers rustled against themselves. The ceiling was blackened and low, crusted up with ice. There was a pattern on the tiles underneath, but not clear enough to make out. I figured the refrigerator had been used for butchering. It was a fitting place to die.

I took a quick report on the boy as I went past. He was naked and he had chains on his hands and on his feet. There was a gag tied over his mouth and lines of cord that connected the chains with his neck. I looked at his eyes. They seemed frozen with fear, blue. His neck had probably been broken. Maybe something had gone wrong. Something like a game. An accident. The refrigeration room opened out at the far end and I had to secure it before I checked him out properly. I held my piece in the right wing with my torch in the left, and went up to the corner.

There was nothing around but a scattering of hooks and chains. They had been recently disturbed. The room was shaped like a capital L and the overhead conveyor system led around the corner on the right, to and from wide warehouse gates at the furthest end. I walked up to them. They were shut, and had not been moved for a long time. Rust and ice on the hinges. I decided I'd seen enough. It was time to deal with the stiff on the meat hook.

As I was on my way back my light picked out a door handle on the corner of the L. I didn't know how I had missed it. I am not someone who usually misses things. The door was made of wood and sat next to a large glass window. It felt as if it had been just magicked up in front of me.

I opened the door and found a switch, flicked it and turned my flashlight off. Some sort of control room. There was a desk and a couple of beaten up vinyl chairs. The equipment on the side looked out of date, like it was from an old film. In front of it was the window, looking out on the ice box. I figured this was where the mechanisms were worked. It was not cold in the room. There was an electric fire in the corner. It was still switched on. I lit a cigarette.

The door at the back of the room was locked. I could not force it. Maybe it just led out onto the waterfront. There were two mugs by the sink. They had a brown liquid in them. There was no mould. I was just about to start cleaning up when I heard a shot. Then two more.

I switched off the light and shut the door silently behind me. Now that I was on my way out of the darkness I could see better. The light was coming in from the warehouse in a belt where the door was open. It looked different from the inside. I walked slowly along the far wall, away from where the gap was. My gun was tight in my wing.

There was another shot. This time near me. There was a thud. The kid on the meat-hook swayed a little. A clean hit. That would give pathology something to think about. I froze against the wall and waited. A body appeared in the doorway. It had no chance.

I fired twice and the figure collapsed onto itself. There was a shot into the darkness. It hit a wall and went God knows where. Then it was quiet. I waited again. There was no movement, no sound.

I approached from the door wall. The caution was unnecessary. The man was dead, cooked. I made a quick check around and put the luger into my holster. It was hot and I could feel it warm against my feathers. The air was fat with the smell of powder. I turned the stiff over with my foot, and I knew him. His name was Spike Koshka, and he pimped in the old quarter. He had a sister, name of Marlene. She was married to Conchitas. This was getting untidy. To have two stiffs in a freezer down on the docks was messy. To have two stiffs with links to old man Steiner and Conchitas was something I could do without. Maybe there was a connection. In my experience there is no such thing as a coincidence.

I stepped over Spike. He had been a good looking boy, but I had blown half his face off. It was a shame. There was nothing that could be done now. It was then I remembered the other shots. I looked up. O'Connor was where I had left him, except he wasn't crying now.

There was blood all round him. It's one thing I still find it quite hard to take. Spike had shot him three times. Twice in the crotch and once in the head. I should have left him behind. If he'd played the level with me, he would still be alive. That wouldn't be any consolation to his old man. There was nothing for me to do. It was time to move.

I stood upright and saw two policeman walking up the aisle towards me. They had me covered. There was nowhere to go. I hadn't heard the sirens. Maybe it was when I was in the freezer. They told me to drop the gun. I did it. I had no choice. I told them to radio Inspector Hamilton in Homicide, but they just laughed.

I can only remember one of them clearly. He was fat with a blonde moustache, rolled over his lip like a hot-dog. His voice was deep and ugly, like the engine of a pick-up. He told me to face the wall.

As I was turning I remember thinking their uniforms looked tight, but it was too late. I felt the butt of a gun slice down on the back of my head and my legs slip out.

"I said it'd be easy," said the fat one.

Marlene told me she wanted to meet at the city zoo, just west off eighteenth. I knew where the zoo was. I said nothing. Her words had sounded desperate, like I wasn't meant to argue, so I left it. It had been a long time. I hadn't seen her since that night at the Grand when she and Conchitas had their little scene, but all I took was one please. She gave time and place and the line went dead. I clicked the tone with my left wing and held onto the receiver with my right. I couldn't be sure how long this was going to take and I didn't want any chances. It's not good for a duck in my position to leave people waiting.

I first met Marlene in eighth grade when her surname was still Koshka. Since then it had gone through more changes than a cross-state express. She had been Marlene Delight, Marlene Honey. Even the Marlene was no fixture. Now she was a Ramires, Marlene Ramires, but I figured she was the same old Marlene underneath. When I was at High School I had a buddy called Spike. Spike was her brother. We played baseball together, chased chicks together, and found ways of getting our hands, or our wings, on bourbon. I guess I was pretty hot on Marlene, but nothing ever happened. There wasn't anything particular special about her, just she was a girl and I knew her. She had the blonde and the legs, the eyes and the smile. That was enough for me. And she was older. Spike got hit by the draft and was killed out there. Marlene and me, we could never be close after that. There was too much to say. Maybe that was why I agreed to her call. Maybe I was still half in love with her.

I checked the slide on my colt and filed it next to my chest. It was getting hot outside but I still took my coat. In this city the rain never needs a second invitation. I took down two slugs of bourbon like it was medicine, put on my hat and headed for the mustang.

I was downtown in twenty. The heat was keeping the cars off the street and I wanted to know what was up. It felt like something big was coming, a storm maybe, and I didn't want to miss out. Ramires was the biggest hood in the Northern districts, and most of what he did now was legit. I wouldn't have touched it if it hadn't been for Marlene. But it was, so there was nothing doing. I parked in a little station-alley off nineteenth, near the back gates to the zoo. If anything went wrong,

I wanted choices of where to fly to. I walked around the front and paid my dime. I was ten early. It was not a problem.

She had said to meet at the bears. I checked it out. She wasn't there. Neither were the bears. I guess the sun was a pain for them with their thick coats. I ripped open a new packet and prised out a cigarette. I lit it and started a stroll. Walking felt good. It gave my mind a chance to play around for possibilities and let me take in the geography. The problem with zoos is that they're always moving things around, like in the big stores, so you never know what you're going to see next. Suddenly I found myself standing at the penguins, watching them. I thought how funny they looked and then guessed that I must look pretty funny to them too. All of us, we're all animals and we all look funny. I ticked a match, started up a cigarette and headed back for the bears.

Fifteen later and Marlene still hadn't shown. I was beginning to feel stupid, on my own, just standing there. There were no bears and I was sticking out. It's not good in my game, with its emphasis on discretion and subtlety. And it was hot. I was going through cigarettes like they were on fire and there was still no sign of the doll. I got the thought that this was a joke or a set-up maybe, but Marlene was sincere as long as I'd known her, and if I was going to get hit I'd be in the pit already and the bears would have come out. Maybe something had happened to her. There was an ices man I had seen by the elephants, so I figured I'd cut myself a break.

When I came back, Marlene had arrived, standing, looking over the edge. She was holding a baby and there was a buggy to her side. This was something new. She had not seen me. I took a lick of my ice and checked out her ass. It was still good. I threw the ice away into some big wire can in front of the tigers and walked up to the bears. I stood next to her and looked where she was looking. "Hi, darling."

"Delane, is that you? What a great surprise." She leant across and kissed me. Her lips burned. I could smell and taste her skin against my beak. "You're late."

"I waited twenty. I just went to get an ice."

She moved away a little, fresh in the chance meeting. Her voice was quick and her lips barely shuffled, "Act like you're telling me something. Make it between three and four."

A life on beds and bars had made her fast. You could tell she hustled sharp. How else could she have hooked someone like Ramires? I told her a little story for three and fifteen. It was not what I'd been doing, but it could have been. I gave her a standard dick run, some shit about bourbon and broads, cops and colts.

She smiled. "Of course. But let me introduce you to Tommy." Tommy was less than a year. A zoo was no place for him, but he didn't look like he'd be making trouble.

"He yours?"

"Don't start it."

He was a pretty kid and he had big smiling eyes. Marlene picked a bottle out of her white patent bag and gave him the plastic nipple. He touched out in the crook of her arm and she slid him into the buggy. She kissed him. "Let's walk the talk."

"It's your call."

Marlene started out with our little play by the bears. It seemed she had it all figured. If someone was on her surveillance, and even if they weren't, she had reasons for the both of us. I was there on a tail, and she and Tommy were doing a zoo run. I had seen them by the bears, and gone over and got them to be my cover. So I didn't stand out too bad. If someone was on her they wouldn't be looking for who I was after. You don't bother to tail someone else's tail. Perhaps I *was* tailing someone else. Perhaps I'm not always on the level. I have to admit I was impressed by the broad. She sure thought it through.

"Okay, so I've got the story. Now what's with it. You're not just here for makin' up fairy tales."

"Yeah, I know that. It's about Tommy."

I took a look at him. He seemed a good kid. "I'm not into child-minding."

"Delane."

"Sorry." Maybe I was kind of jealous for the kid. I don't know.

"I'm not sure he's Silvio's."

"Serious?"

"Yeah." She went to bustle for a cigarette in her bag. I handed over one of mine and burned it with my lighter. I lit one for myself too. She took a hit and let it out. "Not pretty, eh?"

"Well, that depends."

"It's depending right now."

"Tell."

"Do you remember Donny Silver?"

I nodded. I remembered Donny Silver. He was a flash Jewboy from the upstate and Marlene was in love with him. Before Ramires, before Conchitas, before even Marlene Gorgeous. She was proper in love with him, but he was trash. He treated her like shit and she just kept coming back for more. I used to want to kill the guy. I was young then. And I made up speeches to tell Marlene and never said them. It wouldn't have made no difference, I guess. Women are like that. There's no sense in them. The one thing about Silver, though, he was always out of dough. I think he had a habit with the brown or something. When he showed up Marlene just gave him money, all she had, cash for the pimps and all. He had some hold on her. I could never figure it.

"Well, Donny came back and I fucked him. I couldn't stop myself."

I looked at her with questions.

"I didn't want to. Shit, Delane, don't start. I'm through with all that shit now. I'm happy with Silvio. I've got security. It's just."

"Just too much."

"Don't Delane. Please. It wasn't planned or nothing."

"Shit. I'm sorry Marlene."

"He just left again. Like always." She went quiet. We had stopped by the tigers. My ice had melted at the bottom of the trash can. I didn't look at her. I might break what she had to say. "I said I'd never. I meant it this time. It was just Silvio." There was another stop. "And then came Tommy."

"So what's the problem? There's no fucking problem." This was a job for a shrink, not a dick. The broad was just wasting my services.

"I'm not through yet."

"Okay. So what is it? What's the big fucking problem?"

"Some prick, name of Alberti. Y'know him?"

I knew him, all right. He was number two to Ramires but he used to work for O'Connor. One day he turned on the Irishman and sold him out. It was pretty ugly.

"Alberti wants money. Says he knows about Donny. Says he knows about Tommy. Says he's got pictures and all. I don't know what the hell to do, Delane."

"Is Donny in on this?"

"Shit. I hadn't. I guess he could be."

"And how much does Alberti want?"

"Two."

"Thousand?"

"Yeah."

"Can you do that?"

"Just."

"Good."

"But he'll come back. I know it."

"I know it too. And when he's milked you, he'll go running to Ramires."

"Don't say that."

"Shut up. We need time and we don't have a lot of it. Clean up your face and get home. I'm on the case."

My eyes were starting to feel all dusty when the light came on over the veranda. The rain was coming down as thick as mustard and I was glad to be safe in the Buick. I saw Steiner, it had to be Steiner, but the rain was making it hard to be sure. He finished with the door and ran across the street to the blue Cadillac. I caught him in the crossbeam of a truck coming my way. It was Steiner.

I started up the engine and kept my lights off, waiting to see where he was heading. Without so much as a look around he sped off fast down the road in front of me and took a right at the end. I pulled out quickly and followed a block down. It was tough with the rain, but there was no way I was letting him see the tail. Not this time. The Cadillac was in a bright blue so at least it gave me something to work on. He took a left at the next corner down onto East forty-third. I was still a block down, but tight on him, and the rain was beating on the windshield like a drum-major. I slipped the lights at East forty-third and eighteenth, burning it hard, and took the right and then the left onto East forty-four. By fifteenth on crossways I was opposite him again. And now I pretty much had it figured where we were heading. Steiner was on his way to the Rialto and I wouldn't be surprised if the room he wanted was 307.

When I said the numbers in my head, it all started to make sense. It wasn't two cases I was on. It was one. And it was Carmen that put it all together. I wished I hadn't been so dumb when I went round to talk to O'Connor. He had been trying to give me the answers and I was too stupid to see it.

Sure enough, Steiner took the right at eleventh and left me six cars in front of him. I parked fifty yards down from the Rialto on the right and followed him in my mirrors. He didn't have a clue. He just pulled up outside and walked in.

I looked at my watch. McGrath was late. There should have been some unmarked cars at the front, but there was no cover. I could see that from here. I put a cigarette in my beak and lit it. There was no way I was going up there again. Not without back up. Luck is not something best tested twice. Any dick knows that. Fifteen past. Still raining. Steiner had not come down again and there was no sign of McGrath or the boys from Homicide.

Then, suddenly, a shot. Then two more. Like Chinese crackers in the cold Spring air. Without thinking I'm running. Out of the car and up the steps into the hotel. There's a bit of a panic in the plush, red lobby and this isn't helped by the sight of my automatic. I must have drawn it on my way into the hotel. The elevator's used, so I'm taking the stairs.

I'm on the second, still running, when I hear a crash like someone falling down a flight of stairs. I see a man's head hit the carpeted floor in front of me and quickly check him out. His jaw's bleeding from the stone steps. It's the guy in the fake cop's uniform. The one with the ginger beard. I wait for the recognition in his eyes and shoot between them when his hand gets to his gun. Self-defence is just about timing.

Then I'm on the third and I'm standing outside the door. It is quiet, like everything's normal, but maybe I can hear crying. I kick open the door and I'm too late. The room looks nothing like it did two hours ago. There's polythene and cocaine all over the floor in split bags. The cocaine's so thick on the bed, it's looking like cooking salt. Steiner's on my left, lying by the bathroom door with a big hole in his chest. The mirror behind him is smashed at a point and splashed red with blood. In between us, on the bed, Carmen Alberti is lying face up. She looks fucked. She's sobbing like a devotional and her nose and her mouth are coated in powder like she's been rolling in it. There's some shit dripping from her nose all over her top lip and it could be the coke or the crying. I don't know.

I look around. This isn't right. There should be someone else. I take a step forward. And then there's another shot. It clips me on the left wing. I catch the movement and fire twice. The bullets hit Conchitas in the right shoulder and then in the head. His skull bursts like a dysentery, spraying the cream curtains blood. Carmen is screaming. There is another, larger mark on Conchitas's chest, blotting on the white of his vest, visible as he arches backwards onto the floor. He had been lying at the foot of the bed. The door opens behind me and then I'm on the deck behind Conchitas, facing the other way.

"Freeze, Police."

"Don't shoot. It's me, Delane."

I stand up. Carmen is losing it completely. She's trying to eat her hands in between kissing Steiner on the mouth. There's blood everywhere. I can see McGrath coming into the room behind the boys with the padding. He's checking out the damage. "Get your wing, did he, Delane?"

"Get the fuck out of my face, McGrath. Get the fuck right out of my face."

I am walking along a path. My feet are tired. I am waddling. The path is made of pebbles. They are mostly white, but there are some single red ones distributed at regularly random intervals. The pebbles are not comfortable to walk on. I have stopped. I am looking down. My webbed feet shine orange on the matt white of the stones. It is an agreeable juxtaposition: the orange on the white. I am inspecting my left foot. There are blisters on it. I come to the conclusion that this path was not designed for ducks. I do not adjust my hat.

I am walking again. The ratio of red pebbles to white pebbles has altered imperceptibly. I notice it. Excellent observation skills are essential in my profession. There are more red pebbles now. At the sides of the path are thick white curbs, fat and curved like pats of butter. They are raised above the path and as wide as they are high. It looks as if they are made of white stone. I resist the desire to check. It may be granite. Beyond the curbs on either side is limitless grass. The grass is green. It is thick and healthy. I am aware of my brain concluding that it must rain frequently here.

I am looking up. The sky is a heavy blue. It is an endless, fat, cobalt blue. All the colours around me are big. They resonate as if they have smugly found an absolute frequency.

Behind me, all I can see is the path. The path is all I can see in front of me. I am able to detect no local disparity in colour, but there are many more red pebbles now. I stop. I pick up a pebble of each colour in my right wing. There seems to be no difference between them. They are comparable in smoothness, size, weight. I suck one in turn. I can ascertain no difference. Perhaps when I was younger I would have been able to find one. I spit them out, violently, behind me. I start to walk again.

It is not only my feet that hurt now. My knees stutter and twinge. My back jars with each forward step. I try to go faster, well aware that there may be no final destination. The only information that hints at one is the changing colour of the pebbles, but I am aware of no precedent which might support my hypothesis. In addition to this, the gradual rate of the transition means that the only evidence I have for it is my memory, which has recently been unreliable. There is probably a fifty:fifty ratio now. I think about stopping to check, to count the number of each colour within a restricted area. I am aware that this might not be very precise and that the result is probably insignificant. It occurs to me that there could be some problems with stones that were on the edge of the sample block. Perhaps I would need more than one sample. I always found statistics difficult. Still walking, I have not even slowed, despite all the thinking. This is pleasing. I smile.

Beyond the grass, which is probably not limitless, are mountains. These are brown isosceles triangles, peaked with white. It is not presumptuous to assume that this is snow. The mountains surround me on all sides, even in front and behind, making a bowl shape, a gigantic crucible. Perhaps I am walking in a flood-plain. This would certainly explain the flatness of the terrain. It would also suggest that there was a river somewhere near. This could be why the grass is so healthy. I do not look for a river. I do not leave the path. I do not know why. The pebbles are now predominantly red. Perhaps they have always been red.

I am walking faster again. My feet have become private. They do not speak to me of their pain. They walk without me. My wings ache with exhaustion. I let my neck back as I walk, to relieve it. This makes my back hurt more. The occasional white pebble punctuates the matt red path like a stray comma. This is how the path has always been. White pebbles are singularities. The red path vibrates against the green grass, complementing it, under this blue space that is perhaps not a colour but an emotion, a preliminary wash.

I can see something at the end of the path. I turn my creaking neck around and am surprised that there is nothing similar conjured behind me. The fearful symmetry has been finally altered. It would have been quite surprising to get closer to something by walking away from it. But life delights in paradoxes and in theories that run counter to intuition. I do not know what is at the end of the path. My eyes are weakening. There seems to be silver, stretching in an arc across the horizon, under the white and brown of the mountains. I cannot guess what it might be. I seem to have lost the childlike power of invention, of imagination. The white pebbles are rare and seem to have been left by accident, perhaps by a vandal, one of these kids who delights in damage. The white stones look like invaders, impurities. Perhaps the people who maintain the path would better spend their time removing rogue stones. Perhaps they are responsible for it. It is a pattern, an order that I do not recognise, that would only become an order in repetition.

My feet still hurt but there is now an end, the hope of an end. This helps. The silver stretches out in front of me. It may be a crescent of steel, some government project. I conceive that it could be a lake. I feel old. There is only one white pebble as far as I can see, and it is behind me. My eyes ache and struggle to focus. I have a cough that wakes me, that brings up blood with the tar black, that scares me in the night. My shooting has lost its precision. I need to drink more to sleep. The nightmares are the same.

The path has ended. It is stopped by a curb of red stone. At some point the curbs have changed from white to red and I failed to notice. Perhaps I could run back and find where they went from white to red. I know that I am too tired. I would not make it. I would probably run past and not notice. Perhaps the curbs were never white. What is this obsession with white? I do not know the colour. I do not know this white. The red of the curb jostles with the green of the grass, providing a contrast. At the end of the path is a lake. My initial suspicion is confirmed. I feel satisfaction. The lake looks cold and calm and beautiful. It appears to be surrounded by a semicircle of mountains. Perhaps there is a cave in the rock in a direct line with the path. A cave to climb out of the water for. A cave in which to sleep.

There are two stone chalices of immense proportions on either side of the end of the path. They stand at twice my height and issue forth flames perhaps twice my height again. The chalices are carved from fawn stone and are inlaid with fantastic and expensive jewels. The scents of rich spices, of incense, blend and eddy in the air. I can make out symbols on the chalices but I cannot read them. The sky is darkening. It is no longer blue. I look over the edge of the curb into the water and see that lichen is growing on the side of the stone that is in the water. I am disgusted by this transgression, this violation of decorum. I take a step back. My stomach retches.

I am tired. I am old. I remove my cigarettes from my coat pocket and place them in the middle of the red curb at the end of the path. My lungs hurt. I place my lighter on top of the cigarettes and briefly conjure my image standing on a street corner in the rain; at a homicide; in my office slamming sours. I cannot hold it. I pull my gun from its holster, check the slide and position it to the left of the cigarettes. I slip my wings, twitching with exhaustion, out of my raincoat and my holster. I put the holster to the left of the automatic. Carefully, I fold the coat and then use it to cover the other effects. Perhaps I could leave my hat on as a final act of defiance. I take it off and try it on top of the coat as an experiment. It looks ghostly without me, alien, not mine. I leave it there. I test the water with a foot. It is very cold and it makes me shiver. I am tired. I am old. I am naked. It is time to swim. ∎